Parasite
The True Story of the Zombie Apocalypse

By Doug Ward

Smashwords Edition

Introduction

Many people tried to understand what made the dead walk. It seemed few had any true science behind their unfounded theories. The radio was full of these people extolling one supposed scientific cause after another. Radiation from outer space, pollutants, cell phones, it seemed every possible influence was explored to some extent. But no one looked at evolution.

I don't mean our evolution. Our lifespan is too long for us to observe this theory in living humans. Although we understand natural selection from the fossil records, the easiest way to see evolution is through bacteria. Their short lives allow us a clear view of how a life form can adapt to meet the demands of a changing environment.

Darwin's theory is what would lead to our modern world's destruction. It would crush our cities, and render most technology useless.

This is the story of how it happened, how I saw and uncovered the true cause of the zombie apocalypse.

Other Fine Books by Doug Ward;

Ward's Laws
Ward's Laws Part 2
Ward's Laws Part 3
Ward's Laws Part 4

**Saving Jebediah; Another True Story from the Zombie
Apocalypse**
Symbiote; The True Story of the Zombie Apocalypse Part 2
Creator; The True Story of the Zombie Apocalypse Part 3
Predator; The True Story of the Zombie Apocalypse Part 4

Acknowledgements
Thank you to all of my friends and family who stood behind me
and pushed me forward. You guys are the best. Special thanks to
Chris Allman for helping me work out some of the bugs (pun
intended,) and also Heather Sandusky, who helped me with some
of the fire truck scenes. I want to thank Max Shaginaw and Scott
Lee for beta reading and J.D. Reed for editing the book (a huge
task!) I would like to give a very big, special thanks to wife, April,
for putting up with the millions of times we discussed zombies. I
want everyone to know that as far as having a Zombie Apocalypse
Action Plan, she's probably the most prepared woman I've ever met.

Chapter 1
Henry

It had been a long night at the office. I told my wife Melissa that I was going to work late to finish my newest paper. I was documenting my findings for the Journal of Natural Science. I didn't think it would literally take all evening, but I got immersed in my work, as usual, and lost all track of time.

Even though I had a laptop and a desktop at home, I liked to do most of my work at school. It was too easy to get distracted at home. In the office of my University lab, I was able to stay focused. No phone calls, no television blaring in the background, I'd even shut off my cell phone so I could be totally absorbed in the task. Furthermore, I had the added benefit of having my test materials on-hand for when I wanted to look at something.

The paper documented my research of Zombie Snails. I was trying to find the evolutionary link pertaining to why the flatworm, *Leucochloridium paradoxum*, evolved to gain the ability to control the common garden snail. We understand that the eggs of the flatworm, being ingested by the snail, caused the latter to become the host. I was interested in how the evolutionary process began.

I know what you're thinking, *"An entomologist, doing the work of a malakologist?"* I found an infected snail and got interested. It just kind of happened.

I saved the document to a flash drive and turned off the task light illuminating my desk. Natural sunlight filtered through my closed blinds, maintaining the room's brightness. I looked at the oversized clock my wife had given me for our tenth anniversary. Melissa said that she bought the present so I could see what time it was. Mel, as I like to call her, thought it would get me home at a decent hour.

It was 7:00 a.m. I was in the doghouse. A quick stop at Starbucks on the way home would go a long way to softening the blow. Melissa loved her cappuccino. So I scooped up my brown corduroy jacket and made for the door.

As I closed the door, I saw the brushed bronze nameplate situated neatly below the glazed glass window.

Dr. Henry Cooper, Ph.D.
Department of Entomology
Slippery Rock University

My mother had been so proud. I can still hear her bursting with pride over the phone when I told her I got the University job. She told me I was going to save the world. I didn't have the heart to correct her.

The glass in the heavy, wooden door rattled as I closed and locked it. I didn't like the name Henry. My coworkers called me Hank. A few even referred to me as Coop. But as for friends, I didn't have any close ones. My work took most of my time. Mel had tried to include me in a few of her friendships, but they always fell apart somehow. I don't blame them. The only thing I was truly focused on was my work. I got anxious when we had parties to attend or even if we were going to spend the evening with another couple. That was time I could be working. Some people might call me a workaholic, but I tend to think that I'm driven. I'm thankful that Melissa understands and still loves me.

It was becoming a warm spring day, the birds chattering all about the tree-lined campus. In the distance, I could hear the wail of a siren. As I walked toward the parking lot, I powered on my iPhone with one hand and fumbled for my keys with the other. I had walked this path for so many years that I didn't need to look up as I navigated my way to the lot where I had parked the day before. As the screen came to life, I looked up and took in my surroundings. Smoke plumed into the sky in the distance, but all else remained normal. A few people were about their morning business; it being early Saturday morning, that was the norm. Much of the student body had probably taken the evening as an opportunity to blow off some steam. The few ambling about were either going home from an all-night party or up early to get some studying in. It looked like the former. In the distance, two people were running and the rest just seemed to lurch about. It looked almost as if they were in hopeless chase of the joggers.

Keys in hand, I thumbed the button to releasing the door to my car, a 2012 Subaru Forester. Mel thought the dark gray color would blend into the road too much, but I loved how it looked and had to have it. As I swung the door open, I noticed some of the

4

students were coming my way. It must have been a wild night. By the way they were walking, it seemed like the party must have just let out.

I plopped into the light gray leather seat and brought the screen of my phone to bear. In simple block letters, I read the words *"No Connection."*

That's odd, I thought. I usually had a great connection. Dropping the phone in the passenger seat I shifted the car into reverse and backed out of my parking place.

As the car arced around, a young man came into view through the rear view mirror. He looked like hell. His clothes and hair were askew, but his skin tone was the worst. He was literally gray. As he lurched toward the rear of my car, I felt compassion. I actually thought about getting out of the car to see if he was ok,but a quick glance at the built-in clock on the dash made those thoughts disappear.

Fifteen minutes had passed and I had to hightail it. I slammed the car's automatic transmission into drive and was on my way. The coffee shop was just a few blocks away, so I whizzed along the back streets, still damp from dew. I passed a few more late-night partygoers on the way to Starbucks. They all had that same gray pallor and walked as though they could barely stand. It must have been a heck of a night.

As I neared my destination, I couldn't believe my luck. There was a parking space open right in front. On a Saturday morning, that was weird, but what was even stranger was the fact that all the spaces in front were open. I swung into the one directly in front and to my disappointment, I saw the reason the spot wasn't filled. There, in the middle of the window, was a sign indicating that the store was closed. I couldn't believe it. I just sat there with my mouth open reading and rereading the same word. Why would a coffee shop be closed on a Saturday morning? My car idled as I thought of what I could do to smooth over the fact that I had not come home last night.

I wasn't worried that she would think I was with another woman. We were beyond that. She knew the only other woman for me would have an exoskeleton and maybe antennae.

I could stop at another place but that would make me even later. Maybe if I go straight home I can start a pot of java before she wakes up. That might be nearly as good as a cup of Starbucks, I lied to myself. I reversed out of the spot and started down the road toward my house.

I saw a few people in the rearview mirror and thought to myself, *Those will be some sad people when they see that the shop is not open.*

I was now closer to where the party had taken place, because there were cars driven up on sidewalks and abandoned on the street. One even had the door open. Man, that guy would be upset when he comes out and finds a dead battery. More people were walking about, but I hardly gave them a second look as I pulled to the side of the road to give a police car, siren blaring, room to pass. The lights reflected off my face as the car flew by. The officer in the passenger seat looked in shock as he locked eyes with me.

I resumed my journey, noticing that people were shuffling toward the road, probably to get a look at where the police car was going. I fumbled for my garage door opener as I deftly maneuvered through the last of the well-traveled streets.

As I pulled into the driveway of our small Cap Cod-style home, I thought better of using the automatic garage door opener. The door was very loud when the chain engaged. The old Sears motor made half of the house vibrate. If I parked outside and entered quietly, I could start a pot of Joe and have time to sneak back and wake Melissa with a kiss.

Turning the ignition to off, I pulled the keys and as silently as possible, exited the vehicle. I was almost on my porch when I spied my neighbor, Phil, walking towards his mailbox, probably for his morning newspaper. It looked like he had just woken up. His pajamas were halfway down his butt and, worst of all, he had no shirt on.

Please don't get me wrong. I like my neighbors, but I was in a hurry and Phil had the habit of being quite long-winded. Being retired and married to the neighborhood gossip can do that to a person. Unfortunately, while I was selecting the front door key, I dropped them. Bending over, I could see out of my peripheral vision that Phil had stopped and was turning my way. He must have heard my keys jingle as they hit the ground. I quickly scooped them up and headed for the door, eyes staying focused straight ahead.

Putting speed before stealth, I had the door unlocked and was through the portal within moments. I tried to look nonchalant about it as not to hurt my neighbor's feelings.

Inside the house, all was still. I could hear the ticking of the old battery-operated clock we had in the hallway to the kitchen, but all else was silent. I was home free, I thought, hanging my jacket on the old hat rack we kept just inside the door. As I crept down the tile hallway, I heard a thump at the front entrance. Shrugging it off, I started forward once again. Two more thumps and I wheeled about, hurrying toward the door. I quietly opened the door and, to my horror, there was Phil. Blood streamed down from the side of his neck. He emitted a low, wet-sounding moan and raised his arms for what I thought was a cry for assistance. As I grabbed his right arm and reached with my free hand to help him, his head shot forward, snapping teeth mere inches from my face. His jaws continued to bite as my reaching for help turned into struggling for control.

I pushed and he pulled, then we slipped in an ever-growing puddle of his blood. His naked back made a slapping noise as it hit the sticky surface. The momentum brought my face dangerously close to his as Phil's jaws continued their quest for my flesh. I struggled to get away as his attention became focused on my wrist, which had gotten close to his snapping maw. The blood was making things worse as I lost my grip over and over. Somewhere in our struggle, one of us knocked over the hat rack. It slid down the open door frame and landed between our faces. Seizing the moment, I grasped the rack in both hands, my weight pinning his head to the floor. His hands raked at my sides, but I kept up the pressure. Bouncing, I repeatedly bashed his head against the tiled entryway. Blood puddled out, but I kept bouncing and bashing until I felt something in his skull snap. Phil's body went slack, arms plopping into the huge stain of his life's fluid, splashing red onto the walls and door.

I knelt there, weight still pressing on my neighbor's broken skull. Relief flooded my body. No thoughts, just a strong feeling of exhaustion. After a moment, I leaned back and let my body relax. I closed my eyes, blocking the gruesome vision with black.

A sound brought me back from tranquility. A shuffling noise

was followed by a soft moan. My eyes shot open and I saw that old Mrs. Crawford, eyes fixed on me through my open door, was staggering toward me. The Zen moment was over. I shoved Phil's corpse out of the door, which was no easy feat considering his size and that he was all (pardon the pun) dead weight.

Just as I was pushing the door closed, an old, frail wrist shot through the opening. The steel door smashed into the brittle, age-worn bones and snapped it off. The appendage hung, unmoving, from the jam. As I drove the deadbolt home the limb fell to the floor, thudding lightly against the tiles.

I could only stand and stare. It lay in the thickening pool of my deceased neighbor's blood along with my jacket. Not knowing what else to do, I went into the kitchen and retrieved a set of tongs. I used these devices to pick up the severed appendage and walked over to my living room window. Being careful to look both ways, I deposited the limb with a light toss in the shrubs and secured the window latch.

I looked down at my shirt and slacks, covered in blood. Walking into the kitchen, I began to shiver. The trauma was taking its toll. I could hear Mrs. Crawford at the door, trying to gain access. Muffled thumps registered her vain attempts at entry. I stripped off the shirt and dropped it in the garbage can, then continued to the sink. Water ran red down the drain as I washed myself. Had my neighbors been infected by some new disease, something that affected their minds? This renewed my scrubbing. Just as I achieved a nice, rosy-red hue, I glanced into the window glass and saw the coffeemaker reflected there. Mel.

Still dripping, I crept through the house saying her name softly. "Melissa," I called out again, uncertain of what the results might be. Maybe she heard the struggle and was hiding. At the door to our upstairs master bedroom, I paused. Turning the handle slowly, I hoped for the best.

As I swung the door in, nothing happened. I said her name slightly louder. Still nothing. She wasn't home. What did this mean? There was no sign of a struggle, apart from the one I was in earlier. Where did she go?

Chapter 2
Melissa
Yesterday

It was a normal day at work. Phones ringing in cubicles filled the air with a strange, repetitive symphony of sound. The clicking noise of staplers and keyboards only enhanced the effect. I had learned during my first week how to completely block it out. Coworkers bustled to and fro about their individual tasks. We must have resembled a beehive.

I repeatedly told my husband that he should come in and see my place of employment. I'm sure he would have found many similarities to his field of entomology. He had passion for his study of insects that people found hard to understand. Some of my friends openly questioned why I stayed with him. He often forgot appointments, friends, and even my birthday. I literally had to buy him the largest clock in the store so that, maybe, he'd notice what time it was and come home at a reasonable hour.

I swear, if I ever left him, he would move into his University office and would never leave, lost in a world of insects with no human contact.

People didn't understand why I loved him. He's a good man. His job doesn't pay that great, but his heart is in the right place. He does truly love me. It's just his way to lose track of everything else when he becomes immersed in his work. He isn't a knight in shining armor type, but he is a good guy.

I was just about to send him a text, thinking that we could meet for dinner and, maybe, make it into a date night. As I brought my cell phone to life, a scream broke through the routine noises of the Xanthco office.

People rushed toward the elevator as one of the downstairs secretaries nearly fell out of the tiny space holding a wounded shoulder. Blood flowed through her fingers, making short streams down her white blouse until it eventually absorbed as a red stain in the fabric.

"Help me! They're killing each other!" she yelled all at once. Her words were hard to understand because they came out so quickly that they blended together as one.

"What's happening?" and "Who did this?" were some of the questions my coworkers fired back as they surged toward the woman.

I dialed the extension for the first floor to see what was going on. Cradling the phone to my ear, I listened to it ring. It rang about eight times and eventually went to voicemail. I hung up and was about to punch in 911, but a voice stayed my hand.

"911 is down!" came a voice from the crowd.

"What?! How can that happen?" shouted another excitedly.

"It said all their responders were busy and to try again!"

Betsy Wellington and Mitzie Todd tried to get her back into the elevator. "My car is just outside," encouraged Mitzie.

Having none of that, the woman shrugged off their helping hands and slipped back through the crowd. I took my eyes off of her as I redialed the front receptionist desk to see what is going on.

"We need to get you to the hospital," Betsy pleaded.

"I'm not going back down there! They're all crazy!" she said, picking up a Swingline stapler and holding it menacingly in her good hand.

The phone line for the front desk just rang and rang before going to voicemail. I left a brief message explaining that we needed help and replaced the receiver in its cradle.

"Everyone!" boomed a loud voice from the back of the floor. "There's something on the TV. I think something's going on!"

All eyes turned that direction. One of the local Pittsburgh newscasters was speaking and the image on the screen behind him looked like pandemonium. Police, decked out in riot gear, were trying to push back an angry mob who were coming at them with gusto.

As the sound turned up the reporter said, "No one knows why the mob is rioting. There was no sign of any protests, but angry groups are breaking into violence all over the city. We even have reports of people attacking each other in the suburbs and surrounding areas. The hospitals are flooded with wounded. The local authorities are asking that all people stay inside and lock their doors. Do not go outside for any reason." He said all of this with that cool, detached look newscasters get when speaking of wars or disasters. He continued, "The news wire is confirming that this

10

outbreak of criminal violence is happening in many other cities as well as..."

I grabbed Ned Fisher's arm and said, "We have to see what is going on!"

My momentum propelled him toward the front windows. They provided a clear view of the parking lot below. The area was full of cars neatly pulled into each space, but there wasn't a soul around.

We looked around in frustration. I had expected to see angry crowds pounding at the doors, but it was completely still. Not a single person stirred outside.

"Let's go downstairs and see what's happening," Ned suggested, starting off toward the elevator.

I followed his lead, enlisting a large intern to join us. I didn't know his name. He was a young man who had just joined us at Xanthco a few days ago.

We entered the elevator and faced out. Most of the office workers gathered around the television, but a few women were assisting the wounded woman from the lower level who was now lying on the floor.

The doors closed and we felt that familiar falling sensation. As the elevator descended, the Muzak playing over the speakers had a calming effect as the illuminated floor display switched from a three to a two. I felt my nerves relax as we slowed to a stop at the ground floor. The doors opened on the first floor, noisily sliding on their tracks.

The scene before us was one straight from a nightmare. Red blood covered everything. The walls were literally dripping with it. People and body parts were lying in heaps all about. Some coworkers were on their knees feeding on the prone people, while others just wandered about looking disoriented.

A group of five people were eating the front receptionist on the floor directly in front of us. The tone signaling the arrival of the elevator sounded, *"Ding,"* and all eyes turned on us.

I couldn't do anything. I was totally unprepared for the scene before me. I tried to scream but it caught in my throat. Ned immediately started hitting the button for the third, floor. As the cannibals got to their feet, rather unsteadily, they began to slowly shuffle in our direction.

I was frozen in place while Ned was still hitting buttons; having given up on the third he repeatedly struck the one for the second floor. The young intern leaned close to Ned and calmly punched the close door button. The bell sounded its warning as the door began its slow journey closed. We were going to make it. The door would close on this nightmare.

I was beginning to exhale in relief when a blood-soaked hand reached around the tiny opening and halted its progress.

Chapter 3
Henry
Today

I was starting into my second hour of watching the news feeds. The people were sickened all over the place; mostly in cities, but it was happening all around the world. The only concrete connection was that; transmission was by infected people biting others who were not infected. The whole newscast seemed so surreal.

The newscaster sipping from her cup of coffee reminded me. "Mel!" I thought, snapping back to reality. I raced for the cordless phone. Melissa had wanted to ditch our landline, but I couldn't let go of the comfort of a home phone just yet. Checking the answering machine, I saw it flashing one new message. Pressing the play button, a little too hard, I listened to my recorded voice speak our greeting.

"No one is home right now; but, after the beep, leave us a message and we will get back to you as soon as we can."

The machine beeped and my heart skipped a beat, ready to snap into action as soon as she gave the word.

"This is a message from Congressman John R. Noble. Are you aware that the Democrats want to remove God from the classroom..."

I leaned my index finger on the stop button. When prompted, I deleted the message. The red, flashing light winked out and did not return. I picked up the hand device and pushed talk. There was no sound. Not even the rhythmic buzzing of the disconnected signal. I replaced the phone in its charging station and sighed.

Remembering my cell phone, I reached into my left front pants pocket and fished around. Where had I put it? The pit of my stomach seemed to twist. It was in the car.

As I approached the front door, I could hear Mrs. Crawford still thumping at the entrance. Her attempts were half-hearted. She might be losing interest, but if I were 82 and had recently lost a hand, I wouldn't be too patient either.

Looking through the peephole, I could see my neighbor. The floral housecoat she wore stuck to her bloated form by a congealed coating of blood, creating a disgusting caricature Having a background in biology, I was well aware that if a bite spread the disease then it was quite probable that it could be transferred by any bodily fluid. A bite, drool, or even a scratch could be the vehicle, whatever this virus or bacteria would use to propagate itself. All that viruses want to do is to create the next generation of their species.

Even though Mrs. Crawford was small and old, she could be extremely dangerous. I abandoned the idea of a frontal assault on the geriatric corpse and looked out some of the other windows on the ground level. This way I could narrow down my options.

There was a sparse scattering of undead ambling about the neighborhood. I can't believe I was so distracted that a few hours ago I thought these walking corpses were hung-over college students. The way they lurched and, in some cases, were missing a limb or were dragging a leg behind, how oblivious was I? It could have been the lack of sleep or, maybe, the idea that I thought I was in trouble with my wife.

At that moment, I saw the door across the street open and Jim and Marcy's teenage daughter, Jen, walked into view. Dressed for a jog, she had headphones in her ears. She appeared not to notice the dead reacting to her presence as she stretched her hamstrings by touching her fingers to her toes. The music she was listening to must have blocked the sounds of the zombies as they shambled toward her as quickly as their broken forms would allow. I watched helplessly as she straightened, an undead postal worker, her mail bag still slung over his shoulder, approached her from the front. His mouth opened wide, stained red like a six-year-old at a spaghetti dinner. Jen lifted her hands to her head, screaming. She was pumping her legs up and down, shocked and terrified, unsure what to do.

Just as the mail carrier looked like he had her, another jogger, this one undead, took her from behind and planted her, face first, on the lawn. Blood arched out as plague-covered teeth rent flesh from the young girl. I was about to lower the blind when I noticed Mrs. Crawford's bulk cross the road to join the feast.

This is my chance, I thought as I sprinted for the front door. With the zombies distracted, I might be able to get to the car.

Back on the first floor, a quick peek through the spy hole in the

14

door confirmed my belief. I swung the door open and fast-walked around the puddle left from my neighbor's missing limb. I went quickly and quietly to the car. Recovering the phone from the passenger seat, I hastily made my way back to the house. Stealing a glance across the street, I could see that the undead were enjoying their feast. Jen had bought me the time I needed to gain a possible connection to my wife. She had paid with her life, but it wasn't my fault. She was the one who had neglected to watch the TV this morning. She was the one who chose to isolate her senses with loud music. In a way, she had deliberately hampered her chances for survival. *Take that mom! Who said TV was bad for you?*

I closed the door and slammed the deadbolt home with a satisfying click. As I tiptoed around the puddle of my neighbors' congealed blood, I pushed the power button on to wake up my phone. No connection again. The news station had mentioned that cell towers were at capacity, as people tried to contact loved ones. Maybe this was the problem. I slid the cell phone into its usual pocket and wandered into the kitchen. My stomach growled as I poured milk on my cold cereal. Fetching a glass of orange juice and spoon, I took my meal into the living room to check for any updates on the situation.

They were showing live footage of hoards of zombies attacking people on the streets of various cities. Police fired indiscriminately into crowds, trying to contain the violence. A news ticker ran at the bottom of the screen telling all people to stay in their home, not to go outside. It said that the country was under martial law. The weirdest thing was that it included a line saying that the president was alive and well in an undisclosed location. What did I care if he was alive or not? That jerk was probably in a bunker sipping champagne and eating pheasant under glass while I ate Corn Flakes and was being protected by a thin layer of vinyl siding. And I voted for that jerk!

After eating, I went upstairs to our bedroom and sat on my side of the bed. My eyes strayed to the nightstand where a picture of Melissa, beside the shore of Lake Erie, leaned in its stand. She loved that lake. We took pilgrimages to see it at least twice a year. It was our dream to buy a home near the water and retire there.

Mel was out there somewhere. Was she alone? Was she safe? I knew these thoughts were destructive. I had little control over the situation. I lay back onto the bedspread, enveloped in its warmth and comfort. We had just redecorated this room. It took the entire weekend. She helped me strip the wallpaper and then we had painted it a blue-gray. I can still remember her look of terror as she knocked the can of paint off the ladder. It took us hours to get it completely off of the hardwood floors. She always had a smile on her face. Everything would always be ok when I looked into her beautiful, confident eyes.

A scream woke me with a start. The room was still lit by the late afternoon sunlight pouring through the thin window sheers. I sat up and scanned the room for danger. Another call of terror sounded outside. I moved to the window and pulled the thin material of the shears to one side. Mel had insisted that we cover the bedroom windows with curtains, even though I insisted that the angle of visibility wouldn't allow anyone to see us naked. She didn't listen. To be on the safe side, she had hung the material.

Jim was on his front porch trying to hold a struggling Marcy from running onto the lawn as their daughter, Jen, walked slowly toward them, dragging a bloody leg behind. Marcy fought with all her might to run to the animated corpse that formerly was her daughter. She screamed again and I could see, even from across the street, that her face was wet from tears. My neighbor's attempts to hold his wife back failed as she slipped past, ducking under his last futile attempt to grab ahold of her.

Marcy ran, crying, right up to her now-deceased daughter and enveloped her in a comforting embrace. Jen dipped her head and, from what I can imagine, tore out a chunk of her mother's throat. Blood sprayed into the air as the wounded woman dropped to the ground. Jen followed her, dropping to stained knees and continuing the gory feast. I diverted my eyes to Jim, who recoiled in horror, retreating to the open doorway. There he stood, supporting himself on the frame and lowering his head, shoulders visibly heaving as his body racked with sobs.

As he stood there, his daughter lifted her head and started to rise. Jim stood still, not noticing. As his reanimated daughter unsteadily stepped over her prone mother and approached her father, I struggled with the latch on the top of our window. Just as

16

I pushed it open, I could hear a man's voice pleading for Jim to go inside.

"That isn't your daughter anymore, Jim," said the voice. "Get inside and lock the door."

I joined the voice. "Listen to him, Jim. You need to get inside."

Jim's head slowly swiveled up, bringing the lurching corpse into view. After a brief hesitation, he slowly entered the house and, with a last look at his undead daughter, he reluctantly closed the door.

The corpse that I had known as the girl next door raised her blood-soaked hands and began to slap at the closed portal. I leaned out the window and looked to the left, seeing another of my neighbors, Dean Walker, looking back at me from his second-floor window.

There was silence for a moment. We connected. We both knew that the world was coming apart. It was a bond that two humans have when all else is lost. He became distracted and turned, looking inside his house a brief instant, then swung back towards me.

"I have guns," he offered, then, disappeared inside, closing the window behind him.

I didn't know what to do. I kept looking over at Dean's house waiting to see if he would return. I felt very alone. Looking back across the street, I saw that Marcy's corpse was now being devoured by three more of the creatures. They made growling noises as they fought for a good position to dine. The sounds were drawing more of their kind to the feast. But the corpse that was Jen continued pawing at the entrance to her home.

Most people would have turned away from the scene; but, as a trained scientist, I could keep my discomfort compartmentalized and take this moment to study this small segment of their ecology. They were like lions jockeying for a place to feed after the alpha male eats the choicest parts. The strange thing about lions is that the females were the ones who actually hunted, for the most part. Another similarity is that feeding is a hazardous time.

The undead ate their victim slower than a pride of lions would have, but they exhibited some of the same basic habits: growling if another encroached too close to their chosen spot and occasionally swatting or facing off over a choice piece of flesh. After about an hour they began to disperse. In the end, there were about twelve of the creatures that fed on the woman. Many walked away with some part or chunk of the flesh to eat as they left, gnawing on their prize as they lurched, probably in search of another living being.

Only Jen stayed behind, door covered with gore, as she tried to gain entrance. As I scanned the horizon, I could see that smoke was billowing into the sky from multiple areas. Sirens wailed from distant emergency vehicles and the sound of gunshots popped from a myriad of directions.

It was early evening now. I checked my phone and saw that there was still no connection. Worrying about Melissa, I cautiously walked downstairs to check the news. I wondered if it was a localized event and if the police or the National Guard were working to get this under control.

I pushed the power button on the remote and was immediately greeted with a newscaster, dressed in a rumpled gray suit, reporting on the very subject. I didn't recognize the man, but he looked visibly shaken, his hair in disarray and his eyes were open too wide. A ticker at the bottom of the screen scrolled through a variety of safety zones.

"The whole metropolitan area remains under martial law as the strange outbreak sweeps the entire region," he said while wringing his hands over the stack of papers in front of him. "Emergency staff are currently in the field to be joined shortly by National Guard units. A government spokesperson assures us that containment of the strange occurrences of manic homicide should occur shortly and that all persons should stay indoors and away from windows. Do not attempt to go outdoors for any reason." As the harried journalist continued, I decided to turn to a more reliable source of information; the Internet. I typed into the Google search window the words *"zombie outbreak"* and immediately got hundreds of thousands of hits.

Not knowing where to start, I clicked on the top website and the screen filled with pictures of undead attacking people on the street. The header read, *"It is actually happening! The dead are walking and attacking the living."* I spent the next hour pouring over site after site of eyewitness reports of undead biting living people and how the living people turned into more undead. Theories ranged from the end of times to a virus, cosmic

18

rays, and one even speculated that it was a Communist plot.

Mel had insisted I open a Twitter account a few years ago. We even spent a few weeks worth of evenings having brief conversations with people on that social media site. Even though I spent very little time on Twitter, I had hundreds of followers. Many were trying get rich schemes or were pretending they were someone who was famous, but that just added to the fun.

I logged on to my account and the feed was all about the zombie outbreak. People were telling anyone who was reading where to go for a safe place. Others were warning about safe zones that were overrun by the undead. Many were retweets about places that they had never been. They were all just trying to help.

Amid the directions were tweets accusing the government of tampering with biological weapons and other equally absurd accusations. The feed flew by so fast it was hard to read. Every time it refreshed there were fifty to a hundred new tweets. I logged off the site and went to a new page. This website offered a long list of things to do to stay safe and survive the outbreak.

Keep all lights off and fill the bathtub with water were at the top of the list. Shave your head and wear tight clothes so the zombies can't grab you easily were other useful ideas. I thought some of the best were to hole up in Masonic Temples. The reasoning was that they had food but little to no windows. I thought a prison might be better, but I didn't want to have to create a login and password to leave a comment on the site.

A siren rushing past my house brought me to my senses. The man on the television was telling his viewers to isolate anyone who has had an encounter with the infected people. He said to keep the sick in a secure area or to bind them if they had nowhere to secure them.

I couldn't believe this was happening. It was like a dream, and it was certainly a dream I wanted to wake up from. A shot sounded from across the street. I went to the window and saw Jen, still on the porch. She was soon joined by the upper half of her mother, who was scratching at the kick plate at the bottom of the door. I had a bad feeling about what the shot meant, but wholeheartedly hoped I was wrong.

Chapter 4
Melissa
Yesterday

To our horror, the elevator door began to open once again. The hand, holding the left door, slid down, smearing its after-image. When the opening was fully revealed I saw before me Joe, one of our department heads. A piece of his cheek had been torn away, revealing muscle and some of his jawbone. His eyes were white and lifeless and his mouth worked open and closed as he unsteadily started towards our intern. The volunteer pushed his superior, but the bloody man grabbed ahold of the young man's wrist and dragged him to the opening of the elevator.

As the two men locked in struggle, the other cannibalistic coworkers neared the door. Ned and I each snapped out of our first shock and sped into action. I pulled off my heels as my friend side-kicked the nearest threat. The predator, barely able to walk, flew back, taking two of the others with it. I mirrored his technique, sending mine into the pile. The door warning tone sounded once again and the pair rolled toward each other.

Joe and the intern crashed against the back wall of the elevator and slid to the ground as the doors met and the lift began its ascent. We both spun on the demented attacker who was wrestling with the young man on the floor. Ned and I each grabbed ahold of our crimson-coated boss as the elevator came to a stop. The doors opened on the second floor, revealing a room full of chaos.

The bell rang as Ned and I froze, looking out at the unbelievable scene. Workers fought other workers, some in pants and others in skirts. Screams of pain erupted from all directions at once. People were pleading for help while others cried like children. The air was heavy with the metallic smell of spilled blood. It seemed to cover almost everything. From toppled cubical walls to scattered paper and other debris, nothing seemed untainted by the red liquid.

Although we were witness to the ghastly event, it seemed that no one noticed us. They were all caught in life or death struggles of their own, many rolling on the ground battling one or more gore-covered attackers.

We watched one very thin man, I believe his name was Bert,

being taken down by three of the crazed maniacs. He shrieked in defeat as his back hit the carpet. Mercifully, his foes blocked our view of his end.

Ned let go of the man we were holding away from the intern so he could hit the door close button. The doors immediately began to slide closed once again. I pulled a little harder on the back of the boss's stained shirt, but the vicious, life-giving liquid caused my hands to slip. The department head lost interest on the intern's face and turning, bit him on the forearm.

The pinned young man howled in pain as his attacker's mouth tore a large chunk of flesh from his appendage. His skin stretched to its limit before tearing in a jagged line. The beast on top of him seemed to lose focus for a moment, slowly chewing his meal. I seized the opportunity and the back of his wet shirt again. I was able to throw Joe off of the young man by heaving with all of my strength.

The infected man stood and, as the doors met, sounding another chime, he looked back at his last opponent. Then, swallowing, he turned toward me. His milky eyes looking at mine set the hairs on the back of my head on end. I stepped backward against the wall, feeling immediately cornered. The former floor head shadowed my movement and was on me at once. I held him back, pushing with all of my might.

My hands wrapped around his throat, locking my elbows in full extension. His collar was sticky from the partially drying blood. Even though I held him at arm's length, the fetid stench coming from his breath brought on a mouthful of bile.

Even though Joe's movements were slow, his strength remained. If Ned wasn't holding the crazed man's shoulders, I wouldn't have been able to keep him at bay for any amount of time. Even with my coworker's help, Joe was getting closer to me by the second. My arms, now bent, shook with the strain of the struggle. Sensing that his next meal was near, the maniac's stained mouth opened and closed in anticipation. White teeth shone as a large gob of spittle flowed over his lip, hanging like a pendulum and spinning in slow circles. Just as I was about to give in to the pressure, the chime sounded again.

Several hands joined my friend's at the back of my attacker. Our embrace broke as they flung him through the opening and onto the floor. Joe moaned in rage at being denied another bite as my friends pinned him against the carpet.

Ned and I turned our attention to the intern who was holding his wounded arm. Rivulets of his blood dripped on the elevator floor. We each grabbed him under his arms and hoisted him to his feet. The youth was so unsteady he felt like dead weight. We leaned him against the wall beside the elevator and, as the doors started to close, Ned reached around and pushed the black plastic flap, opening the doors once again.

Retrieving a stack of files, he wedged them under the nearest door, holding the flap in, and pressed the emergency stop button. "We don't want that thing going back down and bringing more of them upstairs," he said, answering the unspoken question. "We need to block the stairwell."

I nodded while taking a pull on my inhaler. I was still too winded to respond in any other way. We sprinted to the door leading to the fire escape. Ten feet out, I could see the door beginning to open. Ned must have seen it also, because we both quickened our pace to a sprint. We threw our bodies against the widening gap, reversing its direction and slamming it closed.

Looking around for help, I found that we had become isolated from the rest of the group. As the crazy workers from downstairs shoved hard, having found the push bar, the door inched in. We leaned back with all of our strength and the latch clicked again.

"They must be accidentally hitting the push bar," he reasoned. "I can't believe that they can reason how it works. They seem so oblivious."

"There are too many of them," I breathed between ragged breaths. "We have to block the door somehow."

I could hear change jingling as Ned fished around in his pockets with his back to the door. Retrieving a handful of change, he began shoving groups of the coins into the crack near the latch.

"What are you doing?" I asked, thinking he had gone mad.

"It's an old college trick. If I get enough change tightly in the seam between the door and the jamb, it will hold the door closed. We used to trap freshmen in their dorm room this way. It will hold really well."

When he had finished, we gradually released our pressure, being careful not to trust it too fully at first. Hands continued to assault the portal from the other side, but it remained tightly closed.

"See if you can get some guys to watch the door. I'll stay here to keep an eye on it."

With a last look at the coins in the jamb, I hurried to where I had last seen a cluster of people gathered. I could hear men struggling, and assumed this was a group of men holding Joe down.

I found some people near my cubical. One of the women was on the phone, while the others stood silently waiting.

"No luck," she voiced in a low, disappointed tone. "The line just went dead."

"The whole network is down!" another stated lowering her cell phone from her ear.

"Keep trying!" others encouraged, keeping hope alive.

I recruited two of the bigger men to help with the door and sent another to check on the intern and watch the elevator.

Standing for a moment, I tried to collect myself. Everyone was afraid, but none of them had a clue of what was happening beneath their feet. Just as I was coming to grips with the situation, the man I had sent to the elevator returned.

"There was no one there," he reported.

"What about the doors."

"They were closed," he answered, his eyes shying to the ground.

"Crap!" I screamed in frustration, sprinting to the area to verify his story. Not only had we lost control of the elevator, but my shoes were in there.

The floor indicator illuminated the first floor light. I immediately changed direction, stocking covered feet sliding on the carpet. As my toes gained traction, I sped to the last place I had seen Ned. He was still at the door speaking with the two men.

"The elevator is on the first floor. We have to stop it," I warned as I slid to a stop.

The four of us returned to the elevator. It was still at the lower level, having not moved. The white-collar workers began kicking cubicles apart and placing them against the door. After a few layers of them they stacked file cabinets, followed by desks.

Our hopes fell as the indicator light changed from the first to the second floor. We began stacking anything we could to add weight to the barrier. Some of the other workers joined us, finishing our defense.

When we completed it, Ned and I decided to survey our situation. The elevator hadn't moved in a while, so with our hastily built barricade in place I once again felt a small amount of relief. Exhausted, but the need of safety outweighed the want for rest.

Leaving a small group to watch the elevator, we wandered about the floor. Some of the men had bound Joe with computer wires. Wrapped securely with the cables winding about him he looked like a mummy, but he still thrashed about, making feints at anyone nearby. The woman from the first-floor had also been bound after biting two other people. Her mouth, covered with blood and she was acting just like Joe. The intern who had been in the elevator with us was nowhere in sight.

Ned gathered everyone who was available so we could tell them what we had seen. Due to the confusion, many didn't even know that we had gone down there at all. The entire group remained totally silent, drinking in all the details of our tale. The information was grim, but they all had a stake in it, so they gave us their undivided attention.

When we had finished, one of the computer techs named John said, "It sounds like a zombie apocalypse." All heads swiveled his way, "You know, *Night of the Living Dead*?"

The crowd began to murmur among themselves.

Chapter 5
Melissa
Still Yesterday

"I don't think the dead have come back to life," I said, fully confident of the statement. It would be absurd to think that the dead could be walking around. I remembered that old black and white movie and had to almost laugh.

"Dead-looking human beings, biting and eating other humans. Where have I gone wrong?" the computer specialist shot back sarcastically.

"This isn't some B rated movie," I countered. "This is a viral outbreak, maybe a plague that manifests homicidal tendencies." I could see Ned edging his way closer to my antagonist.

"What kind of plague causes people to want to eat other people?"

"My husband had me read a paper on a parasite which makes mice try to have cats eat them. The parasite takes control of the mouse and makes it lose all fear of cats, forcing it to literally crawl into the mouth of a cat." I paused for effect. "This doesn't seem so very different to me."

Ned led John away from the gathering as I answered the few remaining questions. I could see the two speaking somewhat animatedly but thankfully, in hushed tones. John's pudgy face was scarlet as he stated his case, but Ned was getting through to him.

One thing about being trapped in an office is that we may gossip and backstab, but we know how to organize and work as a team. The group of about twenty people began to break off into teams. Some gathered any type of foodstuff for rationing, while others began creating makeshift weapons. We had TV watchers, 911 callers and a small division of people e-mailing from smartphones.

The floor came alive once again. People who could possibly be infected were closely monitored, while the known infected were confined to the floor manager's office, bound and watched to make sure they didn't spread the disease anymore.

It was when we tried to open the big boss's office door that we found him. He had barricaded himself inside. It took three of our largest men to push their way into his office. There, we found him crying, half drunk on a bottle of bourbon. He was lying in the fetal position, his necktie pulled loose and his black suit crumpled like he had slept in it. The effects of the alcohol turned his usually overly tanned skin slightly gray. As he rose unsteadily to his feet, I casually looked him over as well as possible for any sign of possible infection. He looked free of bites, so I chalked it off as being ill from the strong drink. The lousy rat had blocked himself in his office, resigning us to fend for ourselves.

His name was Thaddeus Wentworth, Division Manager and head of Xanthco's northwest district. We always thought he was a good leader until now. It's funny. Until you really need a leader, you never know just who would be best for the job. I was just a cubical jockey, but it seemed most of the workers were reporting to me. Even Ned seemed to defer to my decisions.

I'm not so sure I was the greatest person to lead my coworkers, but it was my new job. Everyone seemed to walk right around Thaddeus and asked for my approval of even the smallest of matters.

Some of the administrative assistants wanted to make help signs for the windows out of pieces of printer paper. Even though I knew you'd probably never be able to see it through the heavily tinted glass, I approved the idea, even encouraged it. I wanted to keep everyone busy, keep their hopes alive and to give them purpose. I approved many silly ideas to this end. I remembered reading a book by Viktor Frankl a long time ago, a Jew who survived a Nazi death camp.

He outlined how many of the survivors who were driven by having a purpose, lived. Some of the people who died seemed to lack this motivation. They gave up. I didn't know if Frankl's theory was sound, but I sure wasn't going to discard any ideas without trying first. We did have people who gave into their despair. Some women and a few men just sat and cried. There were the ones who refused to help, sending texts and continuously dialing and redialing phone numbers of loved ones. But I was successful at motivating most of our group to take part in small tasks to keep them busy.

Watching one of these workers, fingers flying over her QWERTY keyboard, made me think of Henry. I needed to find out if he was ok. I rifled through my purse and pulled out my iPhone. The signal was good so I tried to call him. The line immediately went to voicemail, so I warned him about the viral outbreak, or whatever the news was calling it and told him to get in a safe place. After telling him, I loved him I hung up and sent a text restating the same information.

You have to understand. My husband is a brilliant entomologist; but outside of his field, he's oblivious. He can barely use his cell phone. And as far as being observant, he walks around with his head in the clouds. Don't get me wrong. I love him beyond anything, but he probably was going to miss the message as well as the text I just sent. He just wouldn't see them.

While leaning back in a desk chair, I sent a couple more texts to his phone, as well as some friends'. Neither one of us had any immediate family, so that limited my concerns. No one returned any of my texts. It was about this time that I felt how totally exhausted I was. I looked at the time on my cell phone and saw that it was after three in the morning. We had been at this for over twelve hours with no stop. The mood in the office had also changed. There were no more small jobs to do. Most people were sitting around slumped in their chairs. Some were even lying on the floor. A few looked like they were asleep.

I conferred with Ned and we came up with a sleeping order and set some of our coworkers who weren't asleep to the first watch. I grabbed an old sweater that I kept in my cubicle and used it as a makeshift pillow, covering my upper half with my suit jacket. My feet were a little cold, but all in all, I was decently comfortable.

I didn't sleep as much as rest. Half awake, I found it impossible to actually slumber. Sure, my eyes closed, but I never totally dozed off.

After about two hours, I opened my eyes and gave up. I pulled on my suit jacket and relieved one of the people on the internet. While I was trying to sleep, the network had come back online, so I scanned pages at the CDC and WHO. Both confirmed that they were working to contain this outbreak and gave safety information. There was nothing we didn't already know, but they did confirm that a bite spread the sickness. People should avoid or restrain anyone bitten.

There was also a disturbing paragraph outlining that a severe blow to the head was the only way to kill one of the people stricken with the disease. The federal government imposed martial law. It went on to exonerate anyone who killed one of the infected for the sole purpose of defending oneself or other innocents. This strange legalization of killing through head trauma repeated on every site I visited. Many times in large, bold print and repeated over and over.

After about an hour, I gave up. I called Hank again with the same results. I sent a few more texts describing what I had read with the strange belief that the more messages I sent him, the better the likelihood he would take notice. My poor, self-absorbed, mate. I needed to get to him and maybe even to protect him from himself.

He kind of lives in a bubble, although he does have a certain rugged quality. Being a professor of bugs, as I like to call him, he isn't at all squeamish. He also spends a lot of time outdoors, many times outside of the United States searching for specimens. But he is alone so much and depends on me too much. In many ways, he's like a super smart child. A leader, he is not. The door to the stairs was holding and still being watched by two of the staff. Two others were hastily assigned to the elevator. Although it had gone between floors a few times, still hadn't stopped on ours. The main threat was that we had people who had full-blown cases of the disease and some who were just in the infected stage. The latter, we placed in a conference room, which was the only other room available. The other room was Thaddeus's office, which was where we had the fully infected people bound. We couldn't admit someone who was just potentially sick to that room. It wouldn't be right, so we used the mostly-glass conference room and just had to make that do.

One of the workers bitten by the first-floor girl was being bound now. There wasn't a struggle. She seemed unaware of her situation as two burly fellows tied her up. In moments, she would be transferred to the office as a more secure holding area. It made me shiver, thinking that she, in a short while, would become a violent, flesh-eating, predator. Thankfully, many of my coworkers would sleep through her removal from the glass room. At least her friends would since they were all sleeping at the moment.

Sleep finally took me, leaning back in my chair. One moment I was resting my eyes and the next I was sound asleep.

The noise of the elevator doors opening brought me out of my dream, the signal tone sounded, as if to beckon new passengers, soon after. I don't know how long I was out but my neck ached as I leaned forward. I put a hand on the offending area and tried to rub the knots out of the strained muscles as my mind slowly began to focus.

My moment of disorientation shifted to panic when I figured out what had awakened me. Unseen hands pawed and pushed at the barricade we had built to block the elevator's entrance. Desks and file cabinets shifted as the infected on the other side struggled to gain entrance. The people watching from this side rushed to secure the defense as a file cabinet crashed to the carpet. The racket, as well as possibly seeing glimpses of healthy human flesh, made the occupants of the elevator work harder at clearing a way in. Moans erupted from the tiny enclosure, which were immediately joined by ones at the stairs. Both entryways literally rattled with renewed effort from our foes.

I ran to the pile holding them back and searched for a way to reinforce the slowly moving blockade. It was giving in. Our efforts were merely going to slow them down.

The rest of my coworkers joined us in a semicircle around the barricade. Weapons in hand, we had no choice other than to fight. Metal bars, originally to support cubicle walls, were held like baseball bats and other crude cudgels were brandished as well.

As we waited, I heard one woman speaking to someone, possibly her husband or child, telling them that she loved them. This gave me an idea. My phone was still in my hand. I woke the device and hit the call button. Henry's phone began to ring.

Chapter 6
Henry

Drawing the curtains closed, I jumped as my pocket vibrated, joined by the sound of AC/DC's song, "Thunderstruck." It was Melissa. Hurriedly fishing around in my pocket, I found the animated device and pushed the answer button. As I brought it to my ear, I could hear the sound of static. It was probably a poor connection.

"Hello, Mel?" I asked in a rush.

Her voice was faint and garbled with static. "Hank? Are you ok?" Relief flooded my body. I literally fell back into the chair by the window.

"I'm fine, Honey. Where are you?" I asked as fast as I could get it out.

"I'm at work." I could make out over the crackling. "I'm ok."

"Stay in a safe place," I said. "I'm going to come and get you."

"But they..." I heard what I thought could have been a crash and the line went dead.

My phone had four bars and data and the display told me I had twenty-seven messages as well as nine voice messages.

I listened and read each one, looking for clues to how Melissa was faring. Almost everyone was asking me to call or text her. She said they were trapped at work with infected people outside trying to get in and that they were waiting for the police.

A part of me was in euphoria. My wife was ok. She was alive. I could barely contain myself. But there was also the dread. What if something happened? I took another peek out of my front window. From the look of Jim's front door, I surmised that the undead weren't the best at breaking down barriers, so if she stayed barricaded in Mel would be just fine, but if there were enough zombies? I had to stop my thought process there. She would be fine. I had to find a way to get there. The sunlight outside was fading, but another light caught my eye. The light was on in my car. The door was standing wide open.

"Crap!" I said loudly. I must have left it open when I went out to get my phone. The light was dim, but if I went out soon, maybe the car would still start.

In a frenzy, I searched for things I might need. I needed a weapon. Melissa wasn't fond of guns and in this sleepy college town, I had never felt the need to acquire one. That sure would change if we got out of this mess. The best thing I could find was a butcher knife; the kind that looked like a little ax. I wasn't so sure of it as a weapon, so I also grabbed the biggest knife I could find. Carrying a blade in each hand, I resumed my search. I stuffed some granola bars in my back pocket and snatched a bottle of water out of the fridge. Juggling the two knives and the water, I discarded the bottle, leaving it on the counter in favor of having two hands to fight with.

I thought of grabbing my jacket but seeing it in front of the door soaked in the dried blood puddle made my choice for me. It was probably welded to the tiles anyway.

There was enough dusky light to still see pretty well. I checked all sides of my house for any animated neighbors and, finding none, I felt compelled to make a try for it. The light in my car's interior was dim, but still shining, so that also bolstered my confidence. Jen and Marcy's torso were still across the street, so I would have to make this quick.

The blood in the doorway was dry, so I didn't have to worry about slipping. The congealed pool actually offered a modicum of traction, so I unlocked the deadbolt and moving as fast as stealth would allow I made my way to the yawning car door. I looked in the back seat before entering so I wouldn't have any surprises. Dropping the knives to the passenger seat, I closed the door, being careful to let the door latch slowly to minimize the sound.

The key slid smoothly into the ignition and I involuntarily held my breath as I turned it. The motor made a cranking sound as it struggled to start. In desperation, I turned the key to the off position and tried it again. Nothing. It made the same cranking noise that it made before. It just wouldn't catch. I looked in the rearview mirror and saw that Jen was halfway across the lawn and nearing the street. Her mother's torso, propelling her half body with her hands and arms, was following at a slower pace. The noise had also attracted others. At least two more zombies were ambling toward my car from various directions. In desperation, I tramped on the gas to see if giving it more fuel might do the trick. Nothing.

A hand slapped against the driver's side window. The face of Mrs. Crawford flattened against the glass, jaws working as she tried to find an entrance. Trails of drool followed her mouth's movements as another undead struck the car from the other side. Trying to look nonchalant, I pushed the button engaging the door locks as another joined Mrs. Crawford on her side of the vehicle. What I had thought was a modicum of safety was actually a trap. I was exposed to the creatures, but sheltered for the time being.

I returned my attention to the car. Turning the key with all my strength did no more than any of my previous attempts, but I tried it two more times, nonetheless.

As the depleted battery made its last gasps, my heart dropped. I was a failure. I had spent my life with my head in the clouds. I had no friends and barely knew my neighbors. I hadn't been an attentive husband, but when I was about to make up for my past misdeeds, I had let my wife and myself down. I had failed.

Picking up the knives, I pondered the end. I didn't want to become like those creatures out there. There were speculations that the dead only rose after being attacked by the zombies and bitten by them. Maybe if someone died naturally they wouldn't rise again.

Faces and entire bodies pressed against the vehicle as I contemplated my demise. Mrs. Crawford's stump of an arm drew abstract images in blood red and puss yellow. It was almost as if she didn't notice that the appendage was gone. It was only an inconvenience instead of a crippling wound.

The car's gentle rocking would have felt soothing if it weren't for the things rocking it. The squeal of their flesh sliding against the glass was unnerving. Then came the blast.

I was lost in my morass when the first shot sounded. It was soon followed by a second, then a third. The zombies lost interest in me and focused on the sounds of the attacker. Another blast and then another, the undead seemed like they were thinning out. A man rushed to the passenger side of the car and slammed his hand off the glass three times rapidly.

"Come on Hank!" he called out.

I crawled over the console to the passenger door and threw it open just as another gunshot rang out into the semi-darkness. A revolver was pressed into my hand, causing me to drop one of the knives. I then watched as my neighbor, Dean, shrugged a shotgun off of his shoulder and pumped a shell into the chamber.

"Hurry up!" he ordered. "We got to get back to my place."

I followed his lead, head swiveling left to right. Dean blazed a trail towards his front door. He basically shot at anything that moved. I mimicked his style and wound up nearly shooting Mrs. Crawford's cat. The gun's recoil bucked in my hands but it felt good. It made me feel powerful.

We bolted through his door, slamming it shut so hard I think I felt the walls shake. Dean secured the locks and we both nearly swooned. The house was dark, but the faint glow of candles gave just enough illumination to see by. The drawn curtains and blinds probably blocked any of the dim illumination from escaping and giving him away.

"That was close!" he said while lowering his weapon and walking into his living room.

"Almost too close!" I answered, trying to calm my breathing while following him.

Dean slumped into a well-worn brown recliner and propped the gun against the wall behind him. I chose the end of the couch, setting the pistol on the coffee table as I sat down.

"Thank you, Dean!" I gushed. "You saved my life. I can't believe you did that!"

He just waved it off. "No thanks necessary. I was actually trying to figure out a way to talk to you and the opportunity just sprang up."

I gave him a puzzled look. "Talk to me about what?" I asked as a slow thumping began at the closed door.

"We must've missed one," he said, looking at the door. "You're a doctor, right?"

"A doctor of biology with an emphasis in entomology..." I added.

"Well, it's still the same stuff, Julie is really sick."

My first thought was, *who's Julie?* I had always believed that Dean had lived here alone. He was the crazy single guy who owned way too much camouflage. I really didn't want to tell him I wouldn't be able to help her unless she was a bug. But I couldn't do that, especially after his daring rescue. So I said, "Sure, let's have a look."

Dean turned on a small flashlight and led the way upstairs. He opened their bedroom door, turned on the light, and let me in. I was temporarily blinded by the glow since I wasn't ready for it. My first concern, as I covered my eyes to give them time to adjust, was that it was so bright it would draw undead. But my worry was for naught, as the window was covered with cardboard to prevent the light from getting out. I was very relieved to have normal illumination to aid in my examination.

A low moan issued from the bed, drawing my immediate attention. I could see his girlfriend, Julie, covered to the neck in a thick comforter. Her face was pale and covered in sweat. Eyes, twin slits, blinked rapidly as she tried to focus on me.

"When did the illness start?" I asked with my best medical doctor voice while I leaned closer to look at her drawn face.

"She got sick over night. I thought she'd really tied one on, but I have never seen a hangover that could last the entire next day. I checked on her about an hour ago and thought I had to do something soon."

I placed two fingers at her throat. The skin there was cool and clammy. I could feel her pulse through her carotid artery. I really didn't know what I was doing, but it felt very slow. I nonchalantly reached up and felt mine as a comparison. My pulse was much stronger and faster feeling. I was confident in my finding now that I had something to match hers against.

"Her pulse is a little weak," I stated with as much of a matter of fact attitude as I could. "Can you lend me the flashlight?" I asked Dean, holding out one hand, waiting.

Dean fumbled for the switch and powered the light on before placing it in my outstretched palm. His hand was shaking as he released its weight into my grasp. I then noticed the beam of light was exaggerating the shake of my own hand.

"Look straight ahead," I instructed the young woman in the bed. As I shone the light directly in her right eye, I noticed that it had a very slow reaction to the bright light in her face. In addition, the iris had very little color.

I tested both eyes several times and then asked her to follow the light. She had trouble tracking the beam as I moved it in a few

34

deliberate directions.

"Can you sit up and lean forward?" I asked, half expecting her to say she couldn't. When she began to struggle out of the cotton cocoon Dean and I assisted her with gentle hands on her back. The comforter and sheets fell forward and I could see that Julie had sweat right through the thin fabric of her muscle t-shirt.

I placed an ear against her back and asked her to breathe normally. Having to strain, I could barely distinguish her lungs operating at all. Asking her to exhale and inhale deeply produced only moderately better results. I could see that my neighbor's face bore a look of concern. His hands were folded over his chest as if praying. She was very ill and in need of a real doctor's attention.

"You can lay back down now," I soothed, replacing my hand behind her shoulders to add support. As she began to recline, one of her hands reached out and began to pull the bed cover back over her. The smell nearly knocked me over. She smelled like the dead outside. Worse yet, the bandages on her arm seemed soaked through with dried blood and what looked like puss.

"What happened to your arm?" I asked, trying to quell the tremor of fear in my voice.

"Some guy bit her last night when she was out. It isn't deep. Just a few tooth marks. I put peroxide on it and covered it with gauze after she got home." Dean said, looking me directly in the face.

He knew, or at least suspected, what was happening to his Julie. I wasn't sure, but I thought he must have smelled the wound a few moments ago. It clearly smelled of rotting flesh, just like the zombies outside.

I reached down, speaking in comforting tones, and removed the bandages. As the gauze unwound I nearly gagged. The odor was overwhelming. I unwrapped the last bit of the bandages, revealing an angry red wound. Puss spilled from at least three places where I suspect the man's teeth had broken the surface of her skin. The crimson area was totally surrounded with black, putrefying skin. Jagged lines of black radiated out across her healthy flesh like veins full of venom. Maybe they were. I was way out of my league here.

I doused the wound in more peroxide, which foamed like crazy as it hit her rotting skin, and rewrapped it in fresh bandages. I splashed some more peroxide over my hands to try to sterilize them the best the situation would allow, then dried them on a clean towel. After we tucked Julie back in bed, I motioned Dean outside. He powered the flashlight on and lead the way downstairs.

When we reached the living room, Dean turned and asked, "How is she, Hank?" His eyes were begging for good news.

"I don't know. She really is in bad shape." I lied, not wanting to have to tell him that she was on her way to becoming like the undead outside.

"Who is she?" I blurted out, not sure how to ask with any decorum.

"She's my girlfriend! We've been dating for a few months now," he responded, sounding mildly offended.

"I'm sorry, Dean," I apologized. "I just don't hear all the neighborhood gossip. I spend too much time in the lab."

My neighbor stood facing me with an odd look. After a short moment, he responded. "That's all right. I understand." Clearly, he didn't.

"We need to get her to the hospital," I said, stating what I thought was obvious.

"The news was saying something about the hospitals, but I can't remember what," he murmured. "It's probably not important."

I placed a hand on his shoulder and propelled him toward his kitchen. "Probably that they are in the safe zones. The news was saying that they have a bunch of protected areas set up and were telling people who were in trouble that they could go there." I knew that there was something else. It was something that I was forgetting. I just couldn't put my finger on it.

Dean had an attached garage, which housed a Jeep Liberty. We stuffed the back with a case of warm water and some food from his kitchen. Food, both canned and boxed, all made its way into the rear of the vehicle. It looked like we were going camping. We added some of his weapons and ammunition to the trunk and topped it off with some clean clothes. Dean had a small armory of guns. He kept pulling them out of drawers, closets, and even some places where you would never expect a firearm to dwell. One of the craziest places was a basket by the toilet.

When I asked him about it, he shrugged his shoulders and replied, "Wouldn't want to get caught by some crook while sitting

36

on the crapper! It just wouldn't be right. You're just too vulnerable there... Exposed."

I really couldn't argue with logic like that, so I just nodded and snagged a four pack of toilet paper, just in case.

Before we went upstairs, Dean handed me a box of bullets for the revolver and two things called speed-loaders. He showed me how the speed-loaders worked and I stashed them in the front pockets of my Dockers. The gun, I tucked in the front of my belt. I was feeling powerful as I looked at the gun stuffed in my pants. Macho. When my eyes met Dean's, he gave me a weird look and said something about getting a holster before I shot off something I might want to keep. I was still clueless when he turned and began ascending the stairs. I guess he meant I might discharge the pistol, hitting myself in the foot?

When we returned to the room, I noticed that the smell had gotten worse. Dean opened a drawer and tossed me what he had retrieved. It was a holster. I guess he really was worried about where I had the gun. I unbuckled my belt and went about affixing the holster. When it was situated, I had to admit that I was looking quite cowboyish. Dean was ready with his girlfriend. She was sitting on the edge of the bed with a robe wrapped around her sweat-covered form. She was looking a little worse, but I brushed that off as the strain of getting out of bed.

As I helped her on her right side, I got a look at her arm again. The bandage was totally soaked through with puss and blood. I thought about taking the time to redo the dressings but decided that the hospital could do better, so I kept my thoughts to myself. Julie moaned a little and offered only a little help as we descended the steps, her feet dragging across each carpeted platform before stepping down to the next. We held the bulk of her weight. She was almost being carried to the car.

When we had reached the bottom of the flight, Julie was almost out cold. Her head listed from side to side. Eyes closed, she did little more than feebly put one foot slowly in front of the other. My hands felt greasy from supporting her. One of my hands was under her armpit while the other was around her waist and I wondered again how this disease was passed from person to person. I could hear faint mumblings and moans mixed with her labored breathing. As her head tilted my direction, her breath caught me directly in the face. It was awful. It smelled much like her wound. I hitched her up a little higher and her face, thankfully, tilted the other way. Hey, she wasn't my girlfriend.

Assisting her to the car wasn't that hard, but getting her inside was a serious task.

Three people couldn't fit in the opening the car door allotted, so my neighbor took her in his arms and sat her on the rear seat. Julie immediately sprawled out over the entire back seat area. Dean folded her legs up and propped her feet on the little room remaining. With the door closed, we went to the trunk. We divvied the weapons into two duffel bags and dumped a little food and some water bottles in each. Ammunition followed and, when finished, we closed the back and piled in the front.

"Umm... Aren't you going to open the garage door?" He said with a sideways look.

I returned his look, but mine was laced with fear. "You don't have an electric opener?"

"Yeah," he said with a meaningful look at me. "You!"

"Who in this modern world doesn't have an electric garage door opener? What are you? A Neanderthal?" I said in total disbelief. "I'll bet you have a smart phone!"

"Just open the door," Dean shot back. He clearly wanted to get on his way to the hospital.

I slowly opened the passenger side and exited, nearly hitting my head on a snow shovel as I made my way to the single bay's opening. The door was old and probably heavy as all heck, but the worst part is that it might be loud. I had no way of knowing if there would be anyone or anything just outside the door.

Chapter 7
Melissa

I was in mid-sentence with Henry when the infected broke through. Not from the elevator area where we all gathered but from the stairwell. The two coworkers who were watching the stairs door had moved to help us with what we all thought was the most immediate problem. We never saw them coming and as they attacked from behind. We had no defense.

Our line crumpled as they bit and tore their way through. Two or three of them would drop with their prey to rip out large chunks of flesh to devour. Most of us dressed in business casual, but others wore professional clothes or uniforms dictated by their job. I watched as a custodian pulled our receptionist, Judy's, head back. Screaming, she bent to his will, only to feel his teeth penetrating her neck. Blood, pumping in rhythm with her heartbeats, spurted across the room.

A rough hand gripped my wrist and pulled. I tried to twist free, but as I spun about, I saw that it was Ned.

"We gotta get out of here!" he screamed over the chaos.

A loud crash signaled the collapse of the barricade. Some people turned and fled while others fought. All were about to die in the very near future.

"Where to?" I asked, thinking that we were trapped.

Stumped, he looked all about. "Let's try the stairs."

"They're full of infected!" I reminded, breaking his hold on my arm.

I felt a tug on my ankle and, looking down, saw Bernie, the annoying guy from the next cubical. "Help me," he said, red foam bubbling from his lips. Two infected women, having pulled his shirt apart were devouring his midsection. Intestines were spilled all over the floor. With a last tug, his weakened hand dropped off my limb. Eyes rolling up into his head, I knew he no longer needed my help.

"Not anymore," he said, indicating the door, which was hanging open. "Run!"

I tried to run, but my leg was pulled out from beneath me. I felt vise-like pressure on my ankle as I sprawled on the floor. Flipping onto my back, I looked down and saw that Bernie truly didn't need my help. It was his hand that had tripped me.

Head rearing back, the annoying man prepared to take a bite of my leg. His mouth worked the whole time, opening and closing as if in anticipation. As his head began to descend, a flash of light caught my eye as a cubical support caught my former office neighbor in the temple.

His body dropped, covering my lower legs with his bulk. I reached up, meeting a hand halfway. It pulled me free, raising me all the way to my feet. Bernie dropped face first on the carpet, its nape wicking up a spreading wet stain.

We shot through what was a battle scene. Arms reached for us, but we dodged the majority, Ned getting his suit coat snagged once by a pot-bellied computer programmer but sliding free of the jacket and leaving it behind. When we crossed the threshold of the door, we immediately started down. Slow-moving bodies lurching up filled the stairs, changing our minds and our direction.

We run up taking two steps at a stride. Ned, in the front, hit the push bar on the door, expecting it to give way to the roof. He bounced back and would have fallen down the stairs if it weren't for me catching him on his rebound.

The dead below continued their awkward march up the stairs. Their progress was slow but had a steady pace. It was already far too late to turn back. Ned struggled at the door, trying to figure out why the push bar wouldn't open the door. Giving out to frustration, he began pounding at the door.

"Go away." came a voice, muffled by the barrier.

"Let us up there or I swear I'll bring all these zombies with us!" Ned called back, as loud and threatening as he could. He punctuated it by striking the metal door with his cubical support as hard as he could.

"How do I know you haven't been bitten?" the voice asked through the door.

"These zombies may not know how to take this door off its hinges, but I sure do." He paused, shrugging his shoulders at me. It was a bluff. After a short pause for effect, Ned continued, "I'd rather leave the door in place, but you're forcing my hand."

The silence above us was drowned out by the moans from below. I could hear the infected approaching us, their feet

40

dragging across each step as they precariously ascended the stairs. The lead one came into view. It paused momentarily as it saw us. Mouth opening wide, a long line of drool ran down his chin, falling to his chest. He moaned encouragement to the ones behind as he once again lurched in our direction.

"Ned!" I urged, making him aware of our situation.

About ten steps below us, the creature's arms were reaching as he locked his eyes on this new meaty prize. There was a metallic clanking sound behind me and the door opened a crack. My coworker seized the opportunity and rammed into the door with everything he had. It flew wide, slamming against something on the other side as I bolted up the last few steps, following my friend. The natural light nearly blinded me as I crossed the threshold.

The door slammed shut and was secured with a chain and padlock. My hand immediately sought out my inhaler. Fumbling to get it out of my jacket pocket, I took a quick pull on the device then hurriedly put it back.

I had never been on the roof before. I walked to the edge, which was surrounded by a low wall. The pea gravel-covered roof was rough on my stocking-covered feet. The stones were hot but not uncomfortable. As I gazed about the wooded scenery, I had to take a moment and marvel at the beauty surrounding my place of employment.

I remembered driving here when I was first interviewing for the position, thinking it was breath-taking, that I would love to have a house in such a setting. But over time, it had just become a place where I worked. I hardly noticed the pretty oaks and maples as I mechanically drove back and forth each weekday. It would have been positively serene if it weren't for the sickened people clambering at the only door to our escape.

No one stirred about the grounds. I guessed that they were all trapped inside the building. The cars in the parking lot were all still lined in neat rows. Everything seemed very normal from the outside.

"It's beautiful up here, isn't it?" came a female voice behind me. A bit startled, I turned and saw Amber, Thaddeus's personal secretary, taking a position beside me. Aside from her auburn hair being a little ruffled, she looked perfect. Her gray business jacket and matching knee-length skirt didn't show one wrinkle. Blouse unbuttoned a little too low for business, I can see why the letch hired her.

For all her outward appearance, she was an incredible administrative assistant. She was positively brilliant. Never let any prejudice tell you that beautiful people are dumb. She had it all and was a sweet person, too. I never got to know her too well, but I would hear the other women putting her down, saying that she only kept her job because of the way she looked.

"Sure is," I answered as I returning to looking at the trees. "Have you ever been up here before?"

She hesitated for a moment, then, softly admitted, "Ted brought me up here right after he hired me."

I felt bad for having asked the question. The jerk had probably tried to take advantage of the young woman up here, so I changed the conversation.

"How are you holding up?"

"Good," she said, sounding happy that I had not pursued the original discussion. "All things considered, I'm doing fine. How about you?"

"I'm surviving," I answered, not noticing the pun.

"Do you think any of the others...?" she asked, leaving the rest of the inquiry hanging as a tear ran down her cheek, marring her perfection.

"I hope so, but I don't know. It was all so crazy."

Amber reached a hand up and wiped the tear away with her index finger. She turned and began walking away from the edge of the building toward the other two. I could see that Thaddeus and Ned were in a heated discussion.

"You jeopardized our lives, you sniveling jerk!" Ned accused.

Our boss looked half crazed. Face still ashen, his eyes nearly bulged out of their sockets as he roared in defense, "I was looking out for our safety."

Amber interposed herself between them, putting her back to Ned and softly taking the other's wildly swinging hands in her own. "It's ok, Ted," she said soothingly. "You were only protecting me. Just let it go."

It was amazing. His rage melted away, leaving him looking exhausted. I took that moment to calm Ned. "They didn't know. It's ok," I explained, also in an even tone. "We need to work together if we are going to survive."

"How are we going to survive up here?" he asked, doubt creeping into his voice for the first time.

I understood his frustration. We were trapped with no visible means of escape. I turned to Thaddeus. "Is there any other way down?"

"No," he said, slumping down on a lone folding chaise lounge chair. "There is no other way."

"Now what are we going to do?" Ned asked, defeated.

"Now we are going to sit here and wait to be rescued," I answered resolutely.

"By who?" he asked, wiping sweat from his forehead with the back of his arm.

He had a good point. This was not a localized event. The news and the internet alluded to the fact that all the emergency resources were strained beyond the breaking point. The National Guard, as well as all the other military branches, were recalled and were trying to regain order. I had no idea where help would come from.

"My husband is on his way!" I said firmly.

"The bug guy? What is he going to do? I know your husband, and a hero he is definitely not!" Now Ned was becoming panicky.

I knew it was a long shot and that he was right, but we all needed to stay calm. "He has been in dangerous situations before," I assured. "He has been deep in rainforests and jungles looking for his specimens and has always survived."

Ned shrugged at my answer, but it seemed to have the desired effect. "I was speaking to him when we were attacked and he sounded fine. He said he was on his way."

"I hope he brings an army!" Ted remarked, head hung low in defeat.

Everyone knew we were in trouble. We could hear the infected pawing at the door to get at us. The four of us were partially safe, protected by the metal door, but nothing was protecting us from the elements. If we were not found soon, we would die from exposure or the lack of food and water.

Chapter 8
Henry

I turned the knob, releasing the twin latches that lock the door in place. They slid free with an audible squeal. My breath caught as I waited a few moments, listening for any sound of undead attracted by the noise. Detecting nothing, I grabbed the handle and prepared to heave it up. Looking back at Dean, I gave the thumbs up, signaling him to start the engine. I wouldn't be caught in a nonfunctioning vehicle again.

The car started on the first crank and was, to my relief, very quiet, so I lifted the heavy door. I wasn't ready for the terrifyingly loud noise of the metal rollers as they rode along their tracks, the sound magnified by the quiet outside and my attempt to keep it that way.

The world outside had changed. As the door reached its apex, I could clearly see the sky filled with the orange glow of distant fires. Sirens called out from every direction as at least a dozen walking dead swiveled toward the racket I had just created by opening the garage. The zombies, who previously were milling about the neighborhood, were now drawn to the only living thing readily available. Me.

I spun and started back toward the passenger side, trailing a hand on the hood, not willing to break my connection with the gently rumbling car. The vibration was reassuring as I rounded the bumper and made my way by the fender. Releasing my hand from sliding across the car, I reached for the door. Something caught my pant leg, pulling me off-balance. I spread my arms as I sprawled to the floor, trying to stay upright. This caused various tools to dislodge from the garage wall and follow me to the ground. Debris pelted me as I rolled to my back, the last of which was the snow shovel banging hard on my shin.

Dean must have turned the headlights on, because twin beams illuminated the front of the garage. I could see Marcy's torso, one hand on my trousers, the other pulling itself toward me.

Holding my revulsion at bay, I grabbed the handle of the shovel and pushed the snow blade against Jen's mom's head. The shovel's edge slid down her face and lodged at the base of her neck, gaining a hold on her collarbone. As she pulled forward, I pushed her back, and we lay for a moment at a stalemate. When I saw a zombie, silhouetted in the headlights, shamble into view, I redoubled my efforts and shoved hard enough to break her grasp. I slid back into a sitting position and, using a hand on the tire, gained my feet once again.

Marcy doggedly slithered toward me, hands, smacking wetly against the cement floor, prompting me to pump my feet in an odd dance to avoid her clutching fingers. My left hand blindly sought the passenger door handle as I continued to dodge my attacker.

Finally, I found my prize and I lifted the handle springing the door's latching mechanism. I swung it open hard, purposefully smacking the door into the prone Marcy's head. I leapt into the seat, dragging the door closed behind me, securing the lock with my free hand just as the next corpse slipped in the gore trailing behind Marcy's upper body. As the zombie slid out of view, Dean dropped the car into drive and punched the gas. The rear end of the Jeep lifted upwards slightly as, I imagine, it drove over a part, or parts, of the two undead inside the now empty garage.

My neighbor accelerated as he drove through the rest of the undead shambling up the driveway. The car rocked with each impact as we barreled our way through the throng. The tires squealed as we pulled onto the road.

Then Dean began to slow the car. What we had seen from the house was nothing. I had heard the term apocalypse, but until now, I had never really understood it. Cars and bodies were here and there. Fires burned unchecked and the undead were everywhere. Any place there was light, the illumination revealed another scene more gruesome than the last. A few blocks down the road, a zombie policeman staggered about near a crashed cruiser with its lights still strobing.

As we drove down the street, many of the walking corpses turned our direction and began to follow in their slow, shuffling gait. Our pace was hampered by debris strewn all about as well as the bodies, both walking and lying still. We wove our way through, avoiding it all, sometimes driving through yards to gain passage around one problem or another.

I leaned my head against the window, watching everything I had ever known come to a screeching halt. This technological world was falling back into the dark ages. Man had put too much stock in technology. We had converted our books, businesses, and lives into a digital format that was being deleted right before our eyes.

As we neared the on-ramp to the highway, a girl ran past, pursued by a larger undead woman. The girl looked about eight years old at the most and was wearing a dirty party dress. Dean and I looked at one another and shared an unspoken word. Stealing a quick look around, I confirmed our present situation. We were alone. Dean had leaned over the seat and checked on Julie. He gave me a solemn look and reached for the door handle.

After exiting the car we looked in the direction the child had taken. A car blocked our view; turned upside down and smoking. Dean called out for the kid to come back. He added that we could help her and that she would be safe. There was no response. She was gone. In the midst of the chaos, we could hear a chorus of distant screams. Turning our gaze toward the noise, I made out a tiny, terror-filled scene. The overpass, as well as the freeway, was swarmed with walking dead. People dragged from their cars were screaming as they passed through shattered glass and were consumed by the dead. The living were trapped as they tried to escape on the fastest route available. As one car stopped, blocked by someone or something in front, it was barred from the rear by another trying to flee in the same direction.

We could see people falling from the bridge where the overpass crossed the road below, not sure if they were live or dead. Whether they were being pushed off the side or jumping in an attempt to escape the gnawing death, which surrounded them, I had no idea. It was a horrible sight.

"I think we should take the side streets to the hospital," Dean suggested.

"I think you're right," I agreed, returning to the yawning passenger door.

I just couldn't lift the latch yet. Taking another look around, I felt reasonably safe, so I continued observing the destruction and chaos all about. It was amazing. Random fires were everywhere. Abandoned and crashed cars joined random junk all over the street. The most disturbing thing was the blood. Spots, smears, pools and spatters were all over. But the blood wasn't the most terrifying part

46

of the scene. It was the lack of bodies that the blood had come from. Bloody hand and footprints were the only tangible human links to the red stains.

The streetlights flickered, drawing us back to reality. It was time to go. Looking at each other, we both lifted the door latches and reclaimed our seats. Dean leaned over the seat to check on Julie. From my quick glance back, I ascertained that she was still sprawled out on the back seat and asleep. I latched my seatbelt and leaned my head against the passenger window. The flickering firelight in the distance danced across my features as I relaxed for a moment, closing my eyes against the bazaar happenings all around me.

The closed car door muted the sounds of the distant highway. I could hear Dean saying soft words of comfort to his girlfriend, soothing things, which seemed to fall on deaf ears. His ministrations were a monolog, which, in a way, was probably just as good for his own fear of her condition.

I heard my neighbor returning to his seat and fastening his own safety belt. The car had been left running. Dean turned to me and told me, "We gotta get to the hospital. Her breathing is really shallow. I could barely tell that she was alive."

I reluctantly opened my eyes. Turning my head, I answered, "She'll be fine." I gave him my most confident look. "Let's get out of this horrible place."

He didn't answer me but put the vehicle in drive and accelerated around the flipped car. Gravel and other debris crunched under our tires as we skirted the obstacle and continued down the road. The walking dead moved to intercept us, breaking off from their siege of living people's homes to try for prey out in the open, only to suffer disappointment by falling behind due to Dean's skillful maneuvering.

It seemed like hours passed by as we wove our way through the various threats. One frightening sight blended into the next, creating one long spectacle. We were lucky the town had a low population. I began to give in to despair.

As we approached St. Joseph's Memorial Hospital, the streets became more crowded with cars and dead. Many of the latter were in pursuit of the few living people in the area, weaving between vehicles and on the tree-lined walkways. As the medical facility came into view, an explosion erupted in the distance, mushrooming out of the medical building's fifth floor.

Dean stomped on the brakes, bringing us to an abrupt stop. "The TV said to avoid the hospitals," he mumbled in a monotone voice, staring straight ahead. The fiery ball rolled skyward as we watched in shock. Black smoke followed in thick billowing clouds, obscuring the facility's floors above. When the explosion first happened, I thought I saw human forms being tossed from the blast, tumbling through the air like dolls.

A man slammed against the windshield, blocking our view and bringing our focus back. Blood flowed from multiple small wounds but mainly one long gash on his forehead. Long rivulets of crimson divided the man's face. Eyes wide, he slapped the flats of his hands repeatedly on the glass in desperation as he begged for aid.

"Help me!" he screamed, his voice a squeal from fear. His hands continued to paw at the windshield. "Get me out of here!" The latter was said as he snapped his head around and screamed again. Three walking dead gained the front of the car and attempted to pull the man to their snapping jaws.

I heard the car doors lock as the victim struggled to get away. Knees slipping against the polished hood, he was being drawn toward his attackers, his eyes shifting between ours as he slid to his demise.

Dean moved the automatic gear shift to reverse and we both spun towards the center of the car, craning our necks to look behind. We were met part way by a snarling Julie. Her eyes were white like her skin and her jaws spread wide. She had turned.

We both screamed as the car shot backward wildly at a high speed. The momentum brought the now undead Julie forward just as fast. My neighbor had casually reached his arm around behind my seat as he had turned to support the twist in his body. His limb was in direct line with his former girlfriend's salivating mouth. I jammed my left hand back as quickly as I could and grabbed a fistful of long, greasy hair, stopping her teeth mere inches from Dean's arm.

Our vehicle slammed into a parked car, snapping us all back into our seats and leaving me holding dripping clumps of hair and scalp. My neighbor had swiveled back into a normal seated

48

position and dropped the gear selector into drive. Punching the gas pedal, we careened forward through the night. Our momentum kept the zombie Julie pressed against the rear seat, but as the pressure normalized, she once again came forward.

Just as I aimed a hand for her forehead again the car crashed, stopping us immediately. The female's forward movement, accelerated by the impact, hurled her past us and through the windshield. The airbags just missed her as they deployed, enveloping us in their pillow-like embrace then immediately deflating.

Years of wearing safety belts had kept us from joining Julie in a crumpled form, neck twisted awkwardly, lying on the hood. The front of the car was nearly wrapped around the base of a huge oak tree. Smoke poured from the front of the vehicle and the air smelled of antifreeze as we recovered our wits in our seats.

A scream in the distance, as well as approaching moans, brought us to our senses. "We've got to get out of here," I urged.

"We're sitting ducks," he agreed, unbuckling and opening the door.

It took me a few minutes to unfasten my restraint, having been twisted around due to the impact. My back was sore and the door took a few shoves to make a wide enough opening for me to escape the wrecked vehicle. It groaned so loudly it made my teeth grind, but I guess after the demolition derby we had just participated in the sound of the door resisting my attempts was comparably quiet.

Taking a quick look about, I saw that we were not alone. Dean had opened the trunk and was rummaging around inside. He closed the lid and pressed an L-shaped tire iron into my hands. I could see a short, snub-nosed revolver in his right hand and a duffel bag slung over one shoulder.

"What am I supposed to do with the tire iron?" I asked, hefting its weight in my right hand while shouldering my bag.

"It's a quiet weapon, good in close quarters. I think guns might draw their attention. We gotta find a place to hide," he said, head swiveling as three more lurched into view. Clothes ragged their jerky movements and telltale bloodstains betrayed their intentions. "Follow me!"

I did as he said, shadowing him as he ran, his gun always

pointed forward with his arms fully extended. We ran down the lane, avoiding the streetlights, using picket fences and shrubs as places to rest. Twice, Dean had to shoot his gun. The first time he fired a bullet into the chest of an approaching zombie. "Crap!" he cried, adjusting his aim as the undead nurse continued toward us. The second round took the horror in the head. "The movies were right! Ya gotta shoot them in the head. Who woulda thought that would work?"

"Who would have thought the dead would reanimate?" I countered between ragged breaths. "We can't stay out in the open. We have to find a car or some place where we'll be safe."

My neighbor sat back against the car we were hiding behind. "I was just thinking the same thing. Ya wanna try one of these houses?"

I nodded my agreement, breathing returning to normal. "Which one do you want to try?" I said, sweeping my arm at the houses in our view.

The suburban block was full of mid-sized homes painted in different colors. Each had a covered porch with stairs leading to a small lawn in front. The houses were well maintained. It looked like a traditional neighborhood in some TV sitcom from the 1960's.

Dean was up and moving. He chose a yellow one, its wide front porch decorated with white-painted gingerbread trim. It looked inviting. As we moved, I saw that a few of the walkers we had previously been avoiding had taken notice. Our risky move had exposed our presence. Their moans became more urgent as they moved in our direction.

We gained the porch and pounded on the door. The only light inside switching off was our only reward.

"Let us in!" Dean demanded while maintaining his pounding at the door. "They're coming!" The door remained closed.

The dead were slowly but methodically continuing their approach. Our time was running out.

"They aren't going to let us in!" I offered. "We have to try another."

"We should break the door down!" he shot back, turning to gauge how much time we had.

"That won't work. With the door broken in it will only be a matter of time until the zombies make their way in. We would be killing that family as well as ourselves."

"Let's try next door," he said, abandoning the barred entryway and moving to the right side of the porch.

The shambling dead were mostly coming from the opposite direction. We leapt the railing and dropped to the ground. As we crossed the rest of the house's front, a zombie came from between the two houses and crashed headlong into my friend. They went down in a tangle, Dean winding up on the bottom, propped up awkwardly by the duffel over his shoulder. Desperately holding his attackers head away from his own I came up behind the creature and, raising the tire iron, dispatched it with a blow to the head. I could feel the vibration ring through the iron shaft as it struck the skull of the zombie.

As my neighbor pushed the now still corpse off of his body, I just stood there, blood dripping off my weapon. It was a weird feeling, killing. Although the beast would have killed both of us with no remorse, I felt strange. This was the second time I had killed.

Sure I had killed countless insects in the field or lab, but now I was ending the life of something very human. Something inside me changed. The world had changed into a place of survival.

Wiping my tire iron on the grass, we continued to the next porch. I could hear our pursuers making their way behind us. Luckily, they were slow. Dean adjusted the load on his shoulder and we were off again. We gained the next porch and were greeted with the muzzle of a shotgun pointing out of the door, which was opened just a crack.

"Just keep moving on!" said the voice from inside.

"Come on man!" Dean begged. "You gotta let us in!"

The sound of a shell being chambered was his answer.

While we crossed the porch, the barrel followed our movement. We once again made our way to the ground. The walking dead had gained on us. We had to get indoors or we would be through.

Chapter 9
Henry

As we were cutting in front of the last house on the block, Dean cried out, "Jackpot! Follow me!"

He ran right past the stairs leading up to the porch and continued toward the road. There were more walking dead out on the road, meandering about in search of food. As our footfalls went from the deadened silence of the grass-covered lawn to the slapping sound of rubber on pavement, the nearest of the dead took interest and joined in our pursuit.

It looked like our destination was a church of some sort. It was not large and somewhat modern-looking. It wasn't like the old, gothic-style buildings I always pictured from my youth. A lone sedan sat in the parking lot.

As we sprinted across the asphalt lot, I chanced a look over my shoulder. There were at least twenty-five of the creatures shambling behind us. Some hunched or twisted in some form or another, while a few others dragged a foot behind. We were quickly running out of time. The undead walkers following us would never tire. While, on the other hand, we would. I was already nearing my breaking point. I couldn't continue much farther without rest.

Dean didn't break stride as he rammed into the double entry doors. They both swung open, clearing our entrance. I had just passed the threshold as my friend pushed the first door closed, latching both top and bottom in what seemed like a single motion. Just as I tried to slam the other in place, hands on the outside pushed back

"Let me in!" came a desperate high-pitched voice. "Hurry!"

I pulled back on the handle, opening the door part way, and a thin form in a hooded sweatshirt shot by. Not ten feet away was the ghastly menagerie of zombies.

"Close it! Close it!" screamed the high voice.

I shoved the door closed once again, driving both bolts in place as hungry hands pawed at the other side. Their repeated attempts at entry were vibrating through the steel doors. I could almost feel their frustration as the meal that was so close just slipped through their cold dead fingers.

My chest was heaving. I bent at the waist leaning on my knees to allow for easier breathing. Dean and the young man who had joined us were both lying on their backs. I laid my duffel bag containing weapons and food with Dean's. All of us were gasping for breath.

"We need to secure the windows!" I said, taking charge for the first time.

Both the kid and my neighbor began to laugh. "That's the beauty of this place," the young man said between bursts of laughter. "There aren't any windows."

"All churches have windows," I asked, standing back up and walking around, looking for evidence.

"This is a Jehovah's Witness Kingdom Hall," the youth answered, looking at me questioningly. "Not many of them have windows. Something about the devil looking in."

"Wrong. they don't want their worshippers being distracted by looking out windows during sermons," Dean corrected.

"Oh, don't believe the kid," the newcomer said sarcastically. "Just 'cause you're past your prime doesn't mean you got any smarter along the way."

"I ought to throw you right back outside!" stormed my neighbor, arms flailing in a mock show of getting up. "Who the heck are you anyway!"

"Tim, but my friends call me Scud," he said with a satisfied grin while pulling his hood off of his head, letting a long mane of curly blond hair flow free.

"What's a Scud? A big skid mark?" Dean said regaining his feet.

"No. It's a missile, Mr. Wizard," Tim said, facing his antagonist. "Can we put him outside now, Hank?"

There was a crash in the basement. It sounded like pots and pans falling to the floor. We all froze. Dean whipped out his pistol and replaced the spent rounds. He took the lead, immediately motioning us quiet and to follow. We found the door with stairs leading down just off the entry room we were presently in. The lights were on, but clearly, someone or something was down there.

"Please be a raccoon. Please be a raccoon." Dean kept mumbling under his breath as he descended. I was right behind him, tire iron in hand. The steps were that backless kind. I kept picturing something reaching through that open space and grabbing my exposed ankles. I could see myself, both ankles grasped and pitching forward, arms windmilling rapidly, clawing for something to stop my fall.

None of that happened. We made it to the landing, Tim following not far behind. What sounded like a small symphony of plastic cups hitting the floor stopped us dead in our tracks. Eyes wide, we exchanged glances before Dean forged ahead, gun held ready.

We could hear something shuffling around, betrayed by sounds of unknown things crunching under foot. Dean pushed the door open and swiveled hastily to the left. There was a low moan and the gun discharged, followed by the thud of a body dropping to the ground. The smell of gunpowder drifted out of the room.

"Dude!" Tim asked, "one shot?"

Dean got a smug look on his face. "I know. Pretty good, huh?"

"You totally didn't double-tap it!"

We both gave the youth a questioning look.

"How did you guys ever survive this long?" Tim continued. "All the contemporary knowledge about the zombie apocalypse says that you should never assume that the zombie is dead with the first shot. You need to shoot it a second time to be sure it won't rise again."

I had to chime in. "Contemporary knowledge about a zombie apocalypse?"

"There are tons of databases on the subject all over the net," Tim replied.

"How can there be knowledge about something as way out as that?"

Tim grinned, "You're in the middle of it right now, so it can't be that way out."

"I meant that hadn't happened yet!"

"So, what are you, a Doctor or something?"

I offered my hand. "Dr. Henry Cooper. My friends call me Hank."

My neighbor offered his hand. "Dean Walker."

Tim shook both of our hands in turn. After finishing with Dean, he turned towards me and asked, "What do you think is causing this?" When I didn't respond immediately, he added, "You know, the zombies to rise?"

As I mulled over the possible causes, I saw a smile spread across Dean's face. Tim's eyes looked expectant, waiting for the answer to this plague.

"He's not a medical doctor. He's a bug doctor," Dean informed the newcomer.

"Oh!" intoned the youth, eyes lowering, mirroring his disappointment.

"I work in the biology department of the university. My main area of expertise is entomology. Entomology refers to insects. I have also done some specific work in forensic entomology, which investigates the cause of death. Through my knowledge of the life cycles of various insects, I can determine the time and perhaps the location of someone's death."

"So, that's useful how?" Tim lashed back at me. "Are you going to tell me when or where a big, fat, ole' zombie died, just before he eats my face off? I thought you were a real doctor."

That really hurt. I had always been really proud of my profession and position at the university. I had authored and coauthored many papers, but in the midst of this outbreak, my accomplishments were meaningless. I couldn't cure this disease. This plague needed to be solved by highly trained minds like the ones employed by the CDC. Not a bug doctor.

"Hank here had an important job!" Dean said, seeing the situation and coming to my aid. "I wish mine was as important."

My heart rose and fell again, all in the span of one sentence. My next-door neighbor, the man who had saved my life, and I didn't have a clue as to what he did for a living. I was a terrible person.

Tim took up the question, saving me from my embarrassment, "So, what did you do Dean?"

"I am, err, was the manager at Radio Shack."

"I'm trapped in a Jehovah's Witness Kingdom Hall with two nerds. Great!" Tim mocked sarcastically.

"And what did you do for a living?" Dean mocked back playfully. "That's right, just a burden on ole' mom and dad."

The youth just sunk in on himself. Dean immediately knew he had hit some terrible note in this world gone mad.

"I'm sorry, kid." he apologized, moving near enough to put a hand on his shoulder in comfort. "I didn't mean anything. It's just that this world, I'm just not used to it."

Tim looked up at Dean. He was not crying but his eyes were red and glassy. We needed something to distract him, distract us all.

"I wonder if there is a way to look outside." I offered, changing the subject. "See what's going on."

The gloomy mood lessened as we went back to the main floor. We could hear the recent dead pawing against the metal-sheathed door. Carefully, we explored the parts we hadn't yet ventured into, the main assembly room darkened but empty, with no windows on either wall. Behind the area where we supposed the leader would preach from, we found two rooms. The first was just a small chamber where the minister could get ready for his sermon. The other was the jackpot, an office. It had a computer with what looked like camera feeds attached.

Tim flopped into the comfortable-looking, black leather desk chair and moved the mouse, waking the computer from its sleep.

"Dang! They have a login," he exclaimed, exasperated.

There were actually two login accounts. One user, called *Admin*, was password protected. The other was named *guest* and was not password protected but had very little access. There were no camera feeds available on this account.

Tim tried a few feeble attempts at hacking the administrative password, but his random attempts all fell short of the mark. "This is useless!" he growled, shoving the mouse away in defeat.

"Ya wanna let a nerd give it a try?" Dean challenged from his perch, leaning on the back of the chair's high back.

Tim reluctantly gave up the cushy seat and Dean took control. He logged onto the *guest* account.

"You can't do anything from there!" Tim warned. "Everything is locked out!"

"And they say you kids know so much more about computers than us old guys. Take away your GUI and you ain't got nothing," Dean mocked, a grin on his lean face. "They weren't smart enough to lock out the DOS command prompt." His fingers flew across the keys as he typed various words, half of which looked like gibberish. The screen went blue, then a DOS prompt appeared and Dean entered something inside a pair of parenthesis. He then logged out and logged back in using the same word he had typed inside the parenthesis and the administrative account opened.

"How did ya do that, Dean?" marveled Tim in awe.

"I'm a Hack Jedi," Walker said, leaning back while folding his arms behind his head. "Actually, it was easy. In DOS, I told the Windows XP machine, system 32 if you were reading my code, to backup the command program and the screen saver files. Then, I edited the settings so that as the screen saver loads I get a DOS prompt that was totally unprotected. That's where I changed the password. We do things like this all the time. If people actually knew how useless their computer security really was, they'd never shop online again. It would wipe out the entire cyber economy."

"And that, my friend Timmy, is why no job is more important and no man is more intelligent than any other," I added, bringing the lesson to a moral conclusion.

"Then what about the guy who sucks the crap outta my septic tank?" Timmy asked with an impish grin.

"Probably the most important job!" I admonished him, wagging an accusing finger at him.

"Crap!" said Dean.

"Exactly!" I replied.

"No, not crap, poopie crap. I mean crap as in one of the camera feeds is down crap! We can't see a whole side of the building," he explained with overly dramatic arm and hand gestures. "Probably an amateur job. See?" he said while pointing under the desk. "No cable ties. They probably had some DIY parishioner who did the job on the cheap, and now we have to pay for his sloppy work."

"DIY?" I implored, leaning closer to see what he was talking about. The screen showed ten small thumbnails of the various camera's displays. I could tell the camera covering the front by the small army of undead outside.

My neighbor leaned back in his chair once again, this time holding his head in both hands. "DIY! Do it yourself. It's really big with young homeowners or people trying to flip houses. The only problem is sometimes they don't have the technical know-how to do the job right. They fudge the parts they don't understand."

"I don't think it's a big deal. We can still see three sides. That's pretty good," I said enthusiastically, trying to keep our spirits high.

"If the person wasn't such an idiot, we could see entire building! Amateurs! Shoulda left the heavy lifting for us big boys."

Tim rose to his feet. "I'm hungry."

Chapter 10
Melissa

We sat for a while, us on the tar-and-chipped surface while Thaddeus reclined in the chair. The four of us were exhausted mentally and physically from our escape. Our boss looked the worst, visibly still suffering the effects of his alcoholic binge.

Our mood was one of defeat. We were now trapped on the roof with no realistic route of escape in the foreseeable future. With the countryside, if not the world, in chaos from the outbreak, we had only our wits and luck to depend upon.

As I looked at the three others, I thought maybe I should use the same tactics I had before. We needed to get organized.

"Does anybody have any food?" I asked without sounding too hopeful.

No one spoke, but all heads swung side-to-side affirming what I already suspected.

"Water?"

I got the same response.

I had them all empty their pockets to look for something useful. A penknife, some loose change, and wallets were all the effort produced. Of course, Ned and I still had the cubicle supports we had used as weapons, but there was nothing of use other than that.

Everyone except Ted searched the rooftop. Thaddeus, being uncooperative, remained in the folding lounge. An old plastic tarp and a windblown grocery bag were our only finds. The tarp was a temporary patch on the roof. Its edges were tarred to seal it but we removed it and made a temporary shelter, somewhat like a tent. Our cubicle supports and one wall formed the posts. Even though it wasn't hot, the roof gave off waves of heat. We would have gotten sunburned if not for the blue plastic canopy made from the tarp.

As we were searching the roof, I asked Amber why there was a chair up here. She giggled and said Ted liked to come up here and sunbathe. He used to chain the door so no one would find out. Although I was slightly perturbed that he was maintaining his tan on company time, I was happy for the chain and padlock, which probably wouldn't have been here if he hadn't neglected his job by sun worshipping.

We turned off all unnecessary functions on our smartphones, not wanting to waste any remaining battery. Then, we shut them off completely. Even though the phones were mostly useless, it was still our only means of communicating with the outside world. We had to make them last as long as possible.

We saw a helicopter in the distance. Everyone, except Ted, jumped to their feet and raced to the edge, screaming while jumping and waving our hands in the air. But it was too far away to notice us.

Ned walked out into a large open spot on the roof and began dragging his heel around. He was writing something in the gravel. *HELP! WE ARE ALIVE!*

There was nothing else we could do. We were all hungry and extremely thirsty. As it began getting dark, Amber leapt to her feet. "The dew!" she said triumphantly. "We can catch it in the tarp."

As fast as we could, the four of us, Ned forcing Ted to help, set the tarp out to collect rainwater. Using the bag torn into strips, we tied the blue plastic to the wall in a corner. We used my cubicle support to anchor the free corner and had a big square to catch any dew or even rain.

We decided on setting a watch order. On the outside chance someone would come by, I wanted someone awake and alert. Once again, Ted refused to take a turn. Ned began to protest, but with a shake of my head, he let it go. I didn't want to take a chance on him. Even though he was sober at this point, he still looked bad. The lack of water and dehydrating effect of alcohol was really taking its toll on him.

We all settled in except Amber, who had volunteered for the first watch. Exhausted, I had slept little during the first night. Lying on my back, I looked up at the canopy and licked my dry lips, anticipating a little water in the morning.

Chapter 11
Henry

We both looked at him questioningly.

"It's just a statement," the youth said sheepishly. "I can't help it."

"There's a whole kitchen downstairs. I'm sure you'll find something down there," I assured, joining Dean as he cycled through the perimeter cameras.

"There's a zombie down there," Tim said in a small, scared voice.

"I, as you kids would say, busted a cap in its head," my neighbor emphasized with a shooting gesture to his head.

"Are you sure about that, Dean?" I asked, pointing at a thumbnail labeled *Kitchen.*

Dean Walker clicked the mouse on the icon and the thumbnail expanded to fill the screen. It showed a modest kitchen with honey oak cabinets. The floor and Formica counters were strewn with debris. A big, dark spatter covered one wall and a corpse, head drenched in blood, staggered about.

"I told ya to double tap 'em! You never believe one of them is down unless ya do."

Dean's shoulders fell. "Sorry, guys. Let's go get him."

"No," I suggested. "Let's study him. Just for a while."

It was my turn to be on the receiving end of the questioning looks.

"What do ya expect to see?" my neighbor asked.

"I'm not sure. But we have this opportunity. We might as well use it."

Tim leaned over, viewing the walking corpse for the first time. "But I'm still hungry."

"Go through one of the duffel bags in the front room. There's some food inside. Beef jerky and stuff like that."

Over the next few hours, I observed the behavior of the undead beings. I looked for patterns in their behavior. I had Dean show me how to record the cameras so I could save some of what the cameras saw for later viewing.

That night, I could see on the screen that it had rained

outside. It didn't fall very heavily, but it was one of those straight down soakers. It didn't matter at all to the walking dead. They paced about, three still clawing at the door, concerned only with their endless quest for food. Clothes plastered to their bodies, they lurched through puddles, mud or dry pavement, all the same.

I found some notepads with the Kingdom's letterhead printed on each page. An array of pens were stored in a thin top drawer. I noted movements I found interesting or even odd and looked for other undead to replicate them. Compiling page after page of traits and behaviors, I was looking for a pattern to emerge.

I became an expert with the camera software, figuring out how to zoom and create split screens. My favorite was to fill the screen with four large camera views. This way, I could cover most of the zombie activity without having to switch views. Since three cameras outside were in working condition, I was able to watch our friend downstairs as well.

Dean and Tim, after securely locking the basement door, had found an old radio and were listening to various reports of the outbreak around the globe. From time to time, they would come in to give me updates on the news they had heard.

It seems the current theory linked the living dead to an unknown virus, possibly something cooked up in Afghanistan or Iran, because third world countries, as well as less traveled places, had not shown any signs of the virus anywhere. This could be due to the lack of immediate contact from the more advanced countries.

The more advanced countries were the ones completely overrun by the outbreak. The larger the population meant the worse off the people were. While New York and Las Vegas collapsed, small town USA lived on with hardly a bite taken out of it.

I tried my phone a few more times with no success. It seemed everyone in the area was trying to use his or her phone at the same time, using up all the towers' capacity. I checked for text messages and found no current ones. I sent Melissa a text saying that I loved her and that I was fine. I was trying to get to her but was currently trapped at a Jehovah's Witness Kingdom Hall.

In the desk, we found an iPod charger, which Tim and I were using to keep our phones' charges topped off. Dean said he hated Apple products, but when questioned, all he kept saying was that they were "Mac-in-trash." Being a scientist, all I used were Apple products, so when the first iPhone came out my choice was already made. At this point, my neighbor's phone was nearly dead.

The door opened, revealing the dynamic duo. They seemed to have gotten close pretty quickly. While I was watching the cameras, they had explored the rest of the building. They had eaten and even slept.

"Bedtime, Hank," Dean said in his best fatherly voice.

"Aw, dad! I don't wanna!" I complained, trying to sound like a little kid.

"We need to conserve our strength if we want to get out of here. And that means everyone. If you don't rest soon, you won't last if we have to run."

I had to agree. My eyes were getting very heavy and my thoughts were difficult to focus, so I reluctantly agreed and retired to the larger meeting room where the guys had made some makeshift beds. As I lay there, I knew that I was missing something. I couldn't substantiate my hypothesis, but I knew I was on to something. It might be a breakthrough.

I would have thought my sleep would have been full of nightmares. With all the things I had experienced in the last 24 hours, you would think that would be true. But the fact is, I was so tired I think I slept right through the REM cycle and nearly into a coma. When I awoke, it was from one of those paralyzing sleeps where you can't move a muscle. In some ways, you don't want to. I finally broke free of the spell and threw off the blanket. The room was musty smelling but warm. I could hear the guys in the other room.

It sounded like they were having a very good-natured conversation. They were quoting movie lines and debating who was better, Kirk or Picard?

I sat up, letting the blanket slide down my chest, pooling up in my lap. Being in this building was like being in a cave. Although we were safe, we were also completely cut off, unable to immediately sense the weather and other factors you would typically notice in a home with many windows.

Pulling out my cell phone, I checked the signal. It once again told me I was not connected, but I must have been at some point while I slept. I had two new text messages, both from Melissa. One told me she was glad that I was safe and that, although they had some difficulties, she was safe for the time being, as well. The other message said we should continue using text messages because it uses less "tower space" and conserves battery. She ended both messages with *I love you*.

I returned the phone to my front left pocket and stretched. I was happy that she was alive and safe, but I really needed to find a way out of this building and to her. I quickly found that buildings could offer safety, but they could also be traps like was the case with the car. Once inside, it may be difficult to leave. Once the food and potable water was gone, you had no option but to go. It seemed safest to keep moving.

I draped the blanket over my shoulders and unsteadily made my way into the office. The lights were off. The room's sole illumination was the computer screen, casting my friends and their surroundings in dull the colors.

"Spock is the best!" chirped Tim.

"The needs of the many outweigh the needs of the few, or the one!" Dean quoted in his best Spock voice.

"Kirk said the middle part," our young friend corrected.

A pen flew at the youth's head in answer to his correction.

The room was efficiently decorated. Pictures, mostly photographs, filled large frames on most walls. A small library of books spilled from the shelves of twin bookcases. Aside from these items, the room was spartan. There were no knickknacks or even desktop picture frames. Just four seats and a desk occupied the room.

I thought about my current hypothesis, prompting me to ask, "Any news on the radio?"

"Nothing new," Dean answered, craning his neck about to look at me. "The outbreak is still spreading. They keep announcing safe places to go, but it seems to us that a few hours after one opens, it's overrun and they are announcing that it isn't safe anymore."

"Timmy, can you go stand at the front door?" I asked.

"Tim!" He spun in the desk chair. "I hate the name Timmy."

"Tim then. Can you please…" I reasserted, not finishing the question.

"Why?"

"I'll do it!" Dean spat in disgust. "Kids nowadays. You just sit

64

there and be comfy, Skid."

"Skud!"

"Whatever," he said, rolling his eyes. He stomped out of the office and toward the entry.

"I would have done it," grumbled the youth as I pulled a chair up to the computer monitor and switched the camera view to the front door. I could tell that Dean had reached his destination by how the zombies reacted. They could tell that he was near. The three who were already at the door began attacking the outside with a renewed vigor. Two of the nearest wanderers made their way to the blocked entry and joined the others reaching, over shoulders and receiving admonishing bites to their offending limbs as a result. The other undead who had wandered a little further out made no response to my friend's proximity. They continued their aimless pacing.

"That's weird, Hank," Tim breathed. "Did you see that?"

"I sure did. Can you go and tell Dean to come back in here? I think he'll want to see this."

Timmy disappeared, leaving me to my thoughts. "What does this mean?" I wondered.   When the two returned, I played the tape back for Dean and he had the same response the two of us had.

"They know when we are near," he said more to himself than us. "How can that be? I didn't make any noise. There aren't even any windows to give me away."

I stroked my chin, taking a few moments to choose my words to avert unfounded fear. "We humans are just animals. We evolved to a point where we depend on technology more than our instincts." I paused to see if either had any questions or arguments.

Tim raised his hand, as if in school. I grinned at the Pavlovian action and nodded in his direction. He immediately lowered his arm and inhaled.

"My Earth Science teacher used to say the theory of evolution," Timmy made quotation mark gesture with both hands as he said the last three words. "He made it sound like it wasn't true. Are you saying it is?"

"Public education," I stated, shaking my head side to side. "And we wonder why we lag behind other countries in science. Yes, Tim, he was wrong. I doubt he read scientific journals or did any research in his time off."

"No, he was the football coach."

"That's my point," I said. "Many public educators insert their own beliefs into the school's curriculum, unresearched and unfounded as their ideas may be, producing generations of young people who are ignorant of the most common principles of today's scientific world. Evolution has been proven consistent with current results in microbiology, genetics, and even proteonomics.

"How is my teacher allowed to do this?" the youth asked, distraught.

"As an instructor, he shouldn't be allowed, especially from a professional and ethical point. But in some political and religious circles, it is overlooked or often encouraged."

Dean cut in, "So how does this relate to zombies being able to tell I was on the other side of the door?"

"It is possible that in our more primitive state we used senses which later became unnecessary, obsolete. My working hypothesis is that somehow these living dead are able to use senses we have long forgotten. Maybe it is because they are throwbacks. They have no need for technology, only a need to survive, much like early homo sapiens."

"So this is your theory?" asked my neighbor.

"A scientific theory is basically a fact. It has reams of proof attached to it. This is my current hypothesis. It is my working idea which I need to prove."

"I hope you live long enough to publish your paper, Doctor, but we have problems of our own."

I switched the camera view back to the current, real-time view of the front door. One of the zombies had wandered away. There were probably forty others milling about in the parking lot.

"We need food and a plan for escaping this place," Dean continued. I had to agree as my stomach rumbled in protest of being empty.

"I have a plan." Dean strode from the room.

As we stood to follow, Tim leaned close. "I wish you were my teacher, Hank."

I placed a hand on his shoulder and smiled as we exited the office.

Dean was rummaging through his thigh pocket. He produced a permanent marker and dropped to his knees on the floor. He

66

crudely sketched the top floor, and to the side he drew what we remembered of the downstairs.

"Umm... Why do you have a marker?" Tim asked sarcastically.

"I found it in the office," he said, looking hurt. "I'm gonna use it to warn people away from dangerous places. It's not like they're gonna use this as a church again."

We still had the problem of the zombie downstairs. We needed to deal with it. From a small closet, the guys pulled some thick rubber-coated gardener's gloves, a rake, and a snow shovel. I laughed as my neighbor pulled on the hand protection and gave a couple of practice motions with the shovel before taking his place in front of the door to the basement. Timmy was about to back him up until I grabbed ahold of the rake. He looked somewhat relieved as he let the weight of the garden tool-turned-weapon transfer to my hands.

Chapter 12
Melissa

Henry was in the study as the dinner guests began sitting down to the lovely Thanksgiving dinner. I tried to pry him from his studies, but he wouldn't acknowledge me. Everything I tried seemed fruitless. Even shaking him brought no result. He just ignored me.

Angry, I left the room, slamming the French doors behind. This caused the glass, which made up the majority of the twin doors to rattle. The dinner guests were oblivious to my distress, focusing intently on the huge turkey in the middle of the table. Each guest piled heaping mounds of meat on their plates, ignoring everything else. Thick slabs of juicy fowl heaped on the china nearly overflowed onto the table.

Sitting at the table's head, I joined them and placed a napkin on my lap. I grabbed the bowl of steaming broccoli covered with cheese sauce and set it next to my plate. The cheese formed pools on my clean plate as I measured out a portion.

Replacing the bowl, I reached for the sweet potatoes. It was then I noticed our friend Mike shoveling forkfuls of the white meat into his mouth. He crammed impossible amounts of the stuff into his already overly full mouth. Small bits dropped to the table in gobs mixed with healthy amounts of saliva. His mouth literally foamed with the effort of keeping the turkey inside.

As I looked at our other guests, they were all doing the same; wet smacking sounds were nearly deafening as they fought to push more food in and chew at the same time.

Trying to stay calm, I spooned the sweet potatoes onto my plate. The marshmallow topping gave a distinct marbling effect to the serving. As I put the dish back, I saw that my fellow diners had abandoned their plates altogether and were now attacking the turkey with their hands. They made a huge mess ripping the bird apart. Bits of flesh flew as they added handfuls of meat to their overflowing maws. Drool flowed freely down their chins, dripping onto my nice, white linen tablecloth.

I slowly pushed my chair back, placing my napkin on my plate. All heads turned toward me and I saw the hollow stare of their nearly white eyes. Their faces were gray, lips and cheeks covered in saliva and bits of their meal. Mouths still chewing, they all pushed back and stood.

I stifled a scream and began backing away, but they followed me in an awkward, shuffling gait. I ran to the study and tried the door but the handle would not move. I must have broken it when I slammed the door in anger. With the palm of my hand, I slapped at the glass trying to gain my husband's attention. But he sat, head down, totally absorbed in his work.

Our dinner guests were getting uncomfortably close as I grabbed the floor vase next to the door and threw it through the glass. It exploded, shattering glass and ceramic both.

While I crawled through the jagged opening, my dress caught on a sharp shard jutting from the frame. Hands reached for me as I twisted my body in a last ditch effort to gain my freedom. I heard a loud tearing sound as the fabric parted, sending me to my knees at the foot of the desk. I spun about, checking on my pursuers' progress. A woman was pushing her way through the broken mess, her flesh slicing open on the jagged glass that remained in the frame. She didn't seem to notice as her skin and muscle parted, blood flowing from the ragged wounds.

I crawled around the desk to my husband and pulled at his pant leg, but he didn't stir. Poking my head over the top of the workspace, I saw the woman clearing the forbidding entryway as another followed behind.

Whirling on my spouse, I grabbed his shirt front and physically dragged him away from his papers. As his face centered on mine, I saw a pair of vacant, near-white eyes looking back at me. His mouth opened and gleaming white teeth came for me.

I was roughly awakened from my sleep. Quickly, my hand shot out and seized my assailant's wrists. I couldn't see. It was dark.

"It's me, Melissa," Ned assured, somewhat startled. "It's your turn at watch."

My heart was beating wildly as I loosened my hold on his limbs. "It was a dream," I mumbled, regaining my control of reality. "It was only a dream."

"I can take your watch if you want," he offered.

I still felt tired, but I sure as heck didn't want to go back to sleep and relive that dream. "No," I responded. "I'm good."

Still a little shaky, I stood. The air was crisp. Steam emitted from each breath. The only light shining was the moon. I felt the chill in my lungs and pulled my inhaler out of my jacket, I breathed out completely and released the medication as I breathed in again. I couldn't see the counter but I knew it was getting low. I replaced my puffer in the jacket pocket. Feeling my lungs expand once again, I looked back at Ned.

"The power went out about an hour ago," he informed me, placing a hand on my shoulder. "When your eyes adjust, you'll be able to see pretty well, not that there has been anything to see. Are you sure you're ok?"

"Fine, I'm fine." I assured him. "Get some sleep."

Ned took my spot under the tarp as I turned and leaned on the wall. The surface was rough and cold but I stayed that way for a few moments to steady my nerves.

All was quiet. The scenery, tones of gray, was robbed of color by the scant moonlight. Clouds mostly obscured the orb, revealing it only momentarily then blocking it for long periods of time. During one of those times, I looked at the tarp. In its center was a sizable amount of water. It must have rained earlier in the night. The roof left no sign of it having absorbed the precious liquid into its porous surface.

I reached out and scooped out a handful of cold water. Carefully drinking the chill liquid, I savored the small amount as it flowed over my dry lips. A foul, oily taste mixed with the liquid, but I didn't care. I followed that handful with several more. Then, feeling guilty, I stopped myself. We were going to have to share it. I had to think of the others.

Nothing outside stirred, at least nothing I could see. A soft rain fell from the sky, so I retreated to an unoccupied corner of our shelter and watched the big drops fall to the roof.

The sound of the rain on our tarp roof reminded me of camping. Henry and I used to do that a lot. He said he didn't like hotels, but I always suspected he wanted to rough it so he could work during our vacations. He would come back from our trips with specimen bottles full of bugs, mostly beetles. As I looked at spectacular views like the Grand Canyon, he would be looking at the ground in search of some insect or another.

Thinking of my husband, I pulled out my iPhone. Its screen

came to life but there was no connection. My phone was essentially useless. Shutting down the device, I returned it to my pocket. After the rain stopped, I took the time to stretch my legs by walking the perimeter of the roof. The gravel was taking a toll on my stocking-covered feet and my toes ached with the cold, but I couldn't stand just sitting.

Orange stained the bottom clouds, which were now breaking up and becoming more scattered. Color was being gradually restored as night gave way to dawn's light. I walked back to the makeshift shelter to check on the others. As I silently approached the tarp, I could make out my companions locked in sleep's soft embrace.

Amber, legs covered with her jacket, looked angelic, her brow wrinkled in what looked like concentration. I wondered what she was dreaming. Ned snored softly while he lay prone on his back. Ted, still on his lounge chair, had flipped onto his stomach, stretching his jacket, uncomfortably tightening its fit.

It was then that I saw the stain on his cuff, the sleeve covered with blood. My hand shot to my mouth, stifling a cry. I tried to make excuses for the wound, unsure what to do.

I snuck up on Ned and, placing my palm over his mouth, I reawakened him. His eyes shot wide and he started to speak but my hand muffled his attempt. With my other hand, I placed the index finger over my mouth and signaled him to be quiet.

We did the same to Amber. She didn't struggle as Ned had, but rather opened her eyes and followed our silent commands.

I pointed at Ted's resting form and pointing at my wrist. I then redirected them to our boss. Amber's sharp intake of breath told me she had found the meaning behind my pantomime. Ned pointed away from the shelter urging us to a distant point so we could speak.

"Do you think it's a bite wound?" Ned asked when we were as far away as we dared.

"I don't know," I answered. "It sure looks like it is."

"What should we do?" posed Amber, pulling her jacket on against the morning chill.

"I don't know," I said, trying to reason our options through. "Most of the people who were bitten only lasted hours before becoming fully infected. In some cases, it had been minutes or even less. For him, it's been most of a day."

"He sure looked bad yesterday," Amber added.

Ned placed his hands on his hips. "I just thought he was hung over."

"I thought that too," I agreed. "But maybe it was a small bite. That may explain why it took longer to take a hold."

"Listen to us!" Amber chided firmly yet quietly. "We don't even know that he's sick. It might not even be a bite. We just can't condemn him without being sure."

We all nodded in agreement. For the next several minutes, we formulated a plan. His lounge chair was in the back of the shelter. We needed to secure the pool of water above him just in case there was a struggle. Our lips already chapping, we needed the life-sustaining liquid more than food.

Amber and Ned took off their shoes. We then crept to the tarp. Ned stalked to the inside and grabbed twin handfuls of the blue plastic. His arms were spread wide. Amber and I took positions at the far corners, while she untied the corner on the wall, I did the same with the cubicle support. We waited for Ned.

With a mighty heave, Ned pulled both of his corners free of their wall hooks, the strips of aged plastic bag tearing easily under the added strain. Water sloshed in the tarp, some overflowing and pouring over Ted's prone body. We hurried away from the site, the blue plastic dragging across the pebbled surface of the roof. We had preserved most of our prize.

"Ned!" I screamed, my eyes looking past my friend to where Thaddeus was rising from the lounge.

When we had reached the far edge of the roof, the three of us gathered the sides and brought the corners together. Amber gathered them in her outstretched arms, keeping the sides high enough to hold the liquid trapped, as Ned and I turned to face our infected boss.

Thaddeus didn't seem to notice being sopping wet. Empty, white eyes stared, unblinking, at the two of us as the predator shuffled in our direction. Arms raised and mouth empty but chewing, he slowly came forward.

We drew him to the edge of the building, away from our prized water and the person holding it trapped. Ted only cared about who was closest, so he pursued us to the low wall. As he lurched at me, the top of the wall was pressing at my mid thighs. I lunged to the

72

left, but the rounded surface of the pea gravel rolled under my stocking-covered feet, causing me to fall well short of my mark. The cubicle support skidded across the stone surface, well out of reach.

Thaddeus bent at the waist to grab the prey at his feet but was stopped short. Ned had two handfuls of the sick man's jacket between his shoulders. Reeling backward, Ned swung the infected man about toward the edge.

My former boss's arms spun wildly as he struggled to halt his backward momentum. Just as I thought it was over, Ted's calves met the wall, giving him purchase just short of falling. Now steady, Ted turned his attention on Ned, who was right beside him. I saw the cubical support gleaming in the new light. It was too far away, so I abandoned it and tucked my legs under my body, launching myself forward.

As Thaddeus reached for my friend, I leapt feet first. Not thinking about what would happen if I missed, I just acted. My arches met our attacker at his midsection and, kicking out, I propelled him out and over the edge.

As Ted fell, he kept reaching for us. Unaware of his demise, he kept clawing for us until he struck the ground. I looked away as blood pooled around his still body.

Ned placed a hand on my shoulder and sighed, "Thank you."

I could hear Amber crying in the distance.

Chapter 13
Henry

We decided to have Timmy open the door. That way, if the undead occupant of the basement was actually at the top of the stairs, we would be, hopefully, able to bring one or both of our weapons to bear. We hoped to push the zombie down the stairwell; and, if we were lucky, that would create the necessary trauma to the brain area to cause permanent death.

"The needs of the many outweigh the needs of the few," said Tim stoically with a knowing grin.

"Or the one," added Dean. I had no idea what they were talking about.

As the door swung out, we lunged into the breach. The stairs before us were empty. We could hear muffled sounds from the kitchen.

"Here zombie, zombie, zombie..." Dean called out, mimicking a master calling for his dog.

We could hear the dragging gait of our quarry as he passed through the kitchen door we had so carelessly left open. The shuffling sound was muffled by the occasional moan. As the walking dead came into view, my hands tightened on the wooden handle, my sweating palms making a sure grip nearly impossible.

At the foot of the steps, the monster looked down, confused. It was seemingly unable to comprehend how to continue. After a few moments, the zombie tentatively lifted its leg and awkwardly placed it on the first riser. Hand finding the rail it slowly began its ascent.

As the creature neared our position, I gained faith that our plan would work. I quickly wiped my hands on my pants and readied myself for the big push.

When he was still a step away, I could only watch as my neighbor's snow shovel lashed out and caught the slow-moving predator in the throat. The zombie flew out and away, then connected with the steps. Bouncing off the step treads, it rolled from back to neck to head as the being flipped down the stairs.

We kept our distance, not wanting to rush in, but content to wait and see the outcome of the fall. When the beast came to rest at the bottom of the steps, we could clearly see, by the odd direction his neck bent, that he was going to stay dead this time.

Dean fearlessly took the lead once again, his descent slowing as he neared the bottom. Gingerly, he avoided the crumpled heap of the zombie at the base of the stairs., taking great pains to tiptoe around the leg that angled out, blocking the path.

As I mirrored his movements, I could clearly see where Dean had shot the now still undead. The bullet had definitely struck it in the head, but it was more a glancing blow, enough to make it drop but obviously not enough to keep it down.

We made our way to the kitchen and began rifling through the cupboards, sometimes slipping on the debris the undead had knocked on the floor. We avoided the blood-splattered areas from the zombie's earlier head wound, searching only the untainted storage areas, not wanting to take any risks with whatever contamination caused this outbreak.

Most of the cupboards were empty. The few that held anything at all were mostly pots, pans, paper products and empty plastic storage containers. The drawers were held a collection on mix matched cooking utensils, potholders, towels, and wash clothes. Everything had the look of donations. Mismatched handles and many duplicates gave validation to that conclusion.

Timmy went straight for the fridge. "Holy Crap!" he trumpeted, pulling out a large pan covered with aluminum foil. Placing it on the counter, he pulled back the silvery covering, exposing delicious-looking lasagna.

"It looks like they were going to have a party," assessed Dean, pulling out dish after covered dish.

"Keep the door closed. You're letting in the heat," I barked, mimicking my father. The other two just looked at me with this odd, questioning face. "Something my dad used to say," I offered. "He said the same thing about the front door."

We all fell in, ripping open containers. Pierogies, hot sausages, and potato salad were all in abundance, but the best of all were two large pans of fried chicken. My mouth watered in response to the feast before us. It had been at least two days since I had eaten anything of substance. Some beef jerky and a few fruit roll-ups just couldn't keep my hunger at bay.

We fired up one of the old gas stoves, nibbling on cold chicken as we warmed our meal. It was all I could do to wait, the smell nearly driving me mad. It seemed to take forever to heat this bountiful supper.

Cheap, generic soda washed down steaming sporks full of food. I ate like there was no tomorrow, my pants straining against my expanding belly.

We were exhausted when it was over, gasping for breath as if we had exercised something more than our mouths. We methodically repackaged the leftovers and put them back in the fridge. The dishes were all paper and plastic, so we threw them away.

Hunger satisfied, we began our trek back upstairs. Dean paused at the body of the dead Jehovah's Witness, reaching down to pat his pocket areas and, finally, reaching inside one.

"What are you doing there, Dean?" I questioned, Tim nodding at my side.

"Looking for this," he chirped, withdrawing a set of keys. "Maybe they go to that car in the parking lot."

"I thought you were going for his wallet," Tim chirped.

"In the middle of a zombie apocalypse?" responded my neighbor, hurt registering in his voice. "Seriously? What could I do with his wallet? Steal his identity? His milk money?"

"He might have his driver's license in there. We would know who he was."

Dean looked a little deflated. He rolled the formerly living man over and patted his back pocket for his wallet. After a few disgusted looks, while struggling with the tight trousers, he produced a brown leather billfold. He let go of the man, causing the corpse to roll back over. We all stared as the dead man rolled back. It was as if we expected him to rise and attempt to eat one of us.

I patted Dean on the back, showing my appreciation for a job well done. He looked back at me, relieved, before sidestepping the dead man and starting his ascent of the stairs.

We all took seats in the small office. I woke the computer with a tap of the spacebar. The screen came to life, displaying one lone living dead at the door. The parking lot was still full of zombies milling about aimlessly.

Dean dropped the keys on the counter, causing a brief musical jingling. The wallet, he kept, emptying the contents on the side of the desk. It contained the usual; credit and bank cards formed a small pile while pictures formed a different pile.

"Eric Matthews," my neighbor said solemnly, letting the card drop to the walnut stained wooden surface of the desk.

"I wonder if these were his kids?" I added to no one in particular, sliding the pictures apart with my fingertip to view them. "Was this his wife?"

Dean reached out and swept the items back to the area in front of him. "Taking the wallet was a bad idea," he muttered while forming a neat stack out of the contents.

My neighbor reverently restored the contents and closed the billfold. Lowering his left hand, he slid open a desk drawer and dropped the wallet inside. "We may not be able to bury the man, but we can bury this," he softly said while sliding the drawer closed. This act of symbolism seemed to lighten the mood. We felt a measure of closure.

A tear slid down Timmy's face as he left the room. I started to rise, but Dean's hand restrained me. "Let him go."

I understood. The boy had gone through unknown trauma. In this new world, there was little time for mourning. There was only time to survive.

I could hear my phone making a pinging sound as it vibrated in my pocket. I reached over and pressed the home button, activating the slide lock screen. There were two new text messages from Mel. With a quick gesture of my thumb, the screen came to life, a picture of my wife and I distorted by the covering of apps. I activated *Messages* and her recent texts appeared on the screen.

Things are getting bad here. Please hurry, but most of all, be safe! I love you so much. Melissa.

The next one continued the feeling of urgency.

My inhaler is nearly used up. The stress is making me use it up too fast. Hurry.

I read the messages three times before looking at Dean.

"We have to get to my wife. I think she's in trouble." I offered the phone to my friend. Dean read the messages and looked at me, sympathy showing in his eyes.

"We need a plan!" he said boldly, returning the device to my hand.

I tried to call her but, once again, there was no connection. So I settled on writing her a hasty text. *We'll be there as soon as we can Mel. Keep yourself safe. I owe you more than you could ever know and I love you even more! Henry.*

I tried calling her but the connection was already gone. I felt helpless. I had to settle for text messages. I would have done anything to hear Melissa's voice. It would have gone a long way toward making me feel like everything would be all right.

I returned my phone to my left front pocket and resumed my studying of the cameras. I wished we could see the one side of the building. We had no idea what was going on over there. The rest of the area surrounding the Kingdom Hall was visible to us, but we could only guess what the void in our view was holding.

"We have the keys to his car," I offered.

"Eric's car," Dean corrected.

"Eric's car," I repeated. "What we need is a distraction. Something to draw the undead away."

"Let's take another look around. Maybe we can find something we can use for this distraction of yours."

Chapter 14
Melissa

There was a lot of water and we were all severely dehydrated, so we took turns drinking greedily, literally shoving our heads in the cool pool of water and taking long noisy gulps. The water was tainted with the oil from the tar but it didn't matter. It was water and we were all in desperate need.

When we had drunk our fill, we carefully tied the blue tarp closed with Ned's belt. He had to keep a hand on his waist to hold his trousers from falling over his hips. In a melancholy mood from the recent events, we went back to the chair, dejected but not defeated.

With halfhearted attempts at small talk, we tried to get past our funk. There was little to speak about except the outbreak. All other things seemed diminished. Any conversation other than the virus had no bearing on the world today. The only thing that mattered was survival, what was happening here and now.

We still had no food so we just sat, conserving our strength and stamina. Belly full of water, I positively swished every time I moved. But I still felt hungry.

We stayed in the little shade the rooftop offered. The square room-like structure surrounding the doorway offered the best protection from the sun, but it seemed like the infected there could feel our presence. As we approached, they became more active, moaning and pawing at the door.

Even though they were securely barred from our area, it was too unnerving being so close and hearing them as they tried to get to us, to rip into our flesh. So we kept to the low walls surrounding the roof's edge, changing places as the sun moved across the partly cloudy sky.

Early that day, I received a text from Henry. He assured me that he was on his way. It was comforting, but we were losing strength up on this roof. We were in serious trouble.

We slept much of the time. We were always careful to appoint someone to stay awake. It was difficult to keep watch. Even though spring was still young, the days were warm. If we weren't careful, we could suffer a heat stroke or worse. Sticking to the shadows of the low wall forced us to stay in a reclined position. That, combined with the heat made getting drowsy and falling asleep a real possibility while on watch.

The nights got very cold. We rehung the tarp each night to try to add to our water supply. It helped hold some heat in, but we had to huddle together to stay warm. We were very cautious with our water supply. It hadn't rained since the first night and our supply was dwindling. What we caught each night wasn't enough to replenish our supply. At some point, unless it rained, we were going to run out.

We began rationing the second day. The temperature swings were really starting to get to us at that point, freezing to death at night and boiling during the day. Even with water and food, we would eventually die of exposure. Our mood went from bad to worse. Bellies rumbling, we were getting weaker from the lack of food. If I stood too quickly, I got very dizzy. We were in danger of falling over the edge, so we moved our little camp to the stairwell. The infected within seemed to have lost interest in us. We hadn't seen them leaving the building, so we assumed our infected coworkers were still trapped inside.

We hatched crazy schemes to get off of the roof. Thinking that the sick people may have died, we even discussed how we could safely enter the building and make a mad dash for the door. We discussed anything and everything. There were no bad ideas, even though some of them were really, really bad ideas. We considered everything.

"The chain and padlock are still on the door," Ned suggested. "I say we open the door a crack and see what it looks like. They could be all dead inside."

"What if they aren't?" asked Amber in a shaky voice.

"We could try to chain it again," Ned answered, sounding ready to try anything.

"There's an easier way of knowing," I said raising my hand. I struck the flat of my palm against the door several times in succession. The sound echoed down the stairwell.

A chorus of moans answered the noise. They sounded far away at first, but over time they approached the other side of the threshold. Hands pawed at the steel enclosure, trying to find a way to us.

80

"You drew them to us," Ned accused.

"Even if we found a way into the building, they would kill us before we got out of here," I assured my friends. "Remember, the key is on the ground with Ted. If nothing happens by tomorrow morning, I say we cut up the tarp and make a rope. I think it is fairly obvious that we are not going to be rescued"

As my friends both hung their heads, I thought of the last words my husband had spoken over the phone to me. *I'm going to come and get you,* as if he were some hero. Although, he did sound different when he said it. He sounded determined.

I pulled out my inhaler and blew out a long breath. As I drew in the hot humid air I released the medication, inhaling it deep into my lungs. Looking the dispenser unit, I noted that it only had a few more doses of it. Things were about to get a bit dicey.

Hurry, I thought to myself, refusing to believe Henry wouldn't make it.

Chapter 15
Henry

We searched for what seemed like hours. As Timmy and Dean slept their shifts, I continued the hunt for anything we could use to draw the zombies off for just a short while. We needed just enough time to get to Eric's car and race to my wife. My quest was fruitless.

There was no useful way. I even thought that launching balls of ground meat might draw the undead walkers away. It might have worked, too. That is, if we had any way of testing it.

Timmy relieved me, sending me off to bed. It was nearly midnight and I was really sleepy. Dean was snoring under a blanket on the floor. I pulled the remaining blanket over myself and laid my head on a musty-smelling pillow. The floor was hard, but at least it wasn't lumpy. My mind continued working on the puzzle. How could we make the zombies leave the area? I drifted off.

*****

"Everybody up!" Dean was screaming as he flicked the lights on and off repeatedly. "On your feet! Something's happening!"

My heart was pounding as I raced into the office. The computer screen was displaying the camera orientated to the front of the parking lot. The scene was chaos.

A group of bikers had rumbled down the road. The large group of zombies we had drawn to this area, along with others who had heard the loud bikes, met the motorcycle riders in front of our building. The undead blocked the way so well that they forced the motorcycle gang to stop and were even now engaged in battle. Shots ripped through the air as the two groups clashed. Some of the bikers fired guns, while others preferred handheld weapons.

Many of the gang dismounted and fought on foot, brandishing everything from axes to crowbars. One guy had a Samurai sword and must have been a trained martial artist. He met his enemy like a tornado. His spinning kicks and flashing blade cut a path through the gathering undead. His dynamic moves proved useless in the end. The zombies just walked right into his vicious attacks and overwhelmed him.

A black leather-clad bear of a man fought hand to hand. Huge muscles bulged under his bare, hair covered-arms. He punched one tattered-looking zombie right in the mouth.

"What an idiot!" I stated after observing the jaw-breaking haymaker.

"What?" asked Skud.

"That tough guy just punched a zombie in the mouth," I commented. "Nice way to get infected!"

"They do that in movies all the time."

"Movies have writers," I said. "If they want you to live, they just make it so. They don't have to follow any path of logic. They just skip whatever reality they want."

"But it looks cool," the youth intoned.

"Just don't ever do that. The next thing you know, you'll be infected."

The other bikers held their own, dispatching the slower-moving undead, but the sounds of the struggle brought more zombies to join the fray. Shuffling corpses came from all directions. Arms reaching and mouths agape, they surged forward toward the diminishing group.

At some point, the bikers realized they couldn't win this fight. They returned to their bikes and began to leave. Abandoning their dead and wounded, the remaining motorcycle riders tore off in the direction they had come, killing a last few zombies on the way.

"This is our chance!" I exclaimed, stepping over to the duffel bags. We stuffed the little we had gathered into three bags now, each of us bearing one of Dean's shotguns, my revolver holstered at my side. We returned to the computer to see how it looked outside. The undead were moving off, drawn by the bikers. We were long forgotten.

After a few minutes of waiting, we cracked the door and peeked outside. The viewable area seemed clear. The only dead outside were sprawled on the ground.

"Let's go!" shouted Dean, slinging his bag over his shoulder, a long barrel poking out the top.

"Do you have the keys?" I asked, checking.

He produced them with a flourish and a wolfish grin. Timmy and I shouldered our burdens and picked up weapons with our free hand. After a last glance at the computer screen, I followed the youth to the Kingdom Hall's front door.

Dean unlatched one side and kicked the door open and, bringing his shotgun to bear, he tracked one direction, then the other. After determining the area was clear, we made our way toward the car. At no time did my neighbor lower the weapon. Fast-stepping with the gun to his shoulder, he acquired target after target, making sure our progress was safe.

Tim and I copied his technique. I was learning a lot from watching how Dean handled himself in dangerous situations. He never took any situation for granted, always staying on the alert, on the balls of his feet, anticipating trouble.

When we made it to the car, my neighbor glanced in the rear seat area and opened the door. While he fumbled with the ignition, Tim and I covered the area, the youth holding his handgun at arm's length while I used my shotgun. I wondered how many of the surrounding homes held frightened people, hiding from the horror all about them. How many people clung to desperate hope as their meager supplies dwindled to nothing.

"Hurry up!" I urged, feeling exposed standing on the asphalt with corpses lying all around.

"I'm trying," he replied, clearly agitated. "This idiot has keys to everything he's ever owned on this key ring. I can't find the right one."

"You better hurry!" I said, my voice raising a few octaves. "We have company!"

The fact was punctuated by a shot from our young friend's gun. There were a few dead emerging in the distance. Although they were still far away, their condition could be determined by the way they lurched about.

"Hold your fire!" I yelled to Tim. "They're still too far away."

My pulse was hammering as the dead continued their relentless march toward our unprotected place. Dean continued, keys jingling as he sorted through the ring, searching for the correct one.

"It's not here," he spat all at once while exiting the car. "We gotta go back!"

The zombies were getting a little close when we turned and

raced back toward the door. As we neared the entrance, Tim swerved to the side, a little off course.

Just as I was about to see if something was wrong, he said, "There's another car!"

Dean and I changed our course to see what he was talking about. It was a blue Nissan Altima sitting beside the Kingdom Hall, parked on the side that the cameras had not been able to show.

As we sprinted toward the vehicle, Dean said between breaths, "I think this is it! I thought I saw a Nissan keyless fob. His pace slowed as he sorted through the keys while holding his shotgun and running.

The car's lights flashed and we could hear the driver's side door unlock. The lights flashed and the locks sounded even louder as he pushed the button again, unlocking the rest of the doors.

"We're home free!" exclaimed Timmy as our hopes soared.

I chanced a look over my shoulder and saw that we had gained some distance on our pursuers. Just as relief flooded my being, I watched helplessly as our dreams shattered. It seemed to happen in slow motion. Dean stumbled as the bag of weapons slid from his shoulder, causing the keys to slip from that hand. I could see them flash in the sunlight as they cartwheeled through the air, arching toward the car. Then they slid underneath, out of view.

"No!" Dean cried, drawing the word out long in despair. He dove after them, sliding with his momentum as stray cinders ground under his body. Head hitting against the car with a soft thud, my friend immediately started scrambling for the lost keys just out of reach. We still had a few minutes before the walking dead would be on us, so I spun to guard our rear.

"Hurry up, Dean!" I urged once again as the dead bikers began to rise from the ground, swelling the ranks of the zombies surrounding us. "The dead bikers are coming back to life!"

"Screw this!" shouted Tim giving up his position and turning to the car. He flung the rear door wide and started inside. The grasping hands and snapping jaws of the two children inside met him halfway. The youth screamed as he pushed back at his attackers, dodging their mouths as each sought the flesh of his arms. Tim's forward motion reversed as the undead children surged against him.

I watched the motorcycle gang continue to rise. It was surreal.

They seemed disoriented at first but soon began scanning the area for food. Almost immediately, they were hungry. I shot the few closer ones, then heard the struggle beside me.

Swinging around, I was just in time to see the two small zombie children spill to the ground on top of Tim. One started to get to its feet, straddling Tim. It looked up at me and the creature's mouth opened wide, making a horrible squealing sound as it raised its hands toward me. The blast from my shotgun literally vaporized its head in a mist of red. The torso dropped next to the struggling duo.

I reached down and grabbed the other undead child by the collar. The beast immediately whipped its head about, faster than I had imagined it could. It snarled at me through white, gleaming teeth. The only thing keeping the diminutive zombie from biting my exposed arm was Tim, who was both pushing the beast at arm's length and pulling it from me.

I yanked the creature free and sent it sprawling several feet away. As it rose and started toward us, I brought the butt end of the gun down across its gray face, knocking it to the ground. Tim finished it off with a well-placed shot to the head.

"Got 'em!" Dean roared triumphantly from beneath the vehicle. He'd used his gun to pull the elusive keys within reach.

My friend recovered his firearm. Tim and I turned our attention to the newly reanimated motorcycle gang members, who were closing in fast. Tim shot two of the closer ones, dropping one with the first shot and using three more rounds on the second.

My shotgun blasted a hole in another of the walking dead, but it failed to kill the nightmare. As it continued toward us, I pulled the trigger and nothing happened. Dean, back on his feet, blew a good-sized chunk out of the zombie's head and it fell, face first, to the pavement.

"Get in the car!" my neighbor ordered, opening the driver's side door and pitching the bag across to the passenger side. He then hopped in, himself. Tim and I both dove for the back seat, rapidly regretting our decision. The bench-style seat was nearly covered with dried gore. It stank horribly and was immediately magnified as I slammed the door closed, locking out fresh air as soon as it shut.

Tim vomited on himself while holding his arms off the

seat. The smell and a sympathetic response nearly made me empty my stomach, as well. I could hear the car's engine come to life as the first of the undead made contact with the vehicle. Rotting hands pawed at the broken windows, leaving smears and smudges of unknown substances, distorting our view.

Dean started forward at a slow pace, nudging our attackers out of our way. Most of them came at our sides, which must have seemed closer to their intended meals.

"Run them down!" Tim encouraged in a somewhat subdued voice, his color drained from his recent vomiting episode. His eyes were red and watery. "Speed up and splatter them!"

I could see my neighbor's eyes briefly glance back in the rearview mirror. "No, the car wouldn't survive that. We'd probably be good if we were driving a Hummer, but this is a family sedan. We could break down and then we'd be trapped. There would be no escape."

"This sucks!" the youth said in frustration.

"This is smart," I argued. "We need to get out of here and we're committed to this car. If it dies, we all die."

The youth sighed his disapproval. We watched the dead as we drove around the larger clusters. Dean tried his best to avoid contacting any of the slow-moving creatures, but when it was unavoidable, he would graze them gently on the side or nudge them out of our way. We methodically made our way on to the street and soon broke free. Undead followed even as we drove far away.

"Is everybody ok?" I asked, pressing the button to open the window. Clean fresh air flooded into the stench-filled cabin.

"Fine," replied Dean, shooting a hasty look in the mirror again.

"I'm good," said Tim, looking better as his own window lowered.

"Did any of those dead scratch or bite you?" I asked Tim, not knowing how to inject any tact in voicing the question. It was something we had to know. We needed to ascertain any danger posed from one of us becoming infected. Dean's girlfriend destroyed our car and had nearly taken our lives, all because we had tried to save her. I would never voice these thoughts to the man who had saved me from my car, but we had to keep our feelings and emotions in check. The world was now a cold, calculating place, a land where the struggle for survival depended on your personal vigilance.

"I don't think so," he said, raising his arms and showing the exposed flesh. He'd removed the hoodie he had thrown up on and was now in a plain black t-shirt and jeans. "Do you see anything?" he asked, a scared look on his face.

I looked him over the best that I could in the limited space. "You look good. I don't see anything," I said as a look of relief washed away what was one of concern a moment ago. "Just a little road rash from where those children pushed you on the ground. Nothing to be concerned about."

"There were two of them!" he replied in his defense. "They caught me totally off guard."

"I'm sure they did," I agreed sarcastically.

"And I'll bet they were bitten by radioactive spiders, too. That probably gave them super strength," Dean joked, as he deftly avoided an undead crossing guard who was trying to intercept us on the road, stop sign still in hand, her vest coated with liquid long turned brown. No one commented at the comedy of the situation.

"They just caught me unprepared, that's all!"

"Wait a minute," I said, drawing the silliness to a halt. "How did they turn if they were in the car alone? I mean, does anyone who dies come back as one of them. Are we all infected?"

The mood in the car changed. The only sound was the car tires crunching over small debris that Dean couldn't avoid. We drove in silence for a few blocks, each looking out the window at this brave new world and feeling a little more vulnerable. At any moment, any one of us might die and would become a zombie with no chance of a natural death. No one wanted to become one of those creatures. No one wanted to roam this burned-out world seeking flesh to consume.

We passed fewer houses, now more spread out as we left the suburbs and traveled out into more open country. We still saw the occasional zombies, mostly traveling in small groups as if some type of herd mentality was present, ingrained in the undead unconscious mind. They were in the oddest places, in fields, wooded areas, and yards alike. I couldn't help but think that this was no virus. It was something more. But I wasn't sure. I wish I could have examined the undead children and discerned their cause

88

of death. Had they reanimated without being bitten? I needed to experiment and find some form of evidence to confirm my hypothesis.

Mostly, we saw the devastation left in the wake of the walking dead; cars run off the road and lanes blocked by vehicles, wrecked and abandoned. It was funny. People had sat in the right lane and died there instead of crossing over to the opposite lane and going against the traffic. It was part of our instilled sense of thinking, right and wrong; Always stay in the right lane. Dean now spent a good deal of time driving down the wrong lane.

We only passed two other moving vehicles. One was a truck with a bunch of hairy baseball cap-wearing men in the back. They wore camouflage and held serious-looking firearms. They cheered as we drove past, pumping their weapons in the air to punctuate their fervor. The other was a car. It was seriously overloaded. A roof rack was stacked with all forms of luggage. It towered awkwardly above the sedan, pitching dangerously to the side as they passed by on a bend in the road. They looked like a family and they were traveling the direction we had come from. I hope they weren't about to run into the undead we left back there.

As we neared the small town of Grove City, where my wife commuted for work, I felt my anxiety grow again. I looked at my cell phone, but there had been no messages since our last series of texts. There were no bars showing on my phone. The country's infrastructure might be failing.

"You have to tell me where to turn," Dean said, breaking the silence.

"It's up ahead about two more miles," I answered. "How's our gas?"

"Not good," he said, glancing at the display. "We have less than a quarter tank."

The small stores and homes that fringed the town were dark. I wondered if the power had gone out in the area.

The local grocery store's doors were yawning open. One was nearly off its hinges. The store might have been looted. As if to punctuate the thought, a woman ran out with what looked like a pillowcase in her arms. Whatever the sack was it looked stuffed with food. Odd-shaped bulges pushed out at strange angles and a few rectangular boxes poked out of the top.

She was walking at a hurried pace, obviously trying to get back to safety as fast as possible without looking out-of-place. She glanced over at us, turning her package away as if to say, *this is mine. Hands off.* After a long moment, she looked forward again and veered down an alley, right into the arms of two undead who were just emerging onto the sidewalk.

The bag she'd been trying to protect dropped to the ground, dry goods spilling out the top. She tried to flee, but it was too late. A zombie woman who looked like she had suffered a bad burn had a hold of her arm, while another woman pulled back on her hair.

"Stop!" Tim cried out, unlocking his door and preparing to exit the vehicle.

I reached across the seat, putting a hand on his arm to restrain him. "No," I soothed. He looked back, harried. "She is already gone."

As we both turned back to the horror, the woman was on the pavement. Blood arched in spurts as the one holding her hair bit deeply into her neck. Her eyes met mine and she reached out a hand, fingers open, pleading for help.

I closed my eyes, not wanting to see anymore. I had witnessed too much.

Our young companion struck the back of the front seat with a tightly clenched fist and muttered to himself, "We couldda helped her!"

"It was too late. We would have died," our driver replied in a serious voice while pointing in the other direction.

Five more walking dead shuffled into view, each one more horrifying than the next. One was a construction worker who had a long flap of skin dangling from his jaw to his gore-covered orange-vested chest. Missing one arm, his other jerked in time with his lurching movements.

Another was an old woman with a large, distended belly. Her once pretty dress was now soaked in dark blood. Whether the bloody stain was hers or her victim's, we had no way of knowing.

A few blocks away, I said, "Make a right."

Chapter 16
Henry

"That was a fast two miles," remarked Tim, still sitting forward on the crusty seat.

"There's a drug store a few streets away." Tim gave me a questioning look, so I added, "My wife has asthma. Her inhaler is nearly empty, so we need to get her a new one."

The youth gave me a firm nod, determination reflected on his face. As we approached the small outdoor complex, I breathed a sigh of relief. There were no undead in sight. The double doors at the entrance to the pharmacy stood open, as if beckoning us to enter. The shop was flanked on each side by a barbershop and a video store.

"What kinda hick town is this?" Tim replied, making his voice twang with a southern accent.

"What do you mean?" I asked, looking for some telltale sign, a confederate flag or boot shop, something that would suggest a country motif.

"A video store? Really? Haven't they heard of Netflix or the internet?" he said, laced with sarcasm.

Dean glanced back at us in the rearview mirror. "I know what you mean. I saw a car back there with wood panels on its sides. Who does that guy think he is? Barney Rubble?"

Tim cocked his head, meeting his eyes in the reflection. "Who?"

His forehead creasing, Dean turned into the parking lot. "Barney Rubble? The Flintstones? What's up with this generation? They have no respect for the classics!"

We pulled right next to the front doors. The darkness within obscured anything more than twenty feet inside. Dean turned off the car and we readied ourselves to enter the shrouded store. Leaving the shotgun, I pulled the revolver Dean had given me out of the holster and opened the car door.

The pavement crunched under my feet. Garbage was strewn everywhere. A trail of abandoned articles led out of the drug store, probably from people overloaded with their looted goods.

As we neared the door Tim, kicked a bag of cheese curls out of his way. The sudden noise startled Dean and I. Our heads swiveled, first to the discarded package, then to the person who had struck it in the first place.

"What!" he asked in very low tones while shrugging his shoulders.

I put my pointer finger to my lips and mimicked a shushing gesture. I imagine Dean would have done the same, if not for the two flashlights he had to juggle to gain a free hand. The sound of our passing magnified as we entered the silent store. My friend handed me a flashlight as we approached the darkness.

Our lights caused twin beams to knife through the darkness, creating independent lanes of illumination. The shelves were half empty, much of their former contents being on the floor. This probably spoke to the haste of other people's foraging. I made my way to the back of the store.

The only sounds I could hear were of our passing. The crunching of each step, exasperated by the tension in the air, made it sound like an army was walking through. I stepped around a big red stain in the middle of the main aisle. The blood mostly obscured a bunch of snack cakes and their packages, which were ground into the floor. It was all mixed together in a disgusting puddle.

A third beam of light cut through the dimly illuminated aisle as Tim had managed to find a Maglite and some batteries, as well. It was one of those used by law enforcement people in cop shows. I could never figure out why they carried something so large and bulky.

As I neared the pharmacy area I could hear a wet, smacking sound. It appeared that the noise was getting louder as I neared the counter. The hair on the back of my neck rose. Everything seemed all right, but I knew that something was on the other side of that counter. I had a feeling that it was something I didn't want to disturb.

The problem was that my wife needed medication that was also behind the counter. I had to get it. She needed it.

I waved a hand behind me to halt my comrades. When I heard the sounds of movement cease, I tapped the counter with the barrel of what Dean had told me was a Colt .45 revolver. Instantly, a bald, blood-soaked head rose up, chewing on something that hung from its mouth. Its white skull showed through a large rip in the creature's forehead. The flap of torn flesh dangled over one eye.

I raised the pistol, taking careful aim. I was able to kill the zombie at my leisure from the safety of the opposing side of the counter. This was so easy. I literally had time to read the pharmacist's name tag. The horror raised its arms as if to grasp me but was held at bay on his side.

"Stop," Dean said in a hushed, yet commanding, tone. "Don't shoot! The noise of the shot could draw others."

I lowered my weapon just as Tim brushed past me. A ray of light arced through the air, tracing the path his flashlight took on its way toward the zombie's skull. The beam winked out as it came in contact with the undead creature's head. The impact knocked it to the ground.

I guess that's why police carry those heavy flashlights. I made a mental note to try to pick one up as soon as possible. The youth leapt after the floored creature to finish the beast off. Tim drew the flashlight back to deliver the fatal blow. As the light reached its apex, the bulb flicked back on, illuminating another undead moving quickly behind.

I whipped my Colt up, firing without much of an aim. The muzzle flashed. Skin and hair flew from where the bullet struck, but the nightmare continued forward toward our young friend. Tim's light whipped away, arching once more at the undead pharmacist, leaving the new threat hidden in the inky dark. I could see Dean's light track away, scanning the building for new threats as I slid half across the counter trying to draw a bead on the newcomer.

My own flashlight revealed Tim struggling in a pile of gore. It was hard to tell who belonged to what until my young friend pushed his attacker's head away at full arm's length. I nearly pressed the business end of the gun against the side of its long hair. As I pulled the trigger, the room filled with a bright flash. I felt the gun buck in my hand. The bullet made a second loud bang as it slammed through the file cabinets holding filled prescriptions; blood and brains splattered a second later.

Dark liquid ran from the now still corpse's mouth, spilling on Tim's shoulder as he rolled the hideous form to the side. I shined my light both up and down the walkway behind the counter. It was clear. Nothing stirred.

Slipping the rest of the way over the counter, I helped uncover the youth. He favored one arm. A wet stain spread from the other. My heart fell.

"What happened?" I asked, filled with dread and knowing the answer without acknowledging it.

"I don't know," he said, raising the limb and pulling the saturated fabric from the wound beneath while wincing.

I helped him to a seat further back in the pharmacist's work area. Dean took up a position in front of the counter, unwilling to stand behind it with the undead and their victim who had lost her head at some point prior to us coming to this place.

I helped the young kid out of his t-shirt. Shining my flashlight, the wound had the distinctive pattern of a bite.

"How does it look?" Tim asked in a tiny voice. His whole body was shaking.

"Keep pressure on it!" I said in a firm voice while placing his trembling hand over the wound. "I'm going to get some bandages. Lucky for you, this happened in a drug store." I said that with the best grin I could muster. He was a dead man walking.

I found a door near where Tim was sitting and used it to exit into the main part of the store. Calling Dean over, I noticed he had a rectangular box shape in a plastic pharmacy bag secured to his belt.

"What's in the bag?" I asked.

"Something for Timmy," he answered, a grin on his face.

I told him what we needed. Our lights roved half empty shelves as we moved further into the dark store. As we searched, we spoke in hushed tones.

"He got bit?" he said, sounding shocked.

I nodded.

"Can't we do something about it? I mean, you're a doctor, right?"

I shook my head side to side. "Not that kind of doctor. At some point, he will turn."

"Can't we kill the virus? Maybe we can cut out the infection, kinda like sucking out snake venom."

Eyes falling to the floor, I explained while pulling several boxes of gauze off the shelf. "If whatever is causing this illness gets in the bloodstream, it is too late. Blood moves about three feet per second through our veins; it makes a round trip from the heart every minute. The bite punctured veins in his arm. It was too late as soon as it happened."

Dean looked crestfallen. "He is... was so young. What can we do?"

"We will make him as comfortable as possible. Then, when the time is right, we will kill him, mercifully, before he dies. That way he won't turn." I could hear slow, shuffling footsteps at the front of the store.

We returned to Tim's side, my neighbor pushing a bottle of hydrogen peroxide into my hands. Setting my flashlight on a nearby shelf, I hastily fit my hands inside a pair of rubber gloves I found near the gauze and poured some hydrogen peroxide over the wound. Using my best bedside manner, I said reassuring comments as the liquid foamed. I blew on it just like my mother had when I skinned a knee or elbow.

The bleeding had slowed, so I placed a large, wadded ball of gauze over the wound. Winding more around his skinny arm I kept the dressing tight to help stave off further bleeding. A gunshot from behind alerted me to the danger still present.

I sped into action. Retrieving the light, I left Tim in the dark and began scanning the shelves for the right section. Another blast lit the far side of the room, urging me to hasten my pace. I had to keep my head. Slow down. I couldn't blow this chance. Then I saw it.

"We gotta hurry up!"

Grabbing a large plastic bag, I stuffed all the inhalers into it, even some types she didn't use. Another shot ended my greed. I secured the plastic bag to my belt and once again drew my handgun.

"Got it!" I called out.

Dean's light spun in my direction. He met me at our young friend's side. Our lights showed a pale sweating face in obvious pain. He had pulled his shirt back on while I was away.

"We need a back door!" Dean urged as more sounds marked the arrival of other zombies. "We gotta move!"

I lent Tim the support of my arm as we made for the rear of the building. Our two beams found the way out in the darkness. We stopped at the exit, Dean leaning close between us. "I'll take point. You guys stay behind. Reload now. We may not get another chance out there. We fumbled in the minimal light, pulling ammunition out of pants pockets to fuel our weapons.

I snapped my revolver closed and looked up to see a grinning Dean.

"Ready!" he told, more than asked.

"Go!"

He pushed the exit bar, opening the door to the outside world. The light was blinding. We all shaded our eyes with upraised arms, Dean taking the lead position. The way was clear to the right, so we circled the building as few ragged dead followed from the left. We stopped at the corner, and after seeing that the way was clear, we sprinted toward the front of the old video store. At the corner, we stopped again to see if any undead barred our way.

"There are too many of them," Dean said between breaths.

Tim looked much worse for the wear. Blood seeped from the bandages, a few rivulets running freely down his arm. His breath was ragged.

"How many is too many?" I asked, Tim and I sneaking our own peeks.

"Fifteen, maybe twenty. If we can only get to the car. A distraction would be nice. Any motorcycle gangs nearby?"

Our zombie followers started rounding the corner. Their hungry moans increased in urgency as we came into view.

"What are we going to do?" I urged.

Tim drew himself up and point at a poster in the video store's side window. He said, "The needs of the few."

The poster was selling the remastered DVD version of one of the Star Trek movies. Spock was the main image on the display.

"Or the one!" he finished and sprinted out in front of the store.

We both reached to stop him, but he was gone.

Chapter 17
Melissa

This roof was not going to be our death trap! Sitting by the door, I looked over at the tarp and tried to decide how thin I could cut the plastic material so that the strips would still bear our weight. It would need to stretch about three floors, or at least near enough that we would be able to drop to the pavement without risking serious injury. In the world today, an ankle injury would most likely be a death sentence.

The other problem was that we were getting weaker by the moment. The total lack of food for the last few days not only made us dizzy and lethargic, but we were losing our physical strength. If we waited any longer than morning, would we be able to climb down the makeshift rope?

I could hear the infected on the other side of the roof pawing at the steel-sheathed door. Moans escaping through the barrier caused goosebumps to rise on my arms and neck. My friends had retreated to the shady side of the roof.

I checked the edge of the pocketknife to test its sharpness. As I drew it across my fingertip, I didn't even feel the razor-sharp edge dig a little too deep. A drop of blood rose to the surface. A moment later, the sick people on the other side of the door positively attacked the metallic surface. They clawed at the door as if in desperation.

At first, I drew back in terror. But as the situation dawned on me, I became increasingly curious. I guess I'd been hanging around my husband a little too long, because I slowly rose to my feet. Leaning back against the cool surface of the brick wall, I gave myself a few moments for the world to stop spinning, then stepped toward the chained and locked door.

The fury of the predators on the other side increased. I literally thought I could see the metal barring their way vibrating with each attack. Then it dawned on me. It was moving. The doorframe set into the mortar and brick structure was coming loose. Eventually, it would break free, allowing the infected trapped on the other side access to the rooftop and everything there, including us.

I spun on my stocking-covered heel and sprinted for the others.

Chapter 18
Henry

Dean and I watched from around the corner as Tim ran between the ranks of the undead. Arms waving and screaming obscenities, he kept far enough from them to stay safe but close enough to entice them to follow. The young man avoided clusters of zombies but would soon become trapped, as they would eventually close in around him. In his condition, he could only keep up this speed for a short while.

"We should go," I said, looking over my shoulder at the creatures approaching from the rear.

Tears streamed down my friend's face as he locked eyes with me. Wiping his cheeks with the back of his shirtsleeve, he muttered, "We can't waste his sacrifice. He's doing this to give us a chance."

As he rose, I realized the bond the two of them had forged in such a short while. It was something I had never done. Sure, I shared deeper bonds with my wife, but I never experienced this feeling with another man, the strong ties of friendship, camaraderie.

Checking the bag tied to my belt, we broke from our cover. Sprinting in front of the video store, I searched for potential threats. Dean ran at my side doing the same.

The reanimated corpses had followed our young companion. Three of the ones trailing far behind Tim turned at the sound of our approach. But we had the angle on them. We were going to make it.

As we closed to within ten feet of our car, a badly burned zombie stumbled out of the store, blocking the passenger door. Its back was turned toward me. I had far too much forward momentum to change direction now. Lowering my shoulder, I barreled into the disgusting horror just as it turned my way. Its loose, relaxed form crumpled under the collision. Half dried, sticky gore clung to my shoulder as the undead creature flew away from the point of impact.

As the beast crashed to the pavement, I wheeled about, grabbing the door handle and heaving it open. I could hear another approaching as I hopped in the seat. Hands reached through the open door, followed by a snapping maw. I pushed back, trying to clear the way so the door would close.

As I struggled with the undead, I saw the barrel of a shotgun slide past my face. Leaning my head away from the weapon, I anticipated a loud discharge. My heart sank when the gun's hammer merely clicked.

"Crap!" Dean screamed as he withdrew the weapon. My left hand found a grip around the zombie's throat, its dull empty eyes staring into mine. Foul liquid flowed over brown, cracked teeth and out of its gaping mouth. It ran freely down my extended arm as the undead beast's hands raked at me, trying to pull me closer for a taste.

The corpse's skin was slick and hard to hold. My hand was losing its grip as the zombie thrashed about, trying to get free. The weight of its body, combined with its strength, made my locked arm muscles burn from the exertion. I couldn't hold out any longer.

A hand extended past me again, this time holding a familiar snub-nosed revolver. Two loud bangs sounded in succession as the zombie's weight went slack. I kicked with my legs to clear the now still corpse from the door opening. Reaching out, I pulled the car door closed, locking it as soon as it shut.

"That was close," Dean said, slumping back into the driver's seat.

"Almost too close," I replied, leaning back in my own. "Thanks!"

"Don't mention it," he answered good-naturedly. "But we better get moving."

The first of the zombies that were trailing us cleared the corner of the building and were streaming toward our position. Dean started the Nissan and threw it in reverse as I checked the package strapped to my belt.

It was gone. Panic spread through my body. As the car pulled back, I saw the white pharmacy bag lying on the pavement beside the corpse I had battled at the door. The trailing undead were nearly on top of the spot where it lay.

"The inhalers," I yelled, grabbing his shoulder with my left hand while pointing with my right.

"Got it!" he assured, dropping the car into drive and accelerating rapidly. We met the first zombie at the same spot we had parked before. Taking him at the knees, he fell heavily onto the hood of the car. It crumpled under the weight of the creature. Seemingly unaware of its injuries, the zombie never let its one good eye leave the two of us, totally fixated on its prey.

I swung the door open and leaned out, extending myself over my former nemesis. Snagging the bag, I pulled myself back, feeling muscles I hadn't used since childhood burn with the effort. After I slammed the door home, I reached for the locking button while watching the one-eyed undead man's progress. He had crawled over to my side and must have been inches from reaching through the door as it closed. His torso was leaning against the windshield, covering my view with a thick coating of some slimy substance and gore.

Dean put the vehicle in reverse as I depressed the door lock button. A strange whirring sound emitted from the door panel. As the car careened backward, the corpse started to slide until its extended hand reached through the opening window and found a handhold on the window frame. I had hit the wrong button. Two choices, and I hit the wrong freakin' one.

My friend swung the car to the left, still going backward, spilling the reanimated predator off the hood to my side. But the lifeless hand remained fixed on the now wide-open window.

With both hands, I worked the buttons, finally succeeding in locking the door. The window whined, pushing against the corpse's iron grip, unable to slide up. Our car stopped for the briefest second, but it was time enough for its other hand to join the first at the opening. Drawing my pistol, I hammered with the handgrip at the fingers trying to break their hold, but the lifeless being pulled itself forward, pushing with nearly ruined legs.

The automobile shot forward again, causing the zombie to lose ground, but its hands remained firmly planted on the window frame.

"Shoot it! Shoot it!" shouted Dean while he deftly avoided the walking dead who had refilled the parking lot.

I hastily spun the weapon around and fired point-blank into the creature's forehead. Red blood misted as the momentum of the car blew the liquid back, but the corpse remained, dragging along on the side of the car. It took several tries to dislodge the fingers free of their grip in the window's opening, the body kicking wildly as it grated against the pavement. The last digit tore free of our vehicle, sending the lifeless zombie spinning to the road. The car bucked as we drove over some limb. I immediately closed the offending window and slumped back into my seat.

The reassuring silence of the cabin area brought my pulse back to normal. As the undead fell back into the distance, a calm seemed to settle over us. The sacrifice Tim had given us was the reason we were still alive now.

"He knew he was going to turn into one of them," I offered, softly feeling my eyes fill with moisture.

"I know," Dean answered softly. "I hate this new world!" He punctuated the last by striking the steering wheel smartly with the flat of his hand.

We retraced our route to the main road without speaking. Leaving each other to our own solitary grief.

As we pulled out onto the main road once again Dean reminded me to tell him where to turn. I assured him I would and we drove the last few miles in silent remembrance.

Chapter 19
Melissa

My friends rose unsteadily to see what was wrong, Ned wobbling slightly and Amber using the low wall to help her gain some sense of balance. Both looked alarmed.

"What is it?" asked Ned, gaze locked on the door. He had his section of the cubical support in one hand and was pulling Amber to her feet with the other.

"The door is coming loose," I answered, not disclosing my possible part in the problem.

Amber nearly dropped to the roof again. If Ned hadn't shot a quick arm around her waist, she surely would have fallen.

"We're going to die up here!" she sobbed onto his shoulder as she turned into his embrace, shoulders pumping with each new breath.

After a few moments of reassuring the young woman, he broke their embrace and silently crept closer to the secured door. He went as close as he dared, then just as quietly returned to us.

"They seem to have settled down again," he breathed in relief. "I think it is going to be ok. What happened?"

"The whole door was moving," I explained. "It looked like it was coming loose."

"That's impossible! It's made of steel." Amber argued, wiping tears from her eyes.

I shook my head in disagreement. "It was coming loose from its moorings. The whole frame was wiggling."

Ned lowered his head in defeat. "What do you think we should do?"

"We need to step up my plan. We need to get off of this roof."

Because the tarp held our only source of water, we drank as much as we could hold, each taking turns plunging heads into the pool of tar-tainted liquid and guzzling huge amounts. The oily water made our stomachs turn, but it was our last, so we continued to gulp until we could drink no more.

Amber spilled what remained on to the pebbled surface of the roof. The pool spread into a large circle, darkening the area. Looking at the quickly evaporating stain, I knew we were now totally committed to our escape.

We then set about the task of cutting the tarp into strips. Gauging the distance as close as we could, Ned cut through the plastic as evenly as was possible. Each strip was carefully knotted to assure a safe descent.

When the makeshift rope was complete, we stretched it out along the low wall and measured it.

"By my best guess, I think we are about ten feet short," Ned reported.

Amber's eyes opened wide, "What are we going to do now?"

Looking about, my eyes fell on Ned's suit jacket, discarded to one side. "Amber, take off your jacket," I answered, stripping off my own. I retrieved my almost empty inhaler and stuffed it into the waistband of my skirt.

We secured the three pieces of clothing to the bottom of the line. "That should do it!" I said, letting the now complete rope fall to the roof's surface. "We just need a place to secure it."

As we were walking around the perimeter of the building, I heard what sounded like tires on the pavement below.

"Turn right at the next street," I warned Dean.

The car slowed and he followed my direction. The sun was starting to creep toward the horizon as the building my wife worked at came into view. It was a three-story box with dark tinted windows, a small balcony being created by the walls indenting at the corners of the building.

"She's in the third floor on the right side," I explained, examining my phone for any updated information. I still had no connection here.

We drove through the parking lot. Our tires made the occasional popping noise as we rode over bits of debris. From what it looked like, they had very little zombie impact. Most of the were cars parked in neat, tidy rows and it almost looked like a normal day. We drove around to her side of the building and I could faintly make out the words, *Alive inside*. What looked like printer paper made the letters of each word, but it was hard to tell through the heavily tinted windows.

The parking lot and surrounding area looked totally clear, not a zombie in view. I felt relieved but disturbed at the same time. Melissa's messages spoke of her being in danger. When we last spoke, days ago, it sounded bad and the last text said to hurry. One might think she was overreacting, but Mel wasn't prone to that. If anything, she typically understated events. This was strange.

"This is odd," my friend stated as if reading my mind. "Her messages made it sound really bad."

We slowly circled in front of the building. The setting sun was mirrored in the black tinted glass. It almost looked tranquil. We came to a gentle stop in front of her side. It looked like there were no lights on. The power outage was probably widespread.

Exiting the vehicle, we were careful to look around for unwanted visitors. After confirming that the surrounding area was clear, I called out softly, "Hello?"

"Melissa!" Dean cried much louder, the word echoing off the building.

Three heads popped up above the roofline.

"Hank?" came a tentative reply. Then, much more clearly, "Hank!"

I began running for the front door.

"Hank! Stop! The building is full of them!"

I stopped in my tracks, looking at the building suspiciously, the dark tinted windows hiding any sign of what was happening inside.

"What can we do?" I asked, looking back up while using one hand to shield my eyes from the bright contrast of the glare.

"We need a way down. Maybe a rope or something."

Dean and I looked around and saw nothing that could help in the immediate area. We looked at each other, hoping for some spark of an idea. Nothing.

"Any ideas?" I called upward, thinking one of them might have a plan.

"There's a hardware store in town. We think there might be something there."

I couldn't imagine what we could use there. "Maybe we could get some rope?"

"We'll have to see. I don't know how we could get it up to them."

I turned back to the building and once again blocked the reflected sunlight. "Stay there, I have something for you."

As I returned to the car, I could see Dean fishing around in the bag he had brought from his house. He produced three small bottles of water and some cans of food. Getting a little closer to the building, he began tossing them up. They barely made it over the edge of the roofline. The three occupants of the rooftop with much cheering quickly retrieved the supplies.

I pulled out one of the inhalers and tried to duplicate his feat. The cardboard created too much wind resistance, making throwing it that high nearly impossible. Unpacking the inhaler, I had better results. The small, pressurized container arced over the edge of the roof on the first try.

After a few seconds, I heard my wife exclaim, "My puffer!" She appeared at the edge of the roof, holding her prize high in the air. "I love you, Coop!"

"I love you more, Mel!" I replied, grinning. "We'll be back as soon as we figure something out."

When I looked at Dean, his eyes were sad. I felt a pang of sympathy. His live-in girlfriend had succumbed to the zombie infection while I got to keep my wife. It must have felt so unfair. I tried to contain any outward look of joy as we opened the car doors. With a last look over my shoulder, I saw the rooftop dwellers waving in appreciation. I gave a quick wave back and took my seat, closing the door behind me.

"Any idea where this store is?" he asked, starting the car again.

"Not far," I assured. "The other side of town. We bought a ceiling fan there a couple of years ago. It's one of those mom and pop stores."

"Maybe we can get a ladder?"

"A three-story ladder?" I asked, sarcasm dripping from my words.

"Can you think of anything else?" he asked, urging me to do better.

"I liked the rope idea. Maybe we can find a grappling hook," I responded, as I mimicked a twirling motion.

"You'd probably just put your eye out," he joked.

As we approached the main part of town, things were much worse. Since we left our neighborhood, we had mostly been in sparsely populated urban areas. The homes were more spread out, and in some cases separated by long expanses of woods. Now we were entering a town, albeit a very small one. It was more densely populated with the undead, a fact we were becoming all too aware of by the number of zombies roaming the streets. They were everywhere, and as they saw our car, the walking dead began closing in on us.

"We gotta get outta here!" I suggested rather urgently.

"Tell me about it!" Dean agreed, trying to make a U-turn in the middle of the road.

He nudged two animated corpses out of our way, but as we started in the opposite direction it was quite clear that our way out was closing fast.

"I'm gonna ram our way out of here!"

I saw no alternative. He floored the accelerator and we shot forward. Dean tried to avoid striking any of the dead directly, but there were so many that he couldn't avoid all of them. The already dented hood repeatedly took more and more blows until the engine

106

sounded like the fan was banging off something. Steam or smoke rose from the front of the car and we could smell coolant.

We broke from the throng of undead and Dean turned down a side street.

"What are you doing?" I cried as he turned again, this time, down an alley.

"We gotta ditch the car!" he explained hastily, probably due to anxiety. "If we stayed on the main road, they would have followed us. We would've been overwhelmed."

"What are we going to do?"

He whipped us down another road, smoke getting thicker, almost totally obscuring our vision. The car began to make a metallic tapping sound and we slowed considerably.

"Grab anything you want to take. When I yell go, get out and run!"

I dumped my flashlight into my bag and holstered the pistol. I grabbed the shotgun and waited for my friend to give the word. I didn't have long to wait.

The car began to buck violently. Dean stopped the vehicle and put it into park.

"Run!" he yelled. Both doors flew open as one. We exited the car and tore off further down the street as fast as we could go. Zombies lurched into view, drawn by the noise of the car, as we cut between two houses, escaping in relative silence. We sprinted down alleys and across lawns until we were thoroughly lost but also free of any undead associated with the car.

Behind a shrub, I stated between ragged breaths, "This feels familiar."

"Yeah, real *déjà vu*," he agreed, breathing heavily with his hands on his knees.

"Any ideas? We could go door to door again."

"I see a fire station at the end of the next block. That might make a good place to hide out."

We broke from our cover and made for the station. Huge garage doors sat to the right of a big metal door that marked the entrance to the main building. To either side of the station were small storefronts.

Two zombies tried to cut us off. Dean ducked the one's outstretched arms and I struck the other with the stock of my shotgun. Neither of the undead would be denied, though mine had to pick itself up off the pavement before it could resume the chase.

We made it to the brightly painted red door and I gave a yank. Nothing. I pushed and pulled in desperation, trying the latch for all I was worth but still nothing. It held fast. The reanimated creatures were getting closer and we were running out of time when we heard a strange sound.

"Psssttt." I looked back at Dean and we heard it again. "Pssssstt," this time a little louder and more urgent. We looked toward the noise and there, in the thin alley between the buildings, was Batman.

He was hard to make out in the dark alley. From what we could see, the Caped Crusader was pumping an arm, signaling us to follow him. I looked at my friend and he shrugged and started toward the costumed vigilante. I followed as Batman spun and disappeared through a door. As I crossed the threshold, I saw a Spiderman poster taped to the back of the door.

The door closed with a solid, wooden thunk, followed by the two deadbolts and a chain. I nearly dropped to the floor, joining my already discarded belongings. Leaning with both hands on my knees, my chest heaved in ragged gasps. My friend was doing the same.

I craned my neck to take in our surroundings. The room we entered was poorly illuminated, just enough light not to bump into things but not so much as to see too well. Batman pushed the fabric cowl back off of his head. It was then that I noticed how out of shape the Dark Knight was. The black cape and our desperation had concealed his chubby cheeks and large gut. A belly, which protruded awkwardly and possibly painfully over his utility belt, that peeked out from beneath the bulk. Long greasy hair pointed in all directions.

Our savior pulled a thick arm across his face, sopping perspiration from his brow, as he drew in a labored breath. "You guys ok?" he asked voice still shaking in fear.

"Yeah, thank you... Batman?" I offered, not knowing what to say in this bizarre situation.

"Drew," the man in costume corrected as two other costumed heroes entered the room. "We were just goofing around in these suits, seeing how we looked."

"What are you doing!" demanded the first, high-pitched voice squeaking as he turned up the lights. "They might have been bitten!"

Drew turned to us and asked, "Have either one of you been bitten?"

"No," Dean assured

"The zombies were a good twenty yards away. How would they have been bitten?" our hero added sarcastically.

The other two staying back a distance, unsure of how safe it was to approach. It didn't look like they had just tried on the costumes but rather had lived in them. The outfits were stained with sweat and what looked like food. There were also deep wrinkles at their joints. These creases added to the impression that these young men had worn these outfits for at least a few days.

"How do we know they haven't been bitten?" the thin man in a red spandex costume with a lightning bolt challenged again.

Drew looked back at us inquiringly. The man in the Flash outfit puffed out his scrawny chest. Arms on emaciated hips, he struck a rather comical heroic pose. I would have laughed if I weren't the one being accused here.

The other one spoke up, "Make them prove it!" all eyes were drawn his way. He was dressed as that Star Wars guy who rode around in the spaceship with Bigfoot, what I assumed was a toy ray gun holstered at his hip. "One of 'em might be hidin' a bite. We gotta be sure!"

"They have a point," Drew agreed, turning a skeptical eye on us both.

That's how we wound up with our pants around our ankles, spinning in tiny, shuffling circles, under the suspicious scrutiny of three guys in a comic book store. If I thought the world was surreal before, this just put it over the top. The room we were in looked like some twelve-year-old boy's dream room. Comic book posters covered the walls and old mismatched furniture was arranged in a semicircle facing a large LCD television. Snack cake and candy bar wrappers, plus the occasional pizza box, covered the floor, nearly obscuring the dirty, green shag carpet underneath.

As I completed my circle, the young man dressed as The Flash pointed with his finger, "What about under the boxers?"

I raised an eyebrow in question. The others looked at my green plaid underwear and back at their friend. "I think he's clean!" added Drew. "Besides, if either of them were bit down there, they wouldn't have been able to run."

"There would also be blood." Han Solo agreed clearly not wanting any part of us dropping our drawers.

After passing their inspection, we dressed. I didn't know how dirty my clothes were until I had to put them back on. I almost asked for a costume to avoid the feel of the soiled apparel, but just thinking of myself walking around as Spiderman changed my mind, so I pulled on the same socks I had worn for the last several days and laced up my shoes.

The Flash and Han Solo brought in two folding chairs from the other room as Drew offered us some prepackaged snack foods, their colorful wrappers offering tempting images of the type of cream-filled treats concealed inside.

I was about to turn the offered food down, but an encouraging nod from Dean changed my mind. I selected a package of Ho Hos. We all sat around eating, Mylar and plastic making crinkling sounds as the packaging was torn away. The guys in the shop tore into the sugary treats with gusto, each consuming several. Dean even went back for seconds. We shared stories about our experiences with the undead and current news reports.

It seemed that this was Drew's store and that they were hanging out playing Dungeons and Dragons the night it happened. They had just ended a quest and some of the other players had left for home when they saw the first incident. Being comic fanboys, they immediately understood what was happening. They already had a stockpile of junk food for gaming nights but had also taken the initiative to raid the local convince store. With no clerk on duty, they had made off with as much food as they could carry.

Luckily, Drew had also been environmentally conscious and had installed solar panels on the roof. This gave them enough power to run some lights and the computer or television. They could only use one or the other but not both at the same time.

The internet was down. We could only assume that their ISP's backup power had finally given out. The television was very limited with the cable being out. We picked up the three major channels being broadcast over the airwaves. The news they were showing was horrifying. Zombies were everywhere. There was still no sign of what was causing the dead to reanimate. They were still telling people to stay indoors

After about an hour, we figured out that the news was old. It was being broadcast on a loop. We turned off the LCD TV to save power.

"What are we going to do now?" asked the young man dressed as the Flash. We had found out his name was Frank.

"I need some rope or something to get my wife down," I answered.

"When we get her down, I want to find a nice, quiet place to hole up and wait till this thing blows over," added Dean

Frank started to say something, but I cut him off before he could get underway. "It won't blow over," I said firmly, drawing all of their attention. "Whatever is causing this to happen needs to be dealt with. I have a hypothesis, but I need time to prove these initial thoughts. A lab and some specimens would help."

"I'm sure the government will get this under control soon." Frank offered, hope ringing in his words.

"When have they ever had anything under control?" I asked. "Crime, the war on drugs, illegal immigration, or even taxes? Did you know twenty-five million people don't file tax returns? That's out of a little over 300 million Americans. Where are these people? Some of these people are just dodging taxes. Where is the control there?"

"Yeah!" Ben, the young man dressed as Han Solo, agreed enthusiastically. "And what about Roswell?"

"But the CDC?" Dean asked.

"Although the CDC has counterparts in many other countries, we're relying on maybe fifteen odd agencies to come up with some type of answer to this problem. I don't like the odds. We need everyone in the field to work on this problem," I stated.

"The hospitals can help," Drew spoke up hopefully.

"They're overrun. They probably took in the first wave of bite victims and were among the first to go down," Dean said. He folded his arms across his chest and looked at me skeptically. "How can you help the CDC?"

I saw in his face that he was thinking about his girlfriend. I wasn't able to do anything for her, and here I was claiming the ability to help the CDC. "In its beginning, the CDC mostly employed entomologists like myself. They still employ many in my field, as well as an array of others. But first, I have to get my wife off of that roof. They can't last much longer. They could succumb to exposure."

"What if, instead of rope, you used a ladder?" Drew asked, scratching his shaggy mane.

"Too short," I responded quickly.

"You do realize what you were trying to break into next door, don't you?" he said, sarcasm once again dripping from his words.

It took me a moment. Then, Dean and I said together, "A fire truck!"

Chapter 21
Melissa

As I watched Henry drive away, a tear ran down my cheek. I couldn't believe it. That was my husband. He'd made it here!

I couldn't fathom what he was doing with Dean. I didn't think he really knew our neighbor that well. But he had come.

I wondered what happened to Julie. Why wasn't she with them? But I pushed those thoughts from my mind and decided to just be happy that they had made it at all. From what the television had said, it was chaos out there.

My heart swelled with pride. I walked right up to Ned, who was busy using the can opener part of the pocketknife. Amber was standing beside him, nearly jumping up and down in excitement. Both were grinning ear to ear.

Drawing my right fist back, I punched him hard in the arm, nearly causing him to drop the can. My coworkers turned their attention on me, frowning. "Ouch," Ned said, shocked, forgetting the can in his hands. "What was that for?"

"Doubting!" I said accusingly while smiling broadly. "I told you Hank was coming. You made a joke of it. You called him the bug guy."

"I guess I was wrong!" he said while turning back to the can of baked beans. "I'm sorry."

I couldn't blame him. As I watched him working on the lid, I couldn't help thinking that I had harbored some of those same thoughts. I didn't think he would even notice the outbreak. I thought that he would be secured in his lab and never notice that anything out of sorts had happened.

My husband, when focusing on a problem, could be quite oblivious to things happening right in front of him. But I had kept my hopes alive. Pushing back my doubts, I believed he would come. He loved me, and seeing him those few moments ago had renewed my faith and love in him. He had crossed unknown hazards to save me. He had even wanted to rush right inside the building to free me from this perch.

Ned handed the now open can to Amber. She literally snatched it from his outstretched hand and immediately began pouring the contents into her mouth. Ned started on the next one, a can of chicken soup.

As he worked the knife's opener on the top, Amber offered the beans to me. I followed her technique and tilted the can to my lips. I never acquired a taste for baked beans. They always tasted chalky to me. But after a few days with no food, I found the unheated side dish to be one of the most wonderful flavors I'd ever eaten. I had difficulty stopping myself when I reached the limit of my portion. Saving the rest for Ned, I set the can on the roof and waited for my turn at the soup.

Amber delicately dabbed at a small trail of the concentrated liquid with a finger, savoring every drop as she passed the container to me.

When Ned finished opening the last can, which held peaches, he snatched the beans from the roof and consumed his share, followed quickly by the soup. The peaches were so sweet. It was amazing. We were actually having desert.

"I guess we just sit and wait," Amber offered, smoothing her now grimy white blouse.

"Let's get our rope secured so we can have a quick escape route," I countered while glancing back at the loosened door. "We might need another way down."

"Not trusting that your husband will make it back?" Ned asked, arching an eyebrow in shock.

"No," I shot back. "I don't trust the door to hold. I would like to have a backup plan, just in case we need to leave really quickly."

The others agreed, so we spent the last of the hour of the evening readying a Plan "B".

Chapter 22
Henry

"Drew and I are volunteers," offered Frank, excited.

"I wonder if there's a truck in there?" I mused, thinking of all the sirens we had heard from the first responders.

"The new one, I believe, is out," said Drew. "But the one we were selling is probably still in its bay. It was decommissioned, so it wasn't being used."

A thud sounded at the front of the store, followed by another. Our whole group drew weapons and made for the next room. We crept in silence through the darkness of the store, passing by odd shapes silhouetted in the black.

Another series of thuds and something hard striking glass made us freeze in our footsteps. I looked to my right and could faintly make out Ben holding his toy gun in one hand while he looked at me.

I could almost make out a silly grin as he softly said, "Hokey religions and ancient weapons are no match for a good blaster at your side, kid."

I raised my Colt. The hammer clicked as I pulled it back with my thumb. Ben's eyes went wide and his grin turned into a gulp.

Arriving at the front, I could see Dean lifting a corner of a poster covering the door. We could see a human, moonlight silhouetting it against the glass.

It stayed there, thumping against the entryway twice more before moving along. We stayed poised for action some time longer, waiting for the creature to return. When we were reasonably sure the event was over, we quietly returned to the back room and secured the door.

"I think they're former customers, mostly," Dean answered the unasked question. "I recognized at least two of them. They come to the door and it is almost like they don't know how to use it. Then, after a while, they just as mysteriously leave. It's almost as if they're going about their normal routine, mechanically, like a robot."

I added this observation to my mental notes, trying to compile information to solve the world's most pressing problem.

We stayed up another hour or so making plans for the next day. "The truck has a turntable ladder, located behind the cab," Frank explained that locating it there gave it more stability. They both assured us that either one of them could drive it, having moved the vehicle a few times each. When we felt comfortable with our operation, we decided on a watch order and took turns sleeping.

My watch was the last, so toward the end of my shift I was able to explore the front of the shop. Light filtering through tiny gaps in the posters plastering the front windows and door indicated that it was safe to turn on the lights. I still wanted to stay hidden but felt confident that the images covering nearly every square inch of glass would hide my presence.

I never knew there were so many comic books. They lined the walls in alphabetical order, back issues filed behind the more recent ones in the specially designed racks. The center areas had tables for gaming and some were covered with boxes of older back issues, all bagged with white cardboard inserts to keep them from bending.

I had never been in a store like this. There were action figures, t-shirts, and games of all kinds, even movies, some in the form of VHF tapes. It was as if someone had peeked into a typical guy's childhood and placed some of his favorite moments here. I could see why these guys loved this stuff. My moments wandering alone in the shop made it all very clear.

I was browsing through a rack of t-shirts with images ranging from scenes to character logos.

"You might want to change into one of those," Drew said, indicating the rounder by pointing a half-eaten Twinkie. "Your shirt looks like it could stand up by itself." I looked at his outfit and let my rebuttal slide.

"I don't have any money," I said, reaching for a wallet that was conveniently at home.

"You can owe me. Besides, I don't think our currency is good anymore, at least not during a Zombie Apocalypse."

I smiled, pulling out a shirt with a Superman logo. "Why are most of the shirts size small?"

The corners of his mouth rose as he ran a hand through his greasy lock. "You've obviously never seen my patrons. They tend

116

to buy up the larger ones."

Not getting the joke, I stripped off my old, plaid button-down shirt and replaced it with the clean t-shirt. As I dropped the shirt on the floor, I noticed that it did, kind of, stand up. Areas stiff with dry blood and gore retained the shape of my torso. It felt weird to put the crisp new garment over my cruddy body, but it also made me feel a little better. Looking down at my slacks, I wished I could replace those, but at least this was a start.

Drew looked at my pants sympathetically. "I have more costumes upstairs," he offered.

I looked at my new friend and smiled. His own outfit was in need of a change. I could only guess, but I was betting that the outfit he had on was the only Batman suit of that size.

"Do you have anything semi-normal?" I asked in my most diplomatic tone.

"Probably not, but we can go see."

The others were all stirring, so we told Dean where we were going and asked him if he wanted to have a look. One glance down at the front of himself and he was right on our heels.

The upstairs was much like the lower level, posters on the walls and more boxes of comic books. Drew explained that these were the duplicates. In the back were rounders hung with various costumes hanging neatly by size. The windows were all covered with heavy blackout curtains to prevent fading of the fabric.

There were costumes for cartoon characters, science fiction, and superheroes. They were all sorted by size and genre.

"Do any of these getups have regular pants?" Dean asked, going straight to the point.

"Well, the Hulk wears stretchy purple pants, but they're kinda big," Drew said with a shrug. "If a character wears normal pants, then we only supply the other parts; the odd, character-specific parts of their outfit."

We sorted through most of the stuff, but anything we found that came close to what we wanted, the material was far too thin for everyday use, let alone to hold up against your average zombie attack.

As I was finishing up, I noticed Drew and Dean peering out one of the windows. The curtain was pulled back and they were pointing at different things.

"What are you guys doing?" I asked, taking a look out at the bright day.

"The undead don't look up," Drew observed.

"What?" I asked, jockeying for position at the window.

"The zombies, they don't look at anything that isn't on their level. They don't look up."

Of the three undead I could see, none of them seemed to look up. I don't know how this fit into the picture, but it was something to think about.

"If I only had a Batarang," Drew mused. "And the upper body strength to use it."

"You'd what," asked Dean. "Swing across to the next building."

"I'd rather do that then cross on their level," he said an edge to his voice. "I'm scared."

"Would Batman be scared?" I asked, leveling my gaze at him.

Drew dropped his eyes to his feet. "No!"

"Then maybe instead of dressing like him, you should be more like him."

Drew's eyes raised and looked straight into mine. A look of determination steeled his features.

"Let's go down and get ready," I said, finishing my pep talk.

"I'll be down in a minute," Drew said, walking off into a corner of the room.

We descended the stairs and began preparing to cross the street to the fire station. Ben and Frank were whining about having to leave the safety of the comic book shop, making excuses for why we should all stay there.

We made plans the night before and no one had said a word, but now that we were about to set it in motion, these two were getting cold feet. As I was listening to Frank's monolog about the finer points of staying here, Drew slowly appeared. Hand on the rail, he took the last steps to the landing. He had put on a pair of blue jeans but still had the Batman spandex top with attached cape on. The cloth cowl, pushed back off his head, laid back on the cape like a hood. The shirt was neatly tucked into his snug pants. The utility belt completed his ensemble.

"We're almost out of food!" he said in a final sort of way. "If we don't leave now, with them, we'll soon have no food left at all."

"We could all stay here," Ben argued in a pleading voice.

118

"They are leaving, and our best chance at living is to follow them."

Frank puffed out his chest and nearly shouted, "We don't need them! We've survived here since the beginning. We can raid the mini mart again."

"Have you looked outside?" Drew demanded, gesturing toward a wall covered with posters. I wasn't about to point this out because it seemed he was on a roll. "There are ten times the amount of zombies since we looted the convenience store and our weapons suck."

Ben looked down at the Han Solo blaster holstered at his side and seemed to deflate. "I'm scared," he stated in a small voice.

"We're all scared," I added, putting my hand warmly on his shoulder. "But sometimes we have to dig deep down and become like these superheroes that you guys have read so much about. A woman, my wife, and her coworkers are in trouble and even now may be dying of exposure. We need to be their heroes."

I looked into their eyes and they all were clear, shining with an inner light, burning with determination. They all stood taller, even Dean. They were ready.

We stashed all the food and bottled water the guys had left over. I had a little beef jerky and some other dry goods drifting around the bottom of my bag. I believe Dean had the same.

My neighbor passed out the remaining guns we had. The one shotgun he had to clear the jam out of, but the remaining one was fine as well as the rifle.

The guys looked comical with their real weapons. Having never even held a gun that wasn't made of plastic before, they held the lethal steel almost at arm's length.

Each of the new recruits got a crash course on how and when to fire the gun. Dean told them to shoot for the head but to wait till the zombies were close enough to assure a lethal hit.

We each shouldered our bags, the guy's from the comic book store all bearing some type of logo belonging to an admired superhero, and readied our weapons. Drew looked about his shop one last time and then put his eye to the peephole. "Clear!" he said, throwing the bolts free and yanking the door open. It stopped after opening a mere four inches. The chain twanged taut. Hastily, he closed the door and released the final barrier before opening the way once again. This time, it ferociously opened wide, nearly taking Dean with it as it swung to the wall. The drywall crunched under the impact with the doorknob.

We made the short dash to the steel fire hall door. I took the lead, alert to any need for cover fire as Drew unlocked the entryway. I looked over my shoulder as I cleared the threshold. A few of the animated dead had taken notice and were stumbling our way. They moaned hungrily as their shuffling steps brought them closer. All at once, the light was gone. The door had closed so rapidly, it seemed like the blink of an eye, plunging us into darkness.

We waited for a few moments, allowing our eyes to adjust to the shock of the twilight interior of the hall. All I could hear was the rhythmic breathing of the men after our brief sprint. Slowly, my eyes adjusted to the contrast between sunny outside and dusky interior. The door was at the front of the hall. Tables in neat rows spoke of bingo games and spaghetti dinners. The folding metal chairs were all upside down, sitting on top of the tables as if waiting for someone to mop the floor.

"Search for more food and water," I commanded as the little light from high windows became enough for us to navigate with. A slow series of thumps at the door marked the zombies' arrival.

As the three quietly darted down the center aisle toward the kitchen, Drew leaned close. "The keys are in the office," he said in a whisper.

"Go!" I answered, releasing him to his part of the plan.

I watched his bulk disappear into the gloom and started to where I thought the garage bays would be. Twin double doors made way to a huge cavernous garage. I could see where two other vehicles were formerly parked and beyond was our prize; a big, shiny, red fire truck with a telescopic ladder mounted behind its cab. Frank had explained that it was called a 'mid-ship.' This style was more stable for engines with a shorter wheelbase. It looked huge to me as I stepped up to the passenger side of the cab.

The three I had sent for supplies were hot on the heels of Drew, who came jogging toward me with a set of keys dangling from his upraised hands. "Isn't she a beauty?" he cried, more a statement than a question. I raised my fist in victory as the others came into

120

view. They were pulling three carts stacked with food.

Boxes of pasta and jars of sauce filled the top of one of the carts. Cases of water were nearly toppling off of one another.

"They must have been planning a party," Dean remarked, skidding to a halt beside the vehicle.

"We were," answered Frank, sounding glum. "A family lost their home to a fire. We were collecting food for them. There was a spaghetti dinner fundraiser scheduled. I guess they won't need this stuff now."

"Where can we put it all?" I asked, looking at the big square box with the ladder on top.

Drew reached down and opened a massive cargo area. "This thing's covered with cargo holds and they're all empty. Remember, we were going to sell it."

Frank chimed in, "Best of all, the reservoir is still full. It has about a thousand gallons of water inside."

I just marveled at the vehicle for a moment. With that much water, we could drink till we exploded, bathe, or even have clean clothes. That was truly a wonder in this world without power.

We all pitched in, scouring the building for any scrap of edible food. Nothing was left. We packed the cargo holds with anything that we felt would be useful. Pots, pans, tarps, axes; we stored it all. When we finished, I hopped into the passenger side while Drew took the driver's seat.

The three remaining guys piled into the crew seating area behind the front cab. Our pilot checked to make sure everyone was secure.

Drew fired up the massive engine. It roared to life, rumbling with a telltale diesel sound. As he revved the motor, I could feel the vehicle tremble at the power under the hood. I watched as he reached for a garage door opener.

"There's no power," I said loudly before he could depress the button.

"It has a battery backup," he called back, grinning as he pressed the mechanism.

The door's motor engaged and slowly began to rise. Several legs came into view as undead, drawn by our rush to the building, shifted position to the sound of the truck.

As the door reached the zombies' waists, I could see them

banging at the door, unable to figure out how to get to us. They knew something living was inside and redoubled their efforts. As the opening reached shoulder height, the first of the walking corpses entered the garage, heads leaning at awkward angles as the lifeless creatures squirmed to gain access.

At first, it was just a few, the shorter ones, who shuffled toward the idling engine; drawn by the sound, not knowing where their prey hid. As more undead entered the bay, the first wandered away from the rumbling sound and almost immediately saw their quarry in the cab. I guess Drew's earlier observation had a hole in it. The zombies looked up this high.

Cold, grimy hands reached for us, falling way short of even the glass. Soft thuds marked their attempts at breaking through the door. I felt an odd feeling of security in our elevated vantage point, a safe island in a sea of horror.

By the time the door had reached its apex, there was a crowd of the creatures. I was a little concerned that the sheer bulk of their mass would stymie any attempt at us making forward progress. Drew put the automatic transmission in drive and we surged ahead, pushing through the throng with no problem.

The sound of the engine, thankfully, hid the sounds of the undead being crushed under the massive tires of the fire engine. I couldn't even detect any rise or fall as we obviously drove over the zombies who had so thickly packed in the open bay. As we cleared the doors, bright light replaced the gloom of the garage. Walking corpses filed out into the street, drawn by the roar of the truck. In search of an easy meal, they walked right into the path of the massive rescue vehicle.

Some of the living dead, we took head on, their arms reaching forward and hands clutching in anticipation as they shuffled right into the grill. Others lurched right into the side of the big, red truck, either bouncing off or spinning wildly to the ground.

We were all exuberant, giddy with the feeling of not having to fear the undead. Rather, we were issuing a little payback and exacting a small toll on the number of our enemy. Cheering and high fives were exchanged in the crew compartment as the occupants went from watching out the windows to nearly hopping up and down with joy.

As we left the main part of town, the zombies attacking our

moving vehicle dropped to a trickle. The fire engine seemed not to have suffered from the impacts with our nonliving pursuers. Drew didn't change his tactics as he turned slightly to strike a grimy-looking woman whose flower print blouse was plastered to her body, half covered with what looked like dried blood.

"That's twenty points!" he said, pumping his fist in the air.

I gave him a questioning look. "Twenty points?"

"Death Race 2000? You've had to have seen that one, right?"

I tried to remember the movie he was referring to, but my friends in those days were less the drive in and more the library type. "Sorry."

"It's a classic cult film. You gotta see it!" he said enthusiastically.

"The world is a Death Race now. I don't know if we'll ever have time to watch a movie again. Dean and I have been on the run for what seemed like weeks." The reality dawned on me the more I thought about it. It had nearly had been nearly five days since I had seen my wife. Sporadic text messages had filled in the gaps, but we had been so wrapped up in staying alive that I hadn't had much time to think of the person I loved.

Chapter 23
Melissa

The morning dawned brightly and carried with it a breeze. My hair blew with each gust, causing stray ends to fly in front of my eyes. Amber still had her hair pulled back in a clip. Although her clothes had succumbed to some of the grit from the rooftop, her hair and face still looked nearly immaculate.

We were like kids on Christmas day; eagerly anticipating what was, hopefully, coming but trying to stay calm. Each of us knew that we needed to keep our heads about us, to keep our excitement checked. There was a real possibility that they would not make it back.

We sat on the edge of the roof's low wall, all eyes fixed on the tree line where the road entered our view. While the sunlight reflected off of the swaying leaves, we drank the last of the water Dean had tossed up to us.

"Oh, my!" Amber gasped, drawing a hand to her mouth.

Ned and I followed her gaze to a man, obviously infected, who was shambling through the parking lot. He wasn't wearing business clothes, but most of the building's staff had dressed down for casual Friday.

"Is he one of ours?" Ned asked, shielding his eyes for a better view. After a moment's silence, he added, "From our building?"

Now understanding Amber, we shielded our own eyes and tried to make out who he was. The glare made identifying the distant man more difficult.

"I don't think so?" Amber admitted.

"I never saw him," I added, not recognizing him; but in the state he was in, I had no real idea. "Why?"

"I was just hoping that he hadn't figured a way out of the building," he answered. "If they do, it would complicate things."

We watched the sickened man shuffle his way onto the road. He followed the paved surface until he disappeared into the foliage. Acting on Ned's assumption, we walked the perimeter of the building. After circling the entire area, we checked the makeshift rope.

"I think he was alone. Probably just wandered past," he said, as much to sooth his own nerves as to calm us, women.

"We need to be sure," I challenged.

Leaning over the edge of the wall, we couldn't make out the entrance doors. They were inset into the building, providing a small overhang, which came in handy when it was raining.

"We need to hang out a little further so we can see if the doors are still closed," Ned announced.

Amber, being the lightest, volunteered. Ned and I each grabbed a hand and she leaned way out knees perched on the edge of the wall.

"Just a little more," she called out as we let a little more of her hang off of the roof. "A little more." she encouraged.

Ned and I held almost her entire weight as she hung nearly vertical in the open air.

"A tiny bit more," she asked.

A grinding sound gave way to sheer panic as Ned and I lost our footing on the rounded pea gravel. We both slid forward as we dug in, trying to halt our forward progress, both folding at the waist when our feet struck the wall. We pulled back, trying to reel Amber back in. Her scream turned into a cry of pain as one of her legs, having extended back in search of purchase, smacked off of the back edge of the wall.

Heaving with all of our might, we brought our friend back to safety. She immediately dropped to the wall and pulled her wounded limb towards her torso. Amber's hands covered a large, angry-looking split in her shin. Blood oozed beneath her palms as she bit back tears.

The door to the roof immediately erupted. Infected hands striking the surface made the door jump back and forth in its moorings.

I threw the rope over the side as Ned, who had stripped off his dress shirt, wrapped her wound to staunch the bleeding.

"What are you doing?" he called as I tested the rope's anchor point.

"They're going to break through! The smell of blood is driving them into a frenzy."

Looking back over his shoulder, my coworker had to agree.

"Amber goes first!" he stated, dragging the girl to her feet. "You're next!"

I never believed in the women and children first thing, but I wasn't going to argue. We helped Amber over the edge. Wiping her red hands on her skirt, she looked terrified and disparate.

"Do you think it'll hold?" she asked, looking directly into my eyes.

I faked a confident grin and said, "Sure it will. You have nothing to worry about."

Chapter 24
Henry

We were heading down the wooded lane, which lead to Xanthco as a zombie lurched into view ahead of us. The road was twisty and we weren't going fast.

"Just go around it," I suggested, but Drew just continued straight ahead.

The undead man reached both hands up in front, reaching for us as we barreled towards his embrace.

"We don't want to hurt the truck!" I stated more forcefully, remembering how the cars reacted to striking zombies I was just being realistic.

"Alright." he acquiesced. "I'll take him on the side."

At the last moment, Drew turned the big truck and drove into the walking dead man near the fender.

"Happy?" he asked sarcastically.

"Happy," I answered. It had taken most of the ride, but I had finally gotten my driver to understand that vehicles weren't made for the kind of abuse plowing through zombies produced. Over time, they damaged the car, or, in this instance, fire truck, to the point of breaking down. As the beautiful wooded road gave way to the building and parking lot we were both startled to see that someone was trying to climb down a blue rope. Drew swung the truck to a stop just past the spot where the rope dangled.

"Frank, get the ladder into position!" Drew barked in command. "Ben, grab Dean and meet me at the one climbing down the rope!"

Doors flew open and we scattered to our various positions. I was about to hurry to the rope, but Frank grabbed my arm, spinning me around. "Give me a hand!" he stated firmly.

I climbed to the top of the vehicle while Frank stood at the controls for the ladder. He swung the telescoping device up and around, then extended it toward the top of the building.

Meanwhile, the others gathered at the bottom of the rope. It was a woman slowly making her way down, a large bandage wrapped around one of her legs. She screamed as she slid down about five feet, losing her grip on the plastic surface.

"Ben! Give me a hand," the burly man in the Batman shirt and cape demanded as he sprinted toward the side of the truck. Dean looked helpless as he shifted position below the swaying makeshift rope.

A scream erupted from the roof. My heart leapt. It sounded like Melissa. I looked up and saw my wife waving her arms over the edge of the roof.

"They're almost through!" she screamed over and over. I didn't know who they were, but I had a good idea. The ladder extended past the edge of the roof and Melissa nearly jumped on to the rungs. She no sooner had started down the escape route when Mel was joined by a shirtless man.

Relief flooded my being as I watched my wife climb down the ladder. I waited at its base for her to arrive. When she reached the bottom rung, she spun and I enveloped her in as big a hug and kiss as I have ever given her. She melted in my arms.

"You came!" she cried out in joy. "My hero!" She kissed me again, more forcefully this time.

I broke our embrace and stepped back from the ladder to allow the other rescuee to step onto the vehicle. "I'm no hero," I said in all modesty.

She traced a finger across the emblem on my shirt. "You could have fooled me," she said, grinning.

A scream erupted behind us. Snapping our heads around, we saw a person fall into a large tarp held by my three friends. They braced, leaning backward, then jerked forward as the person hit the canvas surface. The tarp broke the unfortunate person's downward momentum enough to survive with no injury. As the person emerged from the cloth, I could see she was a woman.

The guys went to check on her as she stepped on the pavement. Even after her ordeal, you could tell that she was a real looker. The men were smitten, but it was Drew she wrapped her arms around, sobbing. His eyes were wide, like he didn't know what to do. Melissa and I climbed to the ground along with the shirtless guy. We began trotting toward Drew and the woman. Something made me look toward the building. It was probably the muffled pounding noise.

Melissa slowed and then joined me in looking at the dark tinted windows. Countless shadowy forms clawed viciously at the

128

glass. This repeated on the second floor. The third floor, being out of my field of vision, probably was the same.

"Dean!" I called out.

"We got to get out of here!" he answered. I looked in his direction and he was noticing the same thing I did.

"Watch out!" Frank sounded from behind the truck, the ladder almost back in its resting place.

A wet smack sounded to my right. I spun and saw a zombie plastered against the ground. Another smack heralded another one splattering to the pavement.

Looking up I saw that it looked like it was raining undead as they simply stepped off of the roof in pursuit of us.

Dodging the falling zombies, we made for the truck. We all piled into the cab areas. Drew took the driver's seat, while Melissa sat squished in beside me. The doors slammed shut.

"Where's Frank?" Ben screamed. He leaned up into our seat area as if to find him there.

I could hear a muffled voice from outside screaming "Drive, drive!"

"Ned! Where's Ned?" The woman cried out, leaning forward and searching frantically.

I opened my door and leaned out. The shirtless guy, Ned, was on his back as a zombie devoured his midsection. It looked up and I could see that it was the undead man we had hit just before we pulled into the parking lot. A long string of intestines hung from its chewing mouth. He must have survived in the wheel well or something.

I hazarded a look above and saw Frank perched up there, staring wide-eyed.

"Drive!" he yelled, and I slammed the door.

"Frank is up with the ladder," I informed everyone. "He wants us to drive!"

"What about Ned?" the woman in the back seat asked in a high voice.

"He didn't make it."

Both women broke down in tears. I slid an arm around my wife's shoulder and guided her face to my neck. Melissa's shoulders shook in rhythm with her sobs.

The mood in the truck brightened a bit when we stopped and let

Frank get off of the roof and into the truck. His hair was wild from the wind, but he seemed fine, otherwise.

"Where to now?" Drew asked, looking in my direction.

"Let's go where the zombies aren't!" I replied.

"No, seriously. We don't have much gas, so we need to figure out where we're going."

I leaned forward, Mel rolling free of our embrace, and looked at him, "Are you trying to tell me that the tank wasn't full?"

"We're a volunteer fire department. We barely take in enough money to stay open and you think we're going to sell a ladder truck with a full tank?" he shot back.

It made sense. No one buying a used fire truck would check out how much fuel was in the tank. They would be more interested in how serviceable the equipment was and how well the engine and transmission were maintained. This rig probably took a lot of gas, so it would be a waste of money to top it off for the next owner.

"I hadn't thought of that," I conceded. "We need a place to regroup. A safe place! Any ideas?"

"Let's get out of town and head north," Melissa suggested, whipping her eyes. "There are some farms that might be good. They're pretty remote, so maybe there won't be any infected."

"Infected?" Drew asked, starting the vehicle forward once again. "Those aren't people anymore. They're zombies."

She slowly looked up, mouth agape.

"I prefer undead," I added. "It seems that even though they're missing vital organs, they can still function as living beings."

"It can't be," she said softly. Her voice was hollow with disbelief.

"No, it's unlikely. But since we're in the midst of this catastrophe, it seems like it is," I corrected, immediately wishing I hadn't.

Melissa snuggled closer. I could feel her trembling against my side. Even though she pressed tightly against me, she seemed so far away.

"There's a farm ahead," Drew informed us, drawing my attention back to the road. It looked like an Amish dwelling. A buggy with a red triangle on the back sat in front of a big barn, while traditional garments hung on a clothesline, billowing in the

130

breeze.

"Let's go a little further," I encouraged. "They probably have a barn full of undead friends and relatives."

"Ah, so you're a *Walking Dead* fan?" he said through a toothy grin.

"A what?"

Our driver leaned forward. "The TV show? *The Walking Dead*?"

"They have a television show about this?" I asked incredulously.

"Only one of the hottest shows today! Where have you been, living under a rock?"

"No, but I study the things living under rocks," I defended myself. "It's my life's work."

We drove in silence for a while. The rural scenery of sun-dappled trees slid by, leaving us feeling calm once again. Mel seemed to have regained her composure. I was about to ask Drew to turn around when we spotted a factory. It had cinder block walls with no windows on the first floor.

"Pull in there," I suggested, pointing at the building.

"Do you think it's safe?" Melissa asked.

"We're about to find out," Drew stated, pulling the fire truck into the lot. As we circled the building, we found a loading dock and stopped the truck in front of the first bay. There were no cars in the lot and it seemed quiet enough.

We all climbed out of the vehicle, Frank and Ben needed encouragement to exit the safety of the cab. The two were looking everywhere at once, not trusting being out in the open, exposed to danger.

Dean and I checked our weapons while Drew gave the girls axes from one of the compartments. Seeing the look on Amber's face as she eyed the chopping tool, he offered her his shotgun. She looked at the single barrel pump and shook her head, signaling *no*. Hefting the heavy weapon, she gave him a small smile.

Melissa nudged me with an elbow and gave a knowing nod toward the two.

"No," I mouthed in disbelief, but her eager nod made her thoughts clear.

We checked each door in the bay area, Dean taking the lead while I backed him up with my revolver. They were all locked. Circling the building, we found two more exits, each of the metal doors secured from the inside. Finally, we tried the front entrance. Those double doors, mostly glass, were also locked. I tapped at the glass, friends holding a collective breath, but there was no answer from inside. Nothing.

We decided that breaking the glass would be a bad idea, so I suggested we force open the main door in the loading dock area. Frank and Ben were arguing that we should get back into the truck, but after explaining the fuel situation and the peril of being trapped inside a vehicle, they nervously came around to our way of thinking.

Drew produced a crowbar from one of the side compartments and, as gently as he could, pried the barrier open with a loud thump. I leapt into the void, swinging my gun from side to side looking for any attacker drawn by the noise. The way was clear. Nothing stirred.

We entered the bay, our weapons pointing in all directions. Huge windows on the upper level flooded light into the large receiving area. Boxes were neatly stacked in long rows, each sitting on a pallet.

"So far, so good," Dean intoned.

We secured the opening as best we could. The locking mechanism was ruined but we stacked the heaviest boxes we could find to offer resistance against intrusion. Satisfied, we explored the immediate area.

The warehouse was very utilitarian, so there wasn't much to see. Forklifts were parked in orderly rows to one side.

"Talk about obsessive behavior!" I heard Drew say to Amber. "Whoever ran this place was a real neatnik."

Drew was right. The place was immaculate. Carefully laid out yellow caution tape marked the road-like routes the various vehicles used while loading and unloading. Painted lines provided boundaries for the various crates and boxes while unloaded. The place was neat as a pin.

At the end of the bay, we found double doors leading into a work area and a small office. Hanging on a hook inside the office door was a set of keys with a tag reading *Pump Keys*.

I turned to the group and handed the keys to Drew, who was being closely shadowed by Amber. "Drew, why don't you take

132

your boys and check out the gas pumps. Maybe you can fill up the truck."

He nodded and the three filed back the way we had come. Amber followed behind them, her ax at the ready. Frank and Ben spoke rapidly in low tones and gesturing wildly, probably trying to make a case for them to leave us behind or some such nonsense.

They used one of the garage doors leading out of the loading dock. The door made a huge racket, but it seemed no one was around, so it was probably ok. The place seemed abandoned.

We went through the double doors like a tactical team. Dean pulled one open as I rapidly entered, revolver outstretched and tracking with my eyes.

This place was the diametric opposite of the loading area. Well lit from high windows, we could see small bits of plastic everywhere. Large industrial lathes and grinders were at workstations strategically scattered across the floor. The factory was a place where they processed plastic. Large rods of the stuff stuck out of bins to one side of the room. The smell of formaldehyde hung heavily in the air.

"What do you make of this?" I asked Dean.

"Looks like some kind of machine shop." he answered.

I rolled my eyes in frustration. "Really?" I asked sarcastically, "What gave that away?"

"Ummm, the machines," he shot back, picking up on my tone.

After we made sure the floor was clear, we checked the offices on the upper floor. Nothing. We returned to the loading bay to search the boxes for anything useful. I was hoping some of them contained food, but they all contained plastic. Some was in its raw form and needed processed, while others held the finished material. Melissa produced a cargo manifest from the office. It was neatly compiled on a clipboard. She read the contents to each numbered area. There was nothing here of use.

While we were looking over the goods stored in the bay, Drew and his group had unloaded some of our supplies. His haphazard pile looked out-of-place in this highly organized holding area. It made me think of his shop and how it contrasted the place we occupied now.

"Did you find anything?" the former comic book store owner

asked.

"Unless zombies are afraid of plastic, I don't think so," I told him. "How's the truck?"

"Fueled up and ready to go."

Dean scratched his head. "There's no power? How did you get the pump to work?"

A grinned and answered, "During hurricane Katrina, the emergency workers in the disaster areas ran out of fuel. They were forced to use small generators to hotwire gas pumps at local filling stations. After our company found that out, we equipped ourselves with hand pumps. We didn't have the funds for generators, so we went the cheaper route."

"Good thinking!" I replied. "The factory seems empty. The workers probably left when they heard the news. My guess is they went to be with their families."

We searched the darkened offices, this time for anything of use. Many of the drawers in the desks and file cabinets were locked. Once again, we found nothing of use.

The break room was probably the best find. It was somewhat dark, the light coming through the door being its only illumination, but it had some comforts. A candy and two pop machines were off to one side. Chairs, tables, and a few small couches filled the center. It seemed like a good place to plan our next move.

We slumped into the various mismatched seats, Drew and Ben lying on two of the couches.

Amber walked up to one of the soda machines and, setting her ax on the floor, pressed repeatedly on one of the buttons. Nothing happened.

"Shoot!" she responded. "I wish there was some power."

Dean roughly kicked the side of the vending machine in a macho attempt to make it drop the intended soft drink. The only thing it produced was a yelping man who hopped around holding his injured toe.

Drew appeared, brandishing his crowbar. He shoved it roughly into the area near the lock and easily popped the door open. With a grand gesture, he offered Amber her pick of the contents there in.

She positively beamed as she pulled a diet soda free and held it to her chest like a cherished prize.

Frank snatched the bar from Dean, who was openly staring at

the young woman, and used it to open the two remaining vending machines. Ben and Frank immediately started grabbing armloads of pop and candy.

Frank offered a snack cake to Drew, but with a quick look at Amber, he declined the treat. It was Frank's turn to look astonished.

We spent the remainder of the day and much of the evening sharing ideas about what we should do next. Wild ideas about where to go were the main topic of discussion.

"I think we should make for Alaska," mused Dean.

"No way," Amber spoke up, rubbing her arms in a sympathetic gesture of warming them. "It's way too cold up there."

"Exactly!" he said. "The zombies will freeze solid and won't be able to bother us ever again."

I couldn't substantiate his hypothesis, but I couldn't argue his line of thinking, either.

"It's pretty far. We would have to stop for gas a lot."

"What about an island?" Mel said, sounding hopeful.

"We'd have to find a boat and then an island. Then we'd have to hope that there are no zombies walking around on the ocean floor," Ben answered. "I don't think they have to breathe."

The room was getting dark. I watched Frank's head slowly slump forward to his chest. His eyes shot open, then the process would repeat itself. We were all exhausted.

Not trusting that the factory was completely safe, we set a watch order. Each of us would take an hour shift while the others slept. I took the first hour and watched as the others settled into various positions to rest.

The night was quiet. I made a circuit, checking the doors in each area. Nothing stirred inside or out. I was just getting drowsy when a sound brought me back around. It was Ben.

"Anything happening?" he asked, yawning.

"Nothing," I replied through my own sympathetic yawn.

I made my way by flashlight to my makeshift bed. It was more a blanket wadded up on the floor, but at least it was beside my wife. I would sleep so much better being next to her.

It seemed like I had just fallen asleep when I was hastily awakened. Light filtered into the break room through the open door, silhouetting Amber's form.

"There's a man outside!"

Chapter 25
Melissa

Most of us piled out of the room, bombarding Amber with questions, Ben being the only one to stay behind.

"Who is he? Where is he? Is he a zombie?" All blended into a single sound as she stepped back under the assault.

Ben, who had stayed in the break room half asleep, stated loudly, "Tell him we're doing the dishes, to come back later."

Amber just ignored his comment. "I just saw him for a second," she explained. "I don't even know if he is really a he at all," she said, clarifying her first statement.

We decided to take a peak. The person was at the front door, so we used all possible stealth as we approached the glass entryway. Each of us took a quick peek around the receptionist's desk to assuage our curiosity. The person was, in fact, a woman. Her tan pantsuit was covered with the leftover liquids from her last meal as well as, possibly, from herself.

She was standing at the barred doors looking in as if ready to pass through and enter the building. It was really quite eerie. She did not look intimidating and if we didn't know better, we would have let her in and tried to administer some type of aid.

We knew better. She was definitely undead. If we had let her inside, she would have turned immediately on her would-be assistants. We would have fallen victim to whatever it was that caused her current demise.

As a group, we watched and waited. After what seemed like a good half hour she just as mysteriously turned and walked away. Her shuffling gait left a telltale path of blood, marking her passage.

"That is really interesting," Hank remarked offhandedly.

"What do you mean?" I asked.

"It all seems to fit," he responded in his puzzled, yet clinical, way.

"Fit what?"

"Her response seems to indicate a pattern," he explained. "I have observed this pattern before. I will have to add this to my notes."

"Your notes?" I cried out, grabbing his shirtsleeve. "You have been taking notes?"

"Yes, er... of course. Why wouldn't I?" he stammered.

I couldn't believe it. Was he trying to tell me he was studying the life cycle of these undead? "What do you think you are doing?"

"I am trying to figure out why the undead are really undead. What is causing this outbreak. Why they act the way they do. Survive."

I couldn't believe it. He was actually working during a, as Dean had called it, zombie apocalypse. I knew my husband was obsessive about his work, but I couldn't believe he was this far gone.

"I think I have some valid hypothesis about the cause of the outbreak and why the dead are acting the way they do," he added.

"And?" I asked, prompting him.

"I have nothing concrete, mind you, but it looks very much like some type of parasite is the cause of this whole epidemic," he answered. "I won't know until I have conclusive evidence."

Everyone in the hallway stood shocked, totally silent. We stood staring at him in disbelief, unable to process the mere fact that he had spent this whole time he was fighting for survival studying the creatures. observing the undead while fighting for his life.

"Are you saying that you think there could be a cure for them?" I asked, thinking of poor Ned.

"Oh, by no means, no," he responded. "They are quite dead, but something is controlling them."

"The news said that it was a virus or maybe cosmic radiation," Dean added, somewhat shocked, himself.

"I assure you, it is no form of radiation," he soothed. "As for a virus, I wouldn't imagine that was possible, either. A virus certainly controls a person, but this is different. A virus might trick you into sneezing, but one wouldn't kill the host as readily as this does unless it benefitted its offspring."

Stunned silence followed his answer. We had no idea where he was going with this train of thought, but we all wanted to hear what he was thinking.

"This seems more like a parasite," he continued. "Although I am not certain why it is choosing to kill its host. I do have good reason to believe that a parasite is gaining control of the human

138

population."

"Why would it do that?" asked Frank from the back of the crowd.

"Many parasites have the ability to control their hosts. They may need the person to be dead in order to gain enough physical control to make them act the way they do."

"Are they trying to take over the world?" Ben asked, voice high and shaking.

"Oh my, no!" Henry assured. "We are the only beings concerned with the world and material goods. They probably just want to assure their existence. I do have a few thoughts on why they need us to be dead, but I am fairly certain why they want to devour us."

No one spoke. We all wanted to hear the answer, but it seemed no one wanted to voice the real question. Luckily, my husband did it for us.

"Humans would be a great source of protein and through biting us, they not only gain vital sustenance, but they can also transfer and possibly propagate their species."

We were all stunned. My husband had us spellbound. He could have told us the parasites were from Mars and we would have lapped up every word of what he was saying.

Amber spoke up hopefully, "Does this mean you can make a cure?"

Henry actually stumbled at this inquiry. He wasn't stumped, or even considering it. I just don't think he wanted to answer it. "It may be a while before there is a vaccine, if a vaccine is ever created! For now, just don't get bit," he answered gravely.

"The news said the CDC was working on a cure." Dean shot back, trying to begin a debate.

"Sure they are. When do you think they assembled the team?" Hank answered calmly.

"What are you saying?" Drew asked suspiciously.

"I just don't believe everything they tell us."

Dean crossed his arms over his chest. "Why not? The government could have choppered them in at the beginning. What could they gain by not leveling with us?"

"Do you remember what the government said when terrorists were using anthrax?"

Dean shrugged at the question.

"They told the public to get plastic drop cloths and duct tape. They suggested that Americans make a sealed safe room," my husband responded. "What do you think that would have done? Nothing. If it were sealed tight enough, it would have suffocated the occupants. It was a placebo. Nothing more."

"You're kidding me," said Drew, shocked. "I still have eight rolls of the stuff. I'll never go through it all."

"Why did they lie to us?" asked Amber.

"I believe it was so we would feel in control," Henry answered. "That the government had an answer and we were going to be ok."

"So we're going to die?" Frank said to himself. We all felt the same. He only stated what we all were thinking.

"No!" I spoke up in a loud, clear, passionate voice. "We are going to live. I will not lie down and become one of them. I refuse to let those zombies chew on me until I turn. We're going to survive, and maybe even thrive."

The atmosphere changed abruptly. Our group, who had lost hope a moment ago, rallied to my challenge. Hank had been wrong. He shouldn't have divulged what he knew. We were all walking a fine line between survival and just plain giving up. It would have been easy to sit back and drink some Kool-Aid together, to end it all in this world of despair. But I had come too far.

The gathering seemed to break up after that. Some people wandering about the warehouse, while others returned to the lounge. I cornered my husband.

"What are you trying to do?" I asked curtly.

He looked back at me, shocked and clearly not understanding. I ushered him into a dimly lit office.

"You have to give them hope," I explained. "They need something to hold on to. That is why the government told the people to get duct tape and plastic. It may have been a placebo, but it was the best they could do. Would you rather they had given out sugar pills?"

"I can't lie to them," he said in a low voice. Henry seemed almost ashamed. He was actually trying to squirm past me to avoid my line of questioning.

140

Cornering him, I explained, "You don't have to lie, but you also don't have to tell them everything."

His mouth moved, but nothing came out. I know he hadn't considered that. In his career, people shared ideas. He never held things back from me. But this was different. He needed to consider his audience.

I could see that he understood, so I let him past. He quickly disappeared toward the other offices. I left him alone. He deserved a respite.

It's funny. Through the years of our marriage, Henry shied away from the forefront of almost everything. With anything except his career, he had no interest in being a leader. Now, though, Hank was a different person. He was strong, confident, and in control. He was a true leader. I don't know everything that happened on his way to my rescue, but he was now truly heroic. He was my knight in shining armor.

My speech seemed to boost the group's morale, but the time we spent cooped up inside the factory drained the effect daily. Occasionally, what we thought were probably former workers would approach one door or another and make a feeble attempt at entry. The undead would paw at the barred opening; then, after a while, they would just as inexplicably leave.

The third day, I found my husband setting up an office desk in the middle of the loading dock. He had enlisted the help of the men.

"What are you boys doing?" I asked as the men grunted and groaned with the heavy oak furniture.

"Right now, your hubby is trying to give me a hernia," Ben responded as they pushed the desk around to have better light.

"Shouldn't it be a hisnea?" Frank joked good-naturedly.

"I need a place to work," Henry replied, ignoring the comedy routine. "I was trying to use one of the offices, but it was way too dark in there. I was getting eye strain."

"Work?" I shot back, completely taken off guard. "What could you possibly work on?"

He looked a little embarrassed. Head down, he mumbled, "I was in the middle of compiling my notes. They're a mess. Half of them are covered with grime, or worse."

My rage subsided. I actually stood nearly dumbstruck. "And?"

"I came across some things I had nearly forgotten. I firmly believe it's a parasite. I won't be sure until I gain a subject and can get specimens, of course, but from all I have observed, well, it all indicates the presence of a parasitic life form."

"You want to capture a subject? Are you crazy?" I challenged as my rage returned.

He looked shocked this time. "How else will we positively verify my hypotheses?"

"What good would it do?"

"How else could I develop something to stop this?"

He said this as if he was telling me what he wanted for dinner. His tone was calm, if not a little meek.

"A cure?" I asked hopefully.

"No, but maybe something to stop someone from becoming one of them."

We spent the rest of the day trying to devise ways we could block off different sections of the factory. It was Frank's idea. He thought it would be a good idea if we had areas we could secure in the event that we would have to fall back; a contingency plan in the event we are ever overrun.

We took the heavier palettes from the loading dock and piled them up to block off different doorways. The forklifts remained parked beside openings to aid in moving the heavy objects. This way, they could be put in place at a moment's notice.

We found generators but decided against using them at the present. Just knowing that they were available made us all feel a little more comfortable.

The next day, we divided up into teams and searched the area. Finding nothing threatening outside, we stretched a tarp into a circle, leaving the top open. With one group watching, guns at the ready, we shot a stream of water into the air, only to have it mist down inside the enclosed circle. We had made an outdoor shower. Soap from the bathrooms assisted as we, two at a time, scrubbed the grime from our bodies and clothes.

Amber and I went first. When we finished with the icy shower, our clothes were still soaked, so we decided to exit the enclosure in our wet bras and panties. I was a little shy about it, but after some coaxing, we exited. I quickly saw that I had nothing to worry about. All eyes were on Amber.

142

I thought Drew was going to pass out. Amber's eyes immediately sought his out and when she found his, she actually flushed a deep red. She strutted right up to Ben and snatched the hose from his shaking hands.

"Next!" she announced.

After a bit of a delay, another group broke off and we repeated the process. I had to seek Hank out. He was busy recopying his notes onto new paper.

"Time for a bath, stinky boy!" I said like I was his mother.

"Aw, Ma! Do I have to?" he answered in a not so convincing, childlike act.

"Everybody else is doing it!" I urged. "You really stink."

Henry set down his pen and reluctantly followed me outdoors.

Joining the others, I took Amber aside and asked, "Do you have a thing for Drew?"

The young woman blushed again and answered, "Does it show?"

I nodded, "Just a bit."

"I have a thing for nerds. He's so cute," she said, staring at the soaked comic book shop owner. The wet Batman shirt left nothing to the imagination. It clung to his obese form in a most unflattering way.

I looked back at the young beauty. Her hair, already dry from the sunshine, lay perfect against her flawless skin.

"Sure," was all I could say in response to her comment. I guess it took all kinds.

After our clothes were dry, we broke down the tarps and put everything back in the truck in the event we had to leave in a hurry. We wanted to stay outside and enjoy the sunny day. Heck, we wanted to have a barbecue, but calmer heads prevailed and we decided to get back out of sight so we didn't draw any attention.

It was early evening and we were all sitting in the lounge, still reveling in the feel of being mostly clean. Jokes were flying back and forth. Then, Dean, who was on duty watching the front door, burst into the darkened room.

"There's a man outside!" he said, words tumbling out as one.

"Just make sure it doesn't get in," Ben answered, waving him off.

"I think he's alive!"

We all leapt to our feet and followed him to our vantage point behind the receptionist's desk.

"I don't see him," Frank squealed, leaning far beyond our hiding place.

"Out there, in the brush line," Dean explained, pulling the lanky fellow back behind cover.

"I see him," Amber agreed. "He's behind the huge oak."

We all turned our attention to the massive tree. There, in the shadows, was what looked like a man. Even from this distance, he looked ragged, clothes mismatched and hanging from his form. He continued along the tree line, headed toward where we parked the fire truck.

"Tell me you locked the storage compartments," I begged Drew. His blank look told me he hadn't. "Let's give him a few minutes and we'll follow the old sot."

When the allotted time had elapsed, the men slipped out the front doors and after we had secured them, Amber and I raced through the factory to the bay doors. We collected Henry on the way.

Putting our ears against one of the metal garage doors, we heard voices, so we opened the enclosure and saw our friends surrounding what could have been an animated corpse.

Covered in dirt, it was wearing mismatched clothes covered in patches. The only thing that gave him away as being living was that he spoke. He slurred words, but we hadn't, at this point, found an undead that could speak.

"I just saw yer water spout and follered it up here," he said through brown teeth.

"What's your name?" I asked.

"I already told them there fellers," he answered. "It's Box Car Bill. Pleased to meet ya, ma'am," he removed his floppy, sweat-stained hat, displaying a mostly bald head fringed with greasy gray hair.

"Melissa," I answered. "This is Amber and Henry."

We invited him inside. He didn't seem comfortable being indoors. His eyes darted to the high windows and doors. We made a rough circle of chairs near my husband's work area. We didn't yet know enough about him to bring him any further inside.

We spent the rest of the evening exchanging stories and news with what we later learned was a hobo. Bill lived near the tracks that ran up to the factory. He wasn't always alone. A few days ago, his friend, Jumbo, had gotten attacked by a group of townspeople. He had fought them off and escaped but was badly injured. Bill explained that this wasn't strange behavior toward his kind, so he'd thought nothing of it.

Jumbo had gotten worse. He couldn't eat and his skin became really pale.

"He was my only friend," Bill explained, tears running down his cheeks.

"Is that when you got bit?" Henry asked in a clinical voice.

Our entire group's eyes collectively widened in alarm.

Bill didn't miss a beat. "He was really sick. I went to put some more wood on the fire. My back was only turned fer a few minutes. That's when he chomped down on my leg."

Bill bent over and pulled up his right pant leg. It was then that I noticed the large stain. His pants were so many colors that it was hard to make out at first.

A dirty handkerchief bound an angry red wound. Black veins surrounded the immediate area of the injury.

"May I examine it?" Henry asked gently.

"Sure. You a Doc?"

"Yes," Hank assured him. "Dean, can you get the flashlight from my bag?

As Dean rummaged through the duffel, Henry tenderly helped the old man onto the desk. He pushed small piles of papers to one side, clearing a spot for Bill to sit. Ignoring the leg, Hank had the gentleman remove his coat. The stench was nearly unbearable from where I was, but my husband didn't even blink. He produced a pair of rubber gloves from a drawer and, after pulling them on with practiced hands, felt Bill's glands at his jaw, under his ears.

The rest of us left, except for Dean. We wanted to give them some privacy. Our group retreated to the lounge in a melancholy mood. No one spoke. The only thing that brightened my mood was when I saw Amber, who was sitting on the couch with Drew, take his hand in hers.

A short while later, Henry appeared at the door. He slumped down in a chair next to me and hung his head.

"Well?" Frank asked from his reclined position on the couch. He looked quite comical, his long form on the diminutive sofa.

"I believe he is infected," he answered in a whisper. "What troubles me is that he hasn't turned yet."

"What should we do with him?" Drew asked, hand reaching for his shotgun.

"Dean is watching him. We made a bed for him and he went right to sleep."

Frank sat up. "Should we… you know?"

"Kill him?" Henry finished the thought. "At some point, I believe we will have to. But not quite yet."

"We can't just let him live here with us!" Frank shot back.

"We need to study his progression."

"I say we end it now!" Frank encouraged, rising to his feet.

"Go ahead, Frank!" Henry dared harshly. "March right in there and kill him now, in cold blood! Can you do that? Huh?"

The room fell silent. "Or maybe you want to turn him out; let him die outside. Then he can attack us at some point when we're not aware." There was a long pause. My husband sat calmly, waiting for someone to act. When nothing happened, he continued, "I didn't think so. I think it's best if we keep him here, in a controlled environment. We can study the progress of this... disease, for lack of a better term. Then, maybe we can have some answers."

"Is he contagious?" Amber sheepishly asked, as if afraid to incur Henry's wrath.

"By his proximity, I don't believe so. I think it is passed on through an exchange of fluids. But I have no conclusive proof."

We spent the next day on edge. Two people watched Bill at all times. My husband rarely left the room. He found some sterile Pyrex test tubes in the nurse's quarters and a few unused syringes. With these he took samples; puss, blood, and spittle. Each one, he meticulously labeled.

"I need to get to a lab!" he said. "Without the proper equipment, these samples are useless. I can't even refrigerate them. I don't know if they will be any good."

"The closest lab is at the university," I said, stating the obvious.

"I know," he said sullenly. "I just can't figure out why he hasn't changed yet."

I was looking over his notes. "His breath smelled like alcohol."

"Yes," he answered. "He said he was drinking squeeze. I

146

believe it is some type of drink made from Sterno."

I gave him a weird look. "That's funny. My boss, Thaddeus, got drunk when he was bitten. He didn't become one of them for a long time."

Hank grabbed both of my shoulders roughly. "How long did it take?"

"More than a day."

"Why didn't you tell me sooner?" His hands loosened their tight grip somewhat.

"I didn't think it was important." He dropped heavily into his chair. It squeaked under his weight. "I am such a fool!"

"Why," I asked, free of his grip. "What's wrong?"

He sat in silence for a moment, letting the full impact of my words hit him.

"I didn't interview each of you. I was only working from my accounts of the outbreak. Everything happened so fast. I just didn't think of it."

Henry spent the remainder of the day interviewing and, at some points, interrogating us. He only took the occasional break to examine Bill. The line of specimens grew as his patient slipped away. In the late afternoon, the guys bound the unconscious man with duct tape, securing him so he wouldn't be able to move much at all.

Later that night, Bill passed away. The corpse became a struggling, animated copy of his former self. Before Hank and Dean dispatched him, my husband extracted some final specimens. Only Drew remained present, to help if anything went wrong. In a far corner of the loading dock, they put the undead hobo to rest. A single gunshot signaled his demise.

"I need to get to a lab!"

"Have fun with that!" Ben said sarcastically while leaning back in his chair.

"I'm serious!" I said more sternly, hands on hips.

"So am I," Ben barked back while leaning forward in his blue plastic chair. "We're safe here. Heck, if we had some steaks, we could have a cook-out today."

"You're safe now, but when the food sources in the towns surrounding here get scarce, those walking dead will come to places like this."

"When that happens, we'll move." he replied offhandedly.

"When that happens, it'll be too late!" Melissa answered rising to stand at my side. "Henry believes he can make a cure. It might not help those that have already turned, but it may help people when they get bitten. I think we have to try."

Frank entered the room, fresh from his duty of watching the front door. "So, you think YOU can make a cure. I think the CDC is probably doing all they can-"

"We don't even know if the CDC had time to assemble a team," I said, cutting Frank off in mid-sentence. "There may be no one working on this."

"How do you know so much?" Ben shot back.

"Because, in the past, I worked for the CDC!"

"I thought you were a bug doctor?" Drew asked skeptically.

"Entomologists are a part of the CDC. I'm a leading scientist in my field and have been called in before. No one contacted me. That's why I'm so worried."

The arguments stopped. They all looked at me with a new respect: all except Melissa, that is. She looked at me with pride.

We spent the rest of the morning eating and stashing our supplies in the fire truck. We ate like it was our last meal, not knowing when we might get the chance again.

Ben and Frank grumbled to anyone who would listen. They were trying to cause dissent. But the rest of the group understood our situation, and even Drew took my side, putting them both in their place.

When we finished, we climbed aboard the big, diesel rig. Melissa and I squished in the front with Drew in the driver's seat. I tried to get her to sit in the roomy, back crew area, but she wouldn't hear any of it. She just squeezed right in beside me.

The engine came to life on the first crank, the huge machine causing the vehicle to vibrate. That feeling of power came surging back. I felt invincible high up in this cab. Looking back, I saw the broken door we had blocked with boxes. Scrawled on a big box in marker were the words, *Safe inside, no food or zombies.*

We left the factory and backtracked the way we had come. We didn't drive quickly, because we wanted the ability to avoid any obstacles that might appear along the way. The road wasn't as serene as it had been on the way here. The landscape, which had been mostly normal before, was now increasingly populated by the undead.

"Now do you see what I mean?" I asked no one in particular. "We were only going to be safe for a short time."

"We could have blocked the glass doors," argued Frank from the back seat.

"I agree," I played along while watching a woman in what looked like a nightgown try desperately to intercept the fire truck. She was missing an arm, but she didn't seem to notice, "And when the food ran out?"

"Oh," was Drew's only response.

As we neared the outskirts of Slippery Rock, we started to notice something strange. The dead lying in the streets increased. What we had seen before was that the victims were typically hauled down and partly eaten. Later, they rose again, leaving some parts but mostly just a big red stain behind. This was different. There were many dead scattered all about.

"Stop the truck," I told Drew. When the big vehicle came to a halt, I opened the door and leaned out.

These undead were not moving. The closer ones that I could see from my present vantage point all had head wounds, as well as what looked like other gunshot injuries. I could hear distant popping noises. "It seems like somebody is fighting back," I called back.

"Was that gunfire?" Drew asked while leaning around my wife.

149

"Yes," I answered. "It sounds like it's coming from up ahead."
"What do you think?"

I looked around. There were a lot of dead, but they seemed like they were going to stay down. Stepping down into the street, I pulled my revolver and signaled Drew to follow me with the truck.

The diesel engine was loud, mostly drowning out the sounds of battle. After walking a few hundred feet, I could see movement up ahead. Soldiers, of the living and breathing variety, were walking towards me, breaking from hiding places among the buildings.

My heart swelled with joy. The military was taking control. As the five urban camouflage-clad people closed within speaking distance, I signaled my friend to stop the truck and cut the engines. The entire population of the truck spilled out as our group saw salvation in the well-armed soldiers.

One of the soldiers came right up to me. "Are you the leader?" she asked very seriously.

I guess you could call me one of them, yes," I replied, unsure.

"Has anyone had contact with the infected?" she quickly shot back. The questions sounded rehearsed.

"We've all had contact with the undead. Hasn't everyone?" I answered honestly.

"Has anyone been bitten or scratched?" she corrected, sounding a little disgusted at having to simplify the original question.

"No," I said, finally understanding her line of questioning.

"Continue on to the campus. The first dormitory is where we are processing survivors. You will find food and medicine there."

I was about to ask another question, but the soldiers abruptly turned on their heels and started back to their hiding places.

We all returned to our seats. Our mood had risen significantly. The government had stepped up and was taking care of the situation.

We parked out on the street in front of the dorm. Two sentries eyed us suspiciously as we approached the building. Each was holding some type of machine gun.

"Follow me," stated the bigger of the two, leading the way through the door.

As we passed between the full-panel glass double doors, I wondered about our former world. We had taken our safety so lightly that most buildings had full-panel glass doors. In this new world, where we are constantly under siege, it sounds completely ludicrous.

The building was well lit. The guard explained that generators were powering this and two other buildings. His statement was confirmed by the hum of the lights.

"Showers?" asked Amber excitedly.

"Fully functional, ma'am," our guide responded.

Amber clapped her hands together and hugged Drew's meaty arm. Excitement shone on her face. Drew was in pure bliss. He looked like he didn't want to move, for fear that she would never touch him again. In this world of despair, he was the one person I knew who had gained something.

We entered a temporary medical area, each of us ordered to go behind a curtain with a nurse and strip. They inspected us for bites, scratches, and any other manner of possible infection. Afterward, we went to another room for interrogations in curtained enclosures.

The questions ranged from who we were and what our employment was before the outbreak to if we had military training and where we had been and what we had seen.

After he asked the last question, the guard who had posed it excused himself. About twenty minutes later, an officer entered the curtained area where my interrogation had occurred.

The man introduced himself as Colonel O'Neill. He was a middle-aged gentleman in similar urban camouflage. He was medium height and build with short, unkempt, gray hair. Although I could see his rank, he spoke and acted like a regular soldier.

"I understand you are an entomologist?" he asked, sitting on the edge of the table which separated the two chairs in the small enclosure. "What is it you study, exactly?" he inquired setting his military ball cap beside himself on the table.

"Currently, I was studying the evolution of *Leucochloridium Paradoxum* and its effects on the common garden snail," I offered.

"Let's act like I don't know what that *Leucochloridium* thing is," he suggested, obviously wanting the term clarified.

"It is a parasite. A flatworm."

"What does it do?" he continued.

"It takes control of its host," I went further. "It makes the snail do what it wants to do."

"Private Harris says that you have been studying the creatures we have been fighting recently," he went on prodding. "He said you have samples and notes."

I didn't feel as though I had anything to hide, but I limited my response, "Yes, to both of your statements.'

The colonel's eyes narrowed, "Why would you do that? These aren't bugs."

I decided my best option was to continue telling him just what he needed to know. "After observing the undead creature's behaviors, I thought it would be prudent to compile my findings."

"Why?" he said, urging me for more.

"In order to give credence to my hypotheses."

"And that is?" he probed deeper.

I felt cornered. "Listen, Colonel, if I did something wrong?"

O'Neill leaned forward, trying to intimidate me. "You listen, son. We are in the middle of a crisis here, one that is worse than anything we have ever seen before. I need to know exactly what I have as resources so I can use my people to their best potential. What were you doing?"

"Trying to gain an understanding of the cause; how and why people are dying and then coming back to a semblance of life," I said, coming clean.

"You think you're the freaking World Health Organization or something?" he barked back.

"No. But I have worked for the CDC. So, in a way, yes!"

He sat back looking at me in unmasked disbelief. "Are you serious?"

"Yes," I assured him. "We were trying to get to my lab. It's a few buildings away."

I spent the next hour explaining what I believed was happening and what I would need. When Colonel O'Neill realized the full implications of what I was trying to do, he immediately pledged his full support. He dispatched a private to retrieve my samples and place them in a refrigerator.

We made plans for me to gain access to my lab. Luckily, they had already cleared the science building where I worked and I was given a few soldiers to act as guards. He even offered to move my lab here, but I told him that I would work better in the surroundings I was already familiar with.

O'Neill told me that they had begun removing the hostile

152

creatures from this small town so it could serve as a staging area from which to secure other areas. Places like Pittsburgh were too large to attempt recovery at this time, but if they could contain the undead within that area, we could effectively stop the spread of whatever was causing the outbreak.

After eating in the generator-powered dining hall, they led me to my lab. Melissa and Dean refused to let me go without them, so they were my impromptu lab assistants. Three armed guards surrounded us as we traveled to the science hall.

It felt great to be in my lab once again. A portable generator powered some of my lab equipment and a few lights. At first, I gave my lab assistants small, simple jobs; but as time wore on, I ran out of chores for them to do.

I examined the samples from Bill, starting with the first and working toward the ones I had extracted after he had turned. I scribbled my findings on paper, Melissa transferring them on to my Macintosh and then to a flash drive. Dean entered my older notes onto another computer he'd found in an adjoining office. These were also put on flash drives.

I sat back and rubbed my temples, trying to regain some focus. Feeling two hands begin to rub my shoulders, I hoped they weren't Deans. Looking up, I saw my former neighbor standing directly in front of me and sighed in relief.

"Anything wrong?" she asked, pushing her thumbs deeper into my tense muscles.

"The cells have degraded. They should have been refrigerated or, better yet, frozen," I lamented.

"You could only do what you had the means of doing," she soothed. "Are they still useable?"

"Somewhat," I answered, leaning back into her massage. "I believe I have seen the culprit. Bill's blood is swimming with some strange parasite larvae. I've never seen its likes before. His saliva is teeming with the same little guys. Here, let me show you."

I switched on the monitor for my dark-field microscope. I placed a prepared slide into the microscope. The cells became visible on the monitor, lifeless and nearly colorless.

"Observe the thin, string-like creatures between the cells. This, I believe, is the cause of the outbreak." Removing the slide, I put another in its place. "This is the last sample of saliva I took from him. Note the same little guy is present in abundance."

"They're moving. Are they alive?" Melissa asked, Dean and one of the guards looking over her shoulder.

"I believe they still are," I confirmed as I removed the slide. "Do you want to see something interesting?"

They all three nodded, eager to hear more. I switched the slide to the last blood sample.

"Is this from Bill?" Dean asked, clearly puzzled.

"Yes," I confirmed.

"Where is the parasite?" he continued.

"It seems to have abandoned the blood stream. In three samples, I have only found a few dead parasite larvae and none living."

"What does it mean?" the guard asked.

"I don't know," I acknowledged. "It could be that the blood was only a vehicle of transport. It wasn't practical as a means of sustaining them."

Chapter 27
Melissa

It was like Christmas morning. The scalding hot water pounded into the back of my head, sending tiny droplets flying overhead, only to fall as a thin mist. Steam formed a thick cloud, limiting my vision. I breathed in, filling my lungs full of humid air. I would have never thought a hot shower with real bath soap could feel so good.

If the military was offering things like this, I never wanted to leave their protective embrace. There were a few other survivors. Some seemed like they were still in shock. Keeping mostly to their rooms, many only appeared during meal times; and even then, they ate alone. Most of the civilians seemed amicable to friendly conversation. Carefully avoiding discussions about what happened to them for fear of bringing back bad memories, we spoke on a variety of other subjects. It was funny, but current events from a few weeks ago seemed so distant and unimportant.

I spent most of my time in my husband's lab, typing readable documents from his terrible handwriting, washing work areas, and even bringing him dinner. The first day, he showed us some blood and saliva samples on a large monitor. He revealed the parasite that was attacking its human host; but, as of yet, he didn't know where it was living and how to get rid of it.

We stored the information on ten flash drives I'd pilfered from different labs and offices. Dean and I also made ten printed copies in the event we went back off the grid. Colonel O'Neill sent nurses to help Henry, but he turned them all away. Even though they had some expertise in the medical field, he just had too little for them to do.

I dried off and donned a clean set of clothes. These, they gathered from the dorm rooms and had belonged to their former occupants. There was little reason to think that we were doing something wrong. The students who owned the clothes were probably dead or, possibly even now, wandering about in search of their prey.

The shoes were the true gift. My feet had toughened up considerably over my long days on the roof, but when I slipped on a pair of clean socks and a slightly worn pair of Nikes, it seemed like heaven. I never realized how vulnerable I felt not having shoes on. Now I felt more prepared for some reason.

I passed by the others from our little group. They were in the student lounge, surrounded by a large pile of comic books borrowed from a few of the more nerdy student's rooms. Drew wasn't reading, though. He was sitting on a couch with his arm loosely around Amber's shoulder. Drew was changing. He was pulling away from his former passion in light of a new love, Amber. It even looked like he'd dropped a few pounds.

Dean sat alone, to one corner. His look was sullen. He eyed Amber and Drew with a mournful look. I felt for him. He was living with Julie for a little while, and

I believe her death, mixed with the new couple's blossoming relationship, opened recent wounds. He now had some time to let his guard down. He wasn't occupied with trying to keep the group safe. He was finally able to mourn.

I walked up to my former neighbor. The happy couple paused their whispered conversation and watched me as I walked past. "Where's Hank?" I asked.

"He's with O'Neill," he answered without lifting his head. "I think he is giving him a report."

"I'm going outside to sit in the sun," I offered.

"Didn't you get enough of that on the roof?" he asked, humor still intact.

"I just want to enjoy the nice day. Who knows when we will get stuck inside a building again."

Dean glanced at the lovers and then locked eyes with me. "I'm with ya."

We made our way outside and sat under a large maple tree. The shade was cool on this sunny day. I slid off my newly acquired shoes and socks, letting the long grass slide between my toes. It would have been very peaceful if not for the sound of distant gunfire.

"I wish they could stop shooting for a while," I lamented.

"If they did, we would be overrun," he said sarcastically.

"No, I mean I wish it was over. I miss relaxing on a warm summer day."

"There's something wrong here," Dean said. "I just can't put my finger on it."

"I think all of this comfort is making you paranoid," I joked.

His demeanor sobered. "No, I'm serious. Something is not right."

I turned the conversation to more mundane subjects, but I could tell by Dean's look that he was still thinking about what could be amiss. We watched the troops come and go. Some were returning from the battle lines while others went out to join the struggle. It all seemed normal to me, but I had never been a part of a military operation.

After nearly two hours of our somewhat relaxing outing, we saw Henry walking in our direction. He looked tired and a bit out of sorts.

"How did it go?" I asked, rising to my bare feet.

"Fine," Hank replied. "Just fine."

"Are you going back to the lab?" Dean probed, rising to join us.

"No," he said. "I'm going to take a shower and then a nap. There isn't any more we can do at this point."

"What do we do now?" I inquired.

"We wait," he responded.

"For what?" I continued.

"A subject."

I didn't know what to say. Were they waiting for a human specimen?

Henry explained that he had shown Colonel O'Neill his findings. The commander seemed very interested and asked him how we could stop the parasite. Henry told him that without someone performing an autopsy, there was no way of knowing where the parasite set up shop in its human host. Someone would also be needed to perform tests to find some type of compound that could be used to destroy the invader.

My husband said the Colonel got angry when he explained that he had no expertise in this area. O'Neill curtly told him that he was going to have to step up and do things out of necessity, that we all would have to go way beyond what we thought our limitations were to overcome our present situation.

Henry said the military man nearly got violent when he explained that some parasites could be flushed out quickly by natural means, those being ones that made a home in the intestines. But others could take a long time to fully get rid of. The discovery of a cure is a long way off, and even then the process may take longer to work than the patient has to live.

"He just doesn't understand that these things take a lot of time and many highly trained personnel. I'm just one man and am working way outside of my field of expertise," he defended.

"What does he want to do?" Dean asked sympathetically.

"He wants to get me a subject to do further testing on," he mumbled, shoulders slumping under the weight of the responsibility. "I begin interviewing the civilians tonight."

"Interviewing for what?" Dean asked.

"Any specialized skills that may help," he said, then kissed me on the forehead and walked off toward our building.

I watched him as he disappeared inside the door. He looked so defeated. The colonel was asking too much from him.

Chapter 28
Henry

"Thank you. That will be all," I said, dismissing the umpteenth civilian. Rubbing my eyes, I walked to the window. The campus was dark. Only a few lit buildings cast any illumination on the grounds at all. The star-filled sky looked amazing. I had never seen so many stars and constellations. With so little ambient light, the cosmos seemed to open up before my eyes.

"Here's the last," the orderly informed from the door.

Without turning from the incredible view, I answered, "Thank you."

I really didn't want to tear my eyes off of the incredible view. The night was moonless as well as cloudless. It was perfect for stargazing.

Just as I was about to resume my duties as the chief interviewer, I caught movement on the poorly illuminated sidewalk. It looked like four guards were helping a darkly dressed person toward the science hall. I couldn't make out much more. They had shut down the generators in that building, so it was completely dark except for thin beams from the soldier's flashlights.

Distracted by the strange scene, I turned to see a middle-aged woman seated on the other side of the wooden table, her hands folded neatly in her lap. She looked somewhat nervous as she awaited my line of questioning.

"What is your name?" I asked, breaking the ice.

"Pamela, Pamela Mason," she responded, then cleared her throat loudly.

"And what did you do before the outbreak?" I asked, not too hopeful.

"Are you referring to employment?"

"Yes," I clarified. The way she phrased her question made me think she was a teacher or something.

She was looking down at her hands. Her mouth worked for a moment, then she met my eyes. It was as though she was judging me, measuring my humanity. "I was a senior researcher at the University of Pittsburgh. We worked mostly with WHO and the CDC in developing vaccines for seasonal flu viruses, as well as other possible viral outbreaks."

I couldn't believe what I had just heard. If I could have placed any person in camp, it would be someone like her. She was perfect. Jackpot.

"When can you start?" I asked sarcastically.

"Excuse me?"

"I was just kidding," I explained. I think Dean was wearing off on me. "Can you meet me at six a.m. tomorrow to be briefed?"

"I guess so," she hesitantly answered. I could see the reluctance return to her eyes, almost as if she already regretted her affirmation.

"I'll meet you at the front of the Science Center," I said while standing.

I offered her my hand. She had the look of a Christian who had just entered the lion's den. Pamela took my hand and I felt hers tremble slightly in my grasp.

As agreed, after the interviews, I headed off to Old Main, which was Headquarters of Operations. I told the Colonel's secretary that I was here and she motioned me inside. He closed his laptop as I entered, acting like he was waiting for me.

"Any luck?" he asked, sounding hopeful.

"We hit the jackpot," I answered. "Did you know you had a senior researcher for the University of Pittsburgh here in camp?"

"Outstanding!" he said loudly. "I had no idea."

I went into great detail about the process, describing some of the more interesting people and the jobs they had done. When I spoke of Pamela, he sat forward in his seat, grinning ear to ear.

Colonel O'Neill actually walked me to the door. His hand resting on my shoulder, I thought he was going to hug me in joy over the recent events.

I returned to our room. Melissa sat by the window, looking out over the dark courtyard.

"How did it go?" she asked, followed by a long, drawn-out yawn.

"Great. We found our guy, er... gal," I corrected, walking into her embrace.

I could feel her breath on my neck. She smelled like strawberries. How women can find perfumes in such hostile times, I have no idea. The warmth of her body was welcome even on this humid night.

160

"That sounds good," she agreed. "Is she pretty?"

I spent the next hour retelling the interview process to Mel. She enjoyed hearing what people had done for work. When I described Pamela's credentials, she was so impressed she whistled.

"That sounds perfect. Do you think you can create a cure?"

"It's a long shot," I answered. "Dealing with parasites is typically a slow process. But it is possible."

"Why would a parasite want to kill us at all?" she asked, "I thought that they kept us alive so we could spread them around?"

"It depends on their life cycle. Normally, many parasites live quite passively inside their host, quietly attaching to the wall of the intestines and absorbing the nutrients they need to survive. The mature parasites eggs are left to be excreted and the cycle begins again. Many of these parasites have no means of self-propulsion. They must lay in wait of a host to devour and transport them to where they need to be."

"Others, though," I continued, "Kill their host, leaving the corpse for their future host to come in contact with. However, it is uncommon. It's typically more advantageous to keep the host alive so the parasite can pump out many generations to ensure the species' survival. So I guess the short answer is that I don't know."

"Can our immune system fight them off?"

"We are at a serious disadvantage in this war. The life cycle of these tiny invaders is quite short. This means they evolve at such a high rate that we can't keep up with them. The only way of battling a parasite is to flush it out completely or introduce some type of medication, which can kill it. Our body will then absorb the foreign material."

"That is so gross."

"The sad thing is that millions of people have parasites living in them at any given time. They can cause anything from exhaustion to behavioral changes. We have actually lived symbiotically with them for so many generations that some have become part of our genetic code. They are actually written in our DNA."

"You are so smart. I can't believe you love me," she said.

I looked at my wife, amazed. She was so beautiful, she had friends and a wonderful sense of humor. Melissa was truly great. I couldn't see what she saw in dorky old me.

"You're the one who traded down," I answered, taking her in my arms again and kissing her deeply.

We went to bed, the sounds of distant gunfire an ever-present reminder of our precarious situation. I lay holding Melissa as she slept. The rhythm of her breathing felt comforting as my mind filled with puzzles, making sleep elusive.

The alarm clock buzzed, but I had been awake for hours. Something Melissa said kept cycling through my mind. Why would it want to kill us? It didn't make sense. I didn't know what type of parasite our present invader evolved from, but if we could locate where it was living that may indicate who our new guy was before its evolution.

I reached over to the nightstand and switched the offending noise off. Mel pulled the sheet tightly about her neck and mumbled something to me. Kissing her nose, I rose from the bed.

The birds were singing through the open window. The sound of distant gunfire gave an all too familiar accompaniment to their song. I made my way to the shower. Sharing my findings with someone who would understand the technical aspects of my work was exciting. It would be good to have Pamela's expertise in the lab.

Soap and shampoo were a real luxury but finding clean clothes folded crisply on the dresser was a real treat. I had gotten rashes from wearing dirty clothes. The soft, slightly worn fabric of the jeans and t-shirt made me feel like a new man.

Clean and dressed, I went straight to the lab. I would have one of O'Neill's staff bring me something to eat later. He was good about that. He wanted me in my lab and focused on the problem as much as possible, so I didn't think it would be out of line.

The sun was just appearing on the horizon as I met Dr. Mason at the entrance to the science hall. I can understand why she was reluctant to use her title earlier. When someone heard you were a Doctor, they immediately thought you were a medical doctor. I had that same problem, and to tell you the truth, in this post-apocalyptic world, it was more of a burden than anything else.

"Thank you for being prompt," I said, extending my hand. She accepted it cautiously and gave a brief shake.

"You're a hand shaker I see," she observed.

"Force of habit," I apologized, looking at my hand. "I will refrain from now on."

162

We entered the building and two armed guards escorted us to my lab. One of the men entered the room, while the other stationed himself outside the door. Pamela looked at me skeptically. I just shrugged and began disclosing my notes.

As I unveiled the findings, she began to act like a true scientist. Her brow wrinkled as she looked at the tiny larva in the first blood sample. I could see that the puzzle was starting to hook her as she read through the notes I had printed out for her.

While she was reading, I asked the sergeant if he could get some food and coffee delivered. He radioed in our request and they told us it would be on its way.

"Fascinating," she breathed, pushing her glasses more securely to her head. "Where do we go from here?"

"I told the Colonel we needed a subject," I explained.

It was then that the guard stepped forward, a young man with a freshly shaven face. "We have your subject in a room down the hall," he reported.

A shiver of foreboding rifled through me as I turned to him. "Are you serious?"

"Yes, sir. We brought it in last night. When you are ready, I was instructed to take you to it."

I woodenly followed the sergeant through the door, followed by Dr. Mason. Three doors down, he rapped at the door in measured succession. The door opened, revealing two more men with pistols in hand.

"How's our prisoner?" he joked.

"Hungry," the shorter of the two answered jokingly, nodding his head to the far wall.

There, in the brightly lit room, was one of the undead, dressed in blue jeans and a barely recognizable Pittsburgh Steelers t-shirt. The smell in the room was horrendous. When the undead beast saw us, he made a muffled moan and reached for us but handcuffs halted his movement, stopping him in mid stride. Pamela gasped, drawing back from the hideous creature as it tried to open its duct-taped mouth.

"He's all yours, Doc," our young guard offered.

I just stood rooted to the spot. I was way out of my league. I didn't know what to do next.

"I need to speak with the Colonel," I offered to no one in

particular.

The smaller guard walked over to the undead and slammed the butt of his weapon into its midsection. "You're scaring the scientists!" he yelled in mock anger. The creature doubled over briefly, then resumed its attempts at forward motion.

"I'm sorry," he apologized sarcastically. "He doesn't have any manners."

I looked at the bound monster and then at the guard. *We aren't so different from them*, I thought to myself.

"Inform O'Neill that we're on our way," I commanded the young sergeant as I left the room in a rage.

Chapter 29
Melissa

I awoke to an empty bed, my husband leaving earlier a distant, hazy memory from my slumber. The sun shone uncomfortably in my eyes as I rolled over, luxuriating in the soft bed. The thin mattress wasn't the nicest I had ever slept in, but it seemed so wonderful after how I had slept over the last few weeks.

After a few more minutes of sogging, I pried myself from the bed's softness and rummaged for my shower supplies. A commotion in the hallway made me start. Loud, familiar voices shattered the early morning silence.

"I don't care what you say! I'm not going to any training!"

The sounds of a struggle ensued as I hurriedly dressed. As I pulled my crisp, clean t-shirt over my head, letting it drop to my denim waistband, I poked my head out of the doorway.

Ben and Frank were both on the ground. Armed military men were everywhere, surrounding the other civilians.

"ALL civilian males will report for training detail," a massive officer announced emphatically. "There will be no exceptions!"

I saw Amber at her door, looking fearfully at Drew as he left along with the others down the hall. Frank and Ben were literally thrown to their feet and prodded in line with the others.

"What's going on?" I asked Amber as she hurried across the hall into my room.

"The men are being forced to join the army," she said hurriedly. "This isn't right!"

"Something stinks here," I said, mimicking Dean's earlier statement. "We need to speak with Colonel O'Neill."

"We have to stop this," she agreed, eyes still wide, pleading. "Drew isn't cut out for this sort of thing."

I had to agree. The guys from the comic shop were ill-equipped to become part of a fighting force. They were pretty much unfit for anything physical.

Even Henry was. "Hank!" I said loudly, reality setting in. "You don't suppose..."

"I doubt it," Amber countered. "He is too important."

Her words stung. Laced in her reply was the assumption that

the others were of less value, so they would have to go off to fight, but because my husband was a scientist, he would be safe.

I had no retort. She was right. He would be safe; at least, as safe as he could be.

At that moment, I was saved from an awkward moment by a gruff woman's voice calling from the end of the hall.

"All female civilians will immediately report to breakfast. There you will be given your duties for the day."

"You gotta be kidding me!" Amber said loudly. A chorus of grumbling from the others in the hall joined her protest. Amber stepped back outside to join them.

The woman who had issued the announcement ran toward my friend. "What did you say!"

Amber immediately backed down. "Nothing."

"Did you think you were gonna lay your pretty butt around here like it was some kinda fancy hotel," she questioned putting her nose squarely against Amber's.

"Hey!" I said pushing her back. "There's no need to-"

Both of her hands shot forward and up, catching me under my shoulders. Off guard, I hurtled backward and down, unceremoniously onto my bottom.

Amber grabbed my attacker's shirt from the back and started to pull her away, but the military-trained female lifted her arm while spinning around. With this maneuver, she snared one of Amber's arms and twisted it roughly behind her back.

The soldier challenged, "Anyone else want to issue a formal protest?"

I climbed to my feet and joined the others in compliance.

Many of the women in the group openly cried as we left out of the dorm and entered the dining hall. We ate in near silence. A few of our number continued to weep but most simply shoveled food into their mouths robotically.

"What are we going to do?" asked Amber in hushed tones, not looking at me.

I continued to stare ahead at my plate as I replied, "We have to bide our time. Wait for tonight to see if we can all get together and make a plan."

"Why do you think this is happening?"

I couldn't answer. Although it was reasonable that we would

166

have to pull our own weight and share in some of the duties, this treatment was out of hand. And the forced military service had some terrible implications.

"I don't know," I replied, keeping my thoughts to myself. I didn't want to alarm anyone with my wild theories, but I felt like we were in some serious trouble here.

After being fed, we were all given specific duties. They deliberately separated woman who either had arrived together or had become friends here. My guess was that they didn't want women, who were familiar with each other, hatching any kind of rebellion.

They assigned Amber to the cleaning crew. In her case, she was to clean the bathrooms. I couldn't help but think it was a payback for putting her hands on the soldier earlier.

I was given laundry duty. Little did I know what I was in store for! While being ushered out in guarded groups to do our given tasks, I saw Henry in the distance walking my way.

Chapter 30
Henry

It was getting hot outside as I crossed the courtyard, walking quickly toward Old Main and the Colonel's office. I had left the shaken Pamela in my lab to steady her nerves and maybe go over the samples more thoroughly. I saw women leaving the dining hall in guarded groups. I was relieved that they were taking these measures to protect the civilian population.

A familiar face broke from the nearest pack on a course intercepting mine. It was Melissa. One of the women soldiers followed her closely.

"We need to talk!" she said firmly.

I stopped in my tracks. I had heard that tone before. She meant business. The other woman cut between us, and blocked Mel as she spoke.

"They took the guys away!" she said, fighting around the camo-clad woman.

"They're forcing them to join the military!"

"You need to rejoin the group!" Mel's guard cut her short in an authoritative manner.

"Sergeant!" I barked. "Stand down!" Everyone stopped what they were doing and looked at me. "What is going on here?"

"Sir, the-"

"Not you!" I said, cutting her off in mid-sentence.

I turned to Melissa and asked her in a calm voice what was happening. She explained everything. The sergeant stood motionless, not knowing what to do. She flinched slightly when Melissa told me about their earlier altercation. They must have been under some special orders about my treatment.

"My wife is coming with me!" I told the woman who had pushed her earlier.

"No, Henry. I will go with the other women. I'll do my part," she said while glaring at the woman.

"Ok," I conceded. "But you had better tone down your attitude, sergeant! If I hear anything like this again, the Colonel will get more than an earful."

"Yes, sir!" she said crisply.

I thought about making her do some push-ups or something, but I didn't want to push my luck. I didn't know what the limits of my power were, but it seemed to have put some fear into the woman.

The pair left me standing there with my guard. He had stayed a few yards away and hadn't said a word.

"What are your orders pertaining to me?"

He looked at me, debating something, then said, "To keep you safe and happy, sir."

"Not a great start, huh?" I mumbled.

"No sir."

We power-walked the rest of the way to the office, occasional arms fire popping in the distance only fueling my outrage. Conscripting my friends into the army was not something I condoned. When I entered the outer office, the commander's aid tried to stop me from entering the Colonel's office. I bowled past him and threw open the door.

"What are you doing!" O'Neill bellowed, veins in his neck and forehead popping.

"I need to have words with you!" I yelled back, my face heating also.

"Lieutenant, this will only take a second," he said to the man who was standing before his desk. "Please take a seat."

The soldier sat heavily down onto a wooden chair to one side.

"Now, what is your problem?" he continued, locking eyes with me.

"What do you expect me to do with that undead creature in my lab?" I intoned vehemently.

"You asked for a subject," he answered, clearly not understanding.

"But, it's alive," I shot back, now not as self-assured as I had been earlier.

"I thought that's the way you would want him," he said, retaking his own seat.

I hadn't thought of that. I guess the stress of seeing the bound creature attempting to attack us had unhinged me.

"Colonel, I think..."

"Lieutenant, could you wait outside a moment?" he asked. The young man reluctantly stood and exited the room.

After the door closed, I continued. "I am way out of my

element here, Colonel. I don't know where to go from here."

"You will do what you think is the next step," he soothed, his inner politician coming out. "I believe in you, son. You can do this. You have to do this. We're all depending on you. Heck, the world might be depending on you."

His ministrations were working. I was feeling better. "But what if I fail?"

He came around his desk and put an arm around my shoulder. "You won't fail. Now, get back there and do your job."

I turned around and headed for the door. Before I grabbed the handle, I turned once again. "My friends, you're training them for the army?"

"Yes."

"I don't think they are the type-" I began.

"We need men," he answered in a low tone. "We have lost a lot of good men and women battling these infected things. We need people who can go out into the field and help us clear out this town. Everybody will submit to training and work duties. The only exceptions are you and Mason. I want you two totally focused on finding a cure."

"But three of the guys who came in with me are not fit for military life."

"But they were fit enough to survive this long," he reasoned. "We are low on soldiers. Did you see the man I was debriefing when you barged in here?"

I glanced at the door and nodded.

"He lost one of his men getting you that subject you needed. Every soldier we lose to them depletes our ranks and adds to theirs. If we don't get everybody ready, we will lose!"

"But, if they have to storm into buildings, I'm afraid..."

"They will purely be used as backups, pretty much out of harm's way."

"Are you sure?" I asked, feeling relieved and a bit silly.

"Yes, I am. And you can have my word on it."

He offered his hand and I accepted it warmly.

"Now get back to work and find me that cure!"

I was still unsure of how to proceed. As my guard and I walked back to the lab, I mulled over various options.

As I entered the lab, I saw that Pamela was making her own

notes while reviewing the slides. Twin plates of what looked like creamed beef on toast sat untouched on a side table. My stomach churned at the thought, so I resigned to leave them that way.

Dr. Mason and I discussed various ideas on how to go ahead. We settled on a direct method. First, we would take samples and then proceed with an autopsy.

I instructed the four guards on what we had done with Bill, so they tightly bound the creature and I carefully extracted blood, saliva, urine, and even feces. All of these, we carefully stored in a refrigeration unit that had been moved into my lab.

"Have you ever done an autopsy?" I asked Pamela.

"No. Have you?"

I shook my head, indicating I had not, and suggested we get some anatomy books from another office I knew of down the hall.

Thumbing through the pages, we refreshed our memories of what things should look like in the human body; and, keeping the tomes at the ready, we ordered the corpse's execution.

A few moments later, the men carried the now still corpse to a makeshift examination table in an adjacent lab. Doing autopsies would be creepy enough, but in a world where the dead typically got up and tried to eat you, it added a whole new level of creepiness.

We started by cutting away its clothing and examining its outer skin tissue. It was gray, and we found what we believed to be the site of infection; but other than some advanced deterioration, we found nothing of interest.

Next, we proceeded to open its torso. We cut from his sternum to the groin. The stench was so incredibly terrible that we had to rub some Vick's VapoRub under our noses to mask the smell. I could hear the short guard emptying its stomach into a nearby garbage can as we began removing organs and comparing them to the images in the book. As he was having his breakfast, I had this strange sense of karma. The way he had abused the creature, he deserved this.

We took samples from every organ. Unsure of what to look for, we didn't want to waste our chance to study anything that might hold the key.

Our gloved hands covered in bodily fluids, we enlisted one of the older soldiers to label the various samples, dictating what each item should be called so we would have no problem identifying them later.

Pamela was great, offering keen insights as we pulled the various organs from the cadaver. When we concluded with its torso, we moved on to its cranium. Having nothing better, we used a hacksaw to open the top of its head. When we removed it we knew we had found the culprit.

From the creature's brain protruded half-dozen tapeworms covered in blood, probably introduced into the brain fluid from the head trauma induced by one of the guards. Each worm lay slack against the brain. Dr. Mason pulled two of these out with a pair of tweezers and she dropped them into individual vials. Stoppers in place, we removed the brain and probed deeper. We sampled tissue from the nasal cavity, eyes, ears, and salivary glands. We even rolled the corpse over and extracted some spinal fluid.

"I think that's enough," I said, my voice weary.

"I agree," Pamela said, sounding little better. "Let's get a look at the tapeworms. That has to be the cause."

Grinning at her determination, I was also eager to have a look. We placed one of the worms under a microscope and, after some further study, decided that it was dead, the cause of which we could not determine.

We spent the night examining the samples we had taken. We left nothing unchecked; looking in the usual places, then in the unusual, in search of clues to its life cycle.

The soldiers who guarded us were replaced and later those were also relieved, but we worked on, coffee fueling our all night investigation.

A knock at the door brought our work to a halt. It was the Colonel. He looked like he also hadn't slept. His usually crisp uniform was rumpled and he had rings under his eyes. He gave us a cordial grin.

"How goes humanity's greatest hope?"

We exploded into a flood of information, both talking at once. The O'Neill waved both hands in front of his face. "One at a time, please," he begged, somewhat revitalized and grinning fiercely at our excitement.

I deferred to Pamela. "We believe the cause of the outbreak is a flatworm located in the brain of the host. We have found eggs in the victim's salivary glands and actual larvae in the saliva itself. This is quite unusual, but our current hypotheses is that one of the two known tapeworms that invade the host's brain has evolved into this current variety and has altered its typical life cycle in the process."

Colonel O'Neill looked very excited. "Great news! Now how do we prevent it?"

"We don't know yet," I said. "But we believe having the larvae in the saliva itself gives the parasite a much greater chance of transporting its next generation to another host, thus assuring the continuance of its species."

Anger shone through O'Neill's eyes as he spat, "We are well aware of the continuance of its species. Look around. The world is teeming with this parasite. While you guys are sitting in here throwing ideas back and forth, people are dying. We need a cure!"

We both were taken aback, not anticipating his wrath. We had worked through the night and thought we were making headway.

The Colonel rubbed his eyes. "I'm sorry. I didn't mean that. I haven't slept in who knows how long," he apologized. "Why don't you two knock off and get some rest. We all have a lot of work to do."

With that, he turned and left my lab.

"What was all that about?" Pamela asked, looking deflated.

"I'm not sure," I answered. "But I do think he's right. We need some rest, or we might start to make mistakes."

We walked together back to the dorm, still tossing ideas back and forth. When we reached a "T" in the hallway, we went our separate ways. I took a long, hot shower and relaxed my tired muscles. The bed was neatly made and I hated to mess it up, so I just lie down on the comforter and immediately fell asleep.

Chapter 31
Melissa

Zombies were overrunning the world and I was doing my twentieth load of laundry. Something just didn't seem right with that. I felt kind of like Daniel Boone's wife. He spent his life out in the wilderness, hunting, exploring, and having fun, while his wife stayed home and took care of the house and kids. Sure, he'd come home for a few months to visit, just enough time to knock her up again and leave. By today's standards, Daniel Boone would be just another deadbeat dad.

The room was hot and humid. I felt a perpetual glaze of perspiration, making me feel sick. The sound of the sixteen machines whirling about their automated chore made it hard to hear anything. In between loads, they pressed us into maid service, picking up and cleaning in the lounge and other communal areas in the building. Other women, like Amber, were scouring the bathrooms at this very moment.

Any time we were outside, even just going between buildings, we realized the grim reality that the enemy was close. And even though I had a strong desire to do anything but more laundry, it was a sobering thought.

I was on lunch break when I saw Amber. She looked both directions and snuck over to my table.

"You ok?" she asked, looking concerned.

"Fine," I said as my hand unconsciously went down and gave my backside a reassuring rub. "She just bruised my ego a bit. How about you?"

She frowned. "I don't like it here. I agree with Dean. There's something weird going on around here."

"What do you mean?" I asked in a hushed voice.

"We need to get out of here," she said even lower, eyes darting about the room. "It... It isn't safe to talk now. Later."

As I took another bite of my sandwich, I scanned the room casually. There were guards at the inside of each entrance. As I watched them, it occurred to me that they looked more like they were more concerned with keeping us inside than they were of protecting us from an outside threat. They all looked inward.

174

The rest of the day, I spent as much time as possible questioning my fellow inmates. Most had lived here, in Slippery Rock, from the start of the outbreak, while others were newer arrivals like we were. The people who had come here more recently were more accepting of the military treatment, thinking that it was a good trade-off for a secure place to survive the rise of the dead.

The residents who were here from the onset explained their view of events. They informed us that this wasn't the Army. It was the Army National Guard. These people were, for the most part, regular citizens with military training. I also found out that they were working alone, that there was no coordinated effort to contain the major cities. It was all a ruse.

Colonel O'Neill was a local lawyer in his civilian life. This gave me a very unsettled feeling, not that he hadn't been properly trained. I began to question what was he up to? Why was he trying to hold this whole town against an undead invasion? I also began to fear for my husband. What if he was unable to synthesize a cure?

I kept these questions in my head. I would have to wait until later to discuss this with my companions. The waiting was the hardest part.

When our shift ended, Amber and I went to the dining hall. It was the last place my friend wanted to go, but we had our limited choices and we could be with the guys so we joined them there. It was odd. Mostly, we ate in silence. We exchanged meaningful looks over half-hearted forkfuls of spaghetti. The men ate ravenously, all except Dean, who barely touched his plate.

Later, we sat in the grass between buildings, not trusting the close quarters of the dorm to maintain our privacy. So we swatted the occasional mosquito and spoke in hushed tones.

"O'Neill can't hold the town much longer!" Dean said while plucking a blade of the long uncut grass. "We're running low on manpower."

"I don't understand why he's trying to hold the whole town," Drew spoke up. He was lying in the grass with his head nestled in Amber's lap. She softly stroked his mass of unruly brown hair as he spoke. "It's absurd."

"I think he's mad," I challenged. "Or at least deluded. There were rumors that he was going to make a run for office. A congressman."

"He can become the flippin' king, for all I care. This is insane," stated Ben angrily.

"He lived in this town, and maybe he never saw what was happening outside here," I offered. "He had a standing army of sorts and mobilized the citizens shortly after."

Frank's eyes shot open from his near sleep, "What are you saying?"

"Just that if he doesn't know that the whole country isn't going to recover anytime soon, he might be hoping he can come out of this a hero. Another Giuliani."

"She might be right," Amber agreed, pausing her hand on Drew's head. "I heard he was only in the National Guard to further his political aspirations. He was involved in some pretty shady deals."

"It isn't going to work, in any event!" Dean cut in, tossing the blade of grass back to the turf. "If we keep this up much longer, we'll be overrun. It wouldn't be so bad if they used the trained soldiers up front."

Amber and I looked at them, stunned. We didn't know what to say. I tried to form the question, but Ben beat me to it.

"Where do you think we were all day?" he said indignantly.

"You were on the front lines?" I asked. A chorus of bobbing heads confirmed the statement.

"It seems like it's mostly a civilian corps," Dean asserted. "At least, the ones I spoke to were."

"I wonder why no one talked to me," Frank inquired to no one in particular.

"Maybe if you weren't such a nerd!" Ben shot back.

Frank hurled a fist full of rocks at his diminutive friend. Throwing his arms up, Ben deflected most of the pebbles.

"Stop it, or you'll put my eye out!" he cried. "That would be great, a comic book artist with no depth perception."

"So! It's not like it stopped Nick Fury! He can still shoot a gun!" Frank defended himself.

"He's also a cartoon character!" Drew stated, bringing the conversation back to reality. "Besides, he has a special eye patch from SHIELD designed to triangulate distance."

"I can't believe they put you guys in front," Amber restated.

176

"I can't believe they gave these bozos guns," Dean said.

"Listen, guys," I said, trying to change the conversation. "We need to come up with a plan. I think something's wrong here."

"I agree," Drew said. "What are you-"

Shhh. I blew the sound out, silencing the conversation. A group of six armed soldiers walked right up to our gathering.

"Nice little picnic you have here," the huge Sergeant said.

"This isn't a picnic, Sergeant Platz. There isn't any food," stated Dean.

"What did you say, son?" the huge man in command said.

"You said 'nice picnic,' and I just stated that we have no food. Pretty poor picnic if we don't-"

"You think you're funny, son? Well, I'm pretty funny too. All civilian men are to report to their commanding officer in ten minutes!"

"We just got off duty, Sarge," Drew said, sounding tired.

"The Colonel just put you back on duty, so let's get moving!" he goaded.

"Really, guys. We-"

Six machine guns were suddenly trained on us. I could hear clicks as safeties were being disengaged.

"I said NOW!" the sergeant barked.

The guys carefully got to their feet and went off in search of their commanding officer.

Chapter 32
Henry

As evening approached, I rose from the bed, the form of my body leaving a ghost-like imprint on the comforter. I smoothed out the impression, knowing how Melissa liked things neat and traded my old clothes for new ones. After changing I looked into the full-length mirror on the back of the door. I looked like some college leftover in a pair of camouflage pants and an Aéropostale shirt. As I left the building, a soldier broke from behind the desk and followed at my heels.

It was comforting, in a way, being guarded so closely. O'Neill was really taking good care of me, watching out for my safety. It was nice.

When I entered the lab, I saw Dr. Mason hard at work. A wall of books surrounded her. Piles sat everywhere; on the desk, chairs, and even the floor.

My entrance caused her to look up. While removing her glasses with one hand, she rubbed her eyes with the other. She mumbled, "What time is it?"

"About six," I said.

"In the morning?"

"No," I corrected. "In the evening. How long have you been here?"

"About six hours," she answered, replacing her spectacles. "Nice shirt, but you look like the oldest freshmen I've ever seen."

"Thanks, but what are you doing here?" I asked, concerned.

"I don't sleep very well lately and was just too curious," she apologized.

"I understand," I assured her. "Find anything good?"

"No, but I have a theory."

I removed a stack of books from a nearby chair and placed them on the floor. "Let me hear it."

"The thing that puzzled me this whole time was why does a strong trauma to the head kills the infected corpse. Last night, it just kept spinning in my head."

"And?" I asked, encouraging her to continue.

"I believe it has something to do with the blood. As you know, the human brain is floating in fluid. This fluid has a very slight iron content. Our human blood has much more iron. I postulate that the parasite cannot survive in an iron rich environment."

"We did find larvae in the earliest blood samples from Subject Bill," I said.

"That was the problem I was wrestling with, so I came back here and reexamined those samples. The larvae, in all cases, seemed to have begun the maturing process. These young parasites died because they just didn't make the cut. Like sperm, how many die just to ensure that one makes it to the egg? These parasite larvae were unable to leave the bloodstream and begin the journey to the brain because they were somehow unfit."

"Something is missing," I said. "I thought that iron content was high in the brain's tissue? Isn't it an important conductor in the electrical processes of the organ?"

"Indeed," Pamela agreed. "But there are regions that have relatively low concentrations of iron. Interestingly, low iron content in vital brain areas has been thought to be responsible for restless leg syndrome. It compels the individual to move its limbs."

"I don't think that the dead larvae in the blood samples were due to maturation. What if the larvae actually feed on the brain's iron, purposely depleting it in order to create the restless leg syndrome? This would give the flatworm's host the ability of motion. At this point, it would just have to compel the individual to attack and bite."

Dr. Mason nodded at my assumption. "That's good. If the larvae absorbed that much iron during maturation, they may not be able to tolerate any additional amounts. Unable to regulate their absorption of iron may be the mature parasite's weak spot. The blow to the head introduces excess blood, causing the parasite to overload on the iron. That is what actually kills it."

"Great work!" I said, hopes swelling. "But what can we do with this?"

"I don't know," she said, looking back at the book on the desk. "It may be of interest that some people may be immune to the parasite. At least, in theory, people with Parkinson's or Alzheimer's disease should be unable to host this parasite. It is believed that they have an increased amount of iron in their brains."

"Great! So all we have to do is inject all of the zombie's brain cases with iron and they'll all drop dead," I said, almost laughing.

She looked back up at me, obviously not getting my joke. "It seems a blow to the head is still the best-known method for killing the organism."

"It's just too bad that we can't just administer iron pills as a vaccine."

"Agreed," she said. "But iron is toxic."

"I know," I assured her. "I was just dreaming."

"We need to get these findings to the CDC or someone who has specialized teams for this kind of work, but the only place I know of is in the middle of Atlanta."

Pamela looked back down at her book, suddenly becoming overly interested in a diagram. "It's probably impossible. There would be millions of undead between us and them."

"Any better ideas?" I asked.

She didn't answer, seemingly absorbed in her study.

"I'm going to catch O'Neill up on your findings. Do you want to come?"

"You go ahead," she said, returning to her book. "That man gives me the creeps."

I had to admit that she was right. He sure was a slick operator. During our last encounter, he had manipulated me, turned my anger into self-doubt. But I had his number now.

I left and, as could be predicted, a soldier detached from the rest and followed me at a discreet distance. As I traveled along the sidewalk, I couldn't help but notice the campus's condition. Grass, too long neglected, was going to seed. The flowers were wilting under the drought-like conditions. I wiped the sweat from my brow as I increased my gait. It would be dark in another hour or so.

I barged into the outer office and waited for the clerk to receive me. He seemed in a state of disarray. Boxes of equipment were strewn about the normally pristine room.

"The Colonel is not in," he said efficiently.

"Where is he?" I asked. "I need to update him."

"He's in the field conducting operations," he responded hastily. "I can get a message to him."

"Just tell him Dr. Cooper was here with promising news."

"Anything you need me to relay," he asked, recognizing me and suddenly becoming interested.

"Just tell him I was here," I repeated, turning to the door.

I was half way out when he sheepishly called after me, "Did you find a cure?"

I closed the door hard, the glass covering the top half rattling from my effort.

I had one last stop. I wanted to check in with Melissa on the way to the lab. I hadn't spoken to her in over a day and for some reason, I needed to hold her, just for a moment. I wanted to be assured that she was all right.

Clouds were just starting to form on the horizon, prematurely darkening the sky. It looked like rain was on its way from distant Lake Erie. With the heat index of the last few days, I was pretty sure it would be a downpour.

I barreled into the dorm, the soldier still trailing behind. Opening the door to our room, I saw Amber and Mel on the bed holding one another, crying.

"What's wrong?" I demanded, my face heating.

"They took the guys!" Amber cried, tears streaming down her face. "Something's wrong!"

I took them both in an awkward embrace, feeling wet faces on my neck. We stayed that way for a few moments, allowing each to rein in strained emotions.

"Where did they go?" I asked as we freed one another.

"We don't know," Melissa answered, wiping her face. "The guys just got off a shift and were exhausted. Then a group of soldiers came and demanded that they follow. Dean refused, but they aimed their machine guns at the guys and forced them to go."

It all came out too quickly for me to understand the whole story, but I got the gist of what they were saying. Things were falling apart. We needed to find a way out of here.

"You two stay here and pack anything useful," I commanded, kissing Melissa hard on the lips. "Lock the door and wait for the guys. If they show up before I do, come to the lab. We're getting out of here."

"Where are you going?" Melissa cried, holding my arms and restraining me.

"I need to do something at the lab," I explained, prying myself free of her grasp. "I'll be back as soon as I can."

Leaving the room, I tried to look nonchalant as I walked back to my lab. The gunfire was definitely closer now, confirming my belief. It took all of my self-control not to break into a sprint.

My guard still followed me, but I stole some quick glances over my shoulder and noticed he was quite distracted. He was looking everywhere but at me. His head darted toward any sound or shadow. It was growing darker by the minute and thunder boomed from afar.

I calmly entered the science hall and casually made my way to the lab. Inside, Pamela was scanning another book.

"Any last thoughts?" I asked abruptly.

"No," she said in a confused tone, returning my look.

"Start downloading all of the data onto those flash drives," I demanded, indicating the pile of memory sticks.

"What's wrong?" she asked, still sitting behind her fortress of books.

Before I could answer what sounded like a burst from an automatic weapon ripped through the silence. Pamela sprung into action. Bringing the computer screen to life.

"While the files are copying send as many to print as you can," I ordered.

"Way ahead of you," she answered, not looking up from her work.

After I had stashed the written notes and image printouts in an old messenger satchel, I handed her one of the test tubes containing flatworm specimens.

"Where are the guards?" she asked in a scared voice.

"Put one of these in your pocket, as well as a copy of the printouts and a flash drive," I told her, ignoring her last question and focusing on what we had to do.

"Why so many?" she asked at as she removed one memory stick and quickly replaced it with another.

"In case we get separated or lose one."

"Where are we going?"

I hadn't thought of that. Where could we go? Another burst of weapons fire erupted from outside. "Atlanta!"

Her eyes shot wide open as she slammed another memory stick

home in its drive, "Impossible," she stammered.

"What else can we do?" I explained as she continued loading one flash drive after another. "We need facilities, a trained staff. We can't do this alone."

"There is another place," she explained reluctantly. "This place is top secret."

"Where?" I demanded, feeling betrayed. She had never mentioned it before. Didn't she understand that there were no more secrets now that the world had gone down the toilet?

Something crashed in the hallway as she spoke. "In the Allegheny National Forest. Near the dam. There is a-"

Through the partially open door, a monster appeared. Covered in blood, the creature lurched the few steps to where Mason sat. She screamed and moved to flee. Her first step knocked over a large stack of books. As she planted her next step, her footing slipped on the pages of a journal and she fell to the ground.

The undead beast was on her in an instant, teeth ripping a large chunk of flesh from her shoulder. I looked hastily about for a weapon. Seizing the first thing available, I brought a laptop down squarely on its head. The zombie dropped lifeless onto Pamela.

Dropping the destroyed laptop, I grabbed its ankles and dragged the corpse off of her. I knelt beside her as her lifeblood poured from her wound. She looked at me, eyes distant, and breathed something. I mustered all the courage I had and put my ear near hers, watching the blood run freely from her torn flesh, helpless to even apply pressure to the wound for fear of infecting myself.

As she spoke, I had to fight the fear of her turning and taking a bite out of my exposed face. Trembling in horror, I suddenly felt a strong urge to empty my bladder.

Pam's voice was soft, dreamy, as she told me her last words. I knelt, and then stood above her. If you looked at her just right, it almost seemed she was sleeping. I took a few steps away, searching for something to strike her with. I didn't want her to suffer the fate of rising again.

"Where is the cure?!" a familiar voice demanded from the door.

I spun around just in time to be thrown against a bookcase. O'Neill grabbed me by my shirt and lifted me off my feet. He was soaking wet, his hair plastered to his head. "I gave you everything you needed, now where is the cure!" he threatened as my feet dangled. I tried striking him but his grip was like iron.

"There is no cure!" I explained through gritted teeth.

The colonel was unreasonable. He seemed driven by desperation. His eyes were too wide, mouth grinning crazily. "You lie!" he bellowed, pushing me even higher.

At this height, I could clearly see past him. His rage had him focused only on me. I watched in horror as Dr. Pamela Mason rose from the floor and shuffled toward us, her wound still pouring blood as a large stain spread on her shirt. Eyes white, she staggered unsteadily our way.

"Let me down!" I demanded the colonel, trying to buy time.

Pamela's walking corpse opened her mouth wide and bit the back of his neck. Dropping me, he spun and swatted her away. He drew his sidearm and put a single bullet into her forehead.

"Crap!" I muttered.

"Nice try," O'Neill said, calmly aiming his 9mm at me. "You have five seconds to produce the cure or I am going to blow a hole in your oversized brains!"

"Let me explain," I said from the floor.

"One," he counted.

"We now understand its life cycle," I tried to distract him.

"Two."

"The parasite can be killed with iron," I continued. "Some people may be immune."

"Three."

"Five already!" a voice yelled from the door. A burst of automatic gunfire sounded from the same place, striking the colonel in the head. Blood and gore erupted as he dropped to the side, dead.

"You could have gotten here sooner!" I reprimanded a dripping wet Dean.

"It was more dramatic this way," he said jokingly.

I picked up the lamp I had eyed earlier and smashed it angrily on what remained of O'Neill's head.

"I think I already killed him," Dean stated confused.

"It was a doubletap!"

"I put at least five rounds in his head," he argued.

"He was twitching," I remarked, collecting my satchel. "And, besides, it felt good!"

184

I stooped over the still body of Dr. Mason and fished around in her pockets.

"Look who's stealing from the dead now!" Dean accused, chuckling afterward. When he saw that I didn't understand his reference, he continued. "Back at the Kingdom Hall?"

Grinning back I now remembered. He had liberated the car keys from the guy in the downstairs kitchen; Eric. Finding what I was looking for, I led my friend to a side door.

"Where are Drew and the guys?" I asked, looking down the hall.

"I sent them ahead to the dorm. All hell is breaking loose out there. I wanted to make sure the girls were alright."

I didn't know whether to laugh or cry at the thought of those comic book geeks protecting anybody. I just couldn't imagine them defending anything other than a pizza.

"Just like old times," he shouted, pressing a handgun into my grip.

"I hate this part," I added as I switched the safety off.

We hurried down the hall and out into the storm. Lightning strikes briefly illuminating scenes of horror. Soldiers were shooting blindly as the downpour limited their vision. I saw a person being devoured by a small group of undead. They surrounded their meal, kneeling around their screaming, still alive entrée.

We sprinted through the tempest, avoiding anything that moved. Dean ran with precision while I followed his lead.

Moments later we were nearing the dorm, the lights of the entry revealing the undead. As Dean cleared the way using controlled bursts from his weapon I swung my gun from side to side, protecting his back.

"Clear!" he yelled, causing me to change direction and follow him once again. Our wet shoes slid on the tile entry but we quickly recovered and pushed on. Dean turned left at a T-shaped intersection without looking and immediately changed course. Hands instantly followed him as three creatures came quickly into view. Releasing my breath, I shot each at close quarters right in the head.

"Not bad!" he complimented. "Now you lead."

I understood. His gun wasn't the best thing for close quarters. My handgun was much more suited for this type of fighting.

I checked both directions. The one side was clear but there were two undead outside my dorm room looking very excited about what was inside. Raising my gun. I calmly walked toward them, shocked that they hadn't been drawn to the most recent sound of my weapon.

At about ten feet, they turned. I dropped each with another three shots. I pounded at the door with my free hand.

"Anybody home?" Dean called, always the comedian.

The solid wood door nearly flew off its hinges. Melissa jumped into my arms, hooting in joy. As we broke our embrace, her hand brushed my gun.

"That's warm," she observed.

"Because I just shot them," I said, indicating the two dead zombies in the hall.

"He shot three more back there," Dean helped.

"You really are my knight in shining armor!" She grinned, eyes shining in delight.

I passed out the flash drives, instructing everyone in a clear voice that this was our research to this point and that if we got separated, they should share it with anyone who could use it in any way.

Frank and the boys had passed out spare firearms to Amber and Mel and were now checking their own weapons. I heard the sound of Dean checking his as he urged, "I hate to rush this but people we really should be..."

"Moving!" I finished while slapping the revolver's freshly reloaded cylinder closed. "Everybody got everything?"

A chorus of affirmation followed and we raced to the fire escape doors at the end of the hall. Through lightning flashes, we determined our best course, and back into the storm we went.

The wind buffeted the rain off of our faces, obscuring our vision even more as we raced to the motor pool. I watched, through one brief flash of lightning, a lone soldier being ripped apart by a group of zombies. There was no time to help. We were all on our own.

I caught a brief glance of what I believed was Ben bashing a zombie out of Amber's way. The rain made it hard to be sure, but it looked like he struck it with the butt of his automatic weapon. They were there one moment and gone the next, the downpour

186

masking them from my view.

We crouched down behind a hedge. The cars were all parked in the lot and on the road below. The fire truck was there as well as a bunch of Humvees. Many of the military vehicles had various packages piled nearby.

"I knew they were trying to bug out!" I exclaimed, face streaming with water.

"The fire truck is blocked in!" Drew informed us. "What are we going to do?"

"Let's try the Humvees," I suggested. "If they have keys in them, I say they're ours."

No one argued so I lead the way to the lead vehicle. I opened the door and jumped into the driver's seat. After spending a few moments fumbling for the ignition, I found it and a set of keys hanging in place.

"Bingo!" I yelled in triumph while pumping my fist.

Dean came up beside my open door, "The other one has keys too. Let's get moving!" He ran around the vehicle toward the passenger door. A pair of hands came out of the rain and hauled him from his feet.

I jumped back out into the rain and circled the vehicle. A soldier was on top of him and Melissa was blocking my aim. As I screamed for her to move, she fired her own shot.

Chapter 33
Melissa

The rain pounding on the hot ground caused steam to rise. The visibility here was extremely limited. As we crouched behind the hedge I caught sight of the rain streaming across the handgun Frank had given me. It made me wonder if it would still fire if the bullets got wet.

As Henry assessed our transportation situation, I marveled at how he had really come into his own. It had only taken an apocalyptic outbreak to do it, but he was now strong and commanding. Commanding.

We fled from our hiding place and bolted for the vehicles, our weapons swinging toward any unusual movement that came into our minimal sight. Twice I fired. Not knowing if it had any effect, I mentally marked where I saw the motion and kept moving ahead. We passed by the fire truck. It was tightly blocked in. Even with its bulk and power, I doubted it could push its way free. Instead, we headed to the front of the line. Interior lights illuminated the inside of the second Humvee while Hank tried the first.

I took up a position between the two, defending the others as they loaded onboard both of the military transports and started their engines. My heart nearly stopped when Dean ran by out of the pouring rain, slapping my shoulder as he went past.

"Let's go!" he yelled as thunder boomed.

"Right with ya!" I called back, taking a last look behind. As I rounded the Humvee's rear bumper, it struck me. Dean was gone!

I could see by the interior lights that he wasn't inside, so I broadened my field of search. He was on the ground, his back pinned to the pavement by one of those things. My friend struggled to hold it at arm's length, and as a bolt of lightning flashed, I shot.

The creature fell slack in Dean's hands. He threw the now slack horror to the side as another jagged line of lightning illuminated the former undead.

"Karma, bitch!" I spat as I instantly recognized the female soldier. It was the one who had planted me on my butt.

"Just pure karma," I muttered as I helped my friend to his feet.

Dean looked shaken, water streaming across his face. "Thanks," he said loudly but with a flutter in his voice.

"If you two are about done fooling around..." Henry cried from behind, startling both of us in the process.

The sound of the downpour and the boom of thunder blanketed all other noises, but I knew that there were creatures moaning all around us. The rain was masking us from them. They could be a few feet away and wouldn't know we were near.

We hurriedly climbed into the Humvee. I felt a pang of guilt at being dripping wet and sitting in the vehicle, but after rational thought took hold, I dismissed the feeling.

Henry fumbled for the headlights as we sat in the idling Humvee. A deep, resonating rumble threatened to vibrate the teeth right out of my jaws. I felt relieved being in the safety of the sturdy military vehicle.

A loud slap on the small window brought me back to reality. I whipped around in my seat, pointing my gun toward the noise. A young woman had the side of her face pressed against the glass. Her mouth slowly opened and closed as she pressed her grimy cheek against the glass. Her nearly white eye stared at me as she slid her face back and forth trying to find an opening. Her hand drew back and smacked again against the barrier separating us.

I felt sad for her, her once pretty hair now matted with rain. Twigs and bits of refuse were tangled in its mass. The zombie had probably been very beautiful before she turned. She rolled her face horizontally against the window, trying a new angle and making me gasp in revulsion. This side of her face had no flesh. It was a huge, open wound. Hair welded to dried blood, which caked her jaw line. The angry red meat of her face smeared the window with fluids.

Half horrified and half revolted, I tracked her movements with my weapon. The zombie's eyes stayed locked on mine as she continued her search for a way in.

I was afraid to shoot, fearing that the bullet would shatter the glass, exposing me to any other undead which wandered close.

"Can we get out of here?" I asked no one in particular, while my voice quivered uncontrollably.

Just then, another joined the first. This man was bigger, much bigger. When his hand came down on the window it nearly burst inwards.

"Hank?" I urged.

"Crap!" he shouted as he noticed my situation. Henry pushed down on the accelerator causing us to surge forward quickly. The hands of the two squealed loudly, dragging against the glass as it slid away.

Dean leaned between us. "Slow down, Henry. We need to stay in control. Just creep. If we hit a tree, we're screwed."

The vehicle decelerated to a crawl, headlights barely penetrating the heavy rainfall.

"That's it," Dean said, relaxing back into his seat. "This downpour can't last forever. We can go faster when we can see better."

Twin beams of light shone from the other Humvee trailing behind us. As the rain began to let up, my husband increased the speed of the vehicle, slowing only to pass around or nudge walking dead out of our way. In turn, Drew, who was driving the second military vehicle, copied our movements and speed.

"Where are we going?" I asked. I knew we traveling north as a sign for Harrisville passed by.

"Dr. Mason let me in on a little secret," Hank said solemnly. "She told me where there's a secret CDC facility."

"Not the one in Atlanta," She moaned.

"No. Closer," I replied. "In the Allegheny National Forest."

"But there's nothing up there," Dean remarked.

"Exactly," I agreed. "I always thought it was a crazy idea to put a facility which housed so many lethal diseases in the middle of such a densely populated area. It just makes sense that they would have a special pathogens branch in a sparsely populated area."

"I thought you had only been to the Atlanta facility," I queried.

"That's true. I never heard of this place," Henry responded. "She said it was a classified location."

Harrisville is a tiny town. Its main intersection housed a somewhat large convenience store with gas pumps all around. The building was dark, doors yawning wide open.

"Should we stop for gas?" I asked. Henry had a knack for driving and not noticing that we were nearly on empty.

190

"No. We're good," he answered. "I think O'Neill was planning his escape for a while. The tank is full."

As we passed by the convenience store, I noticed a few wet forms shambling about the pump area. They changed direction as our sound and lights caught their attention.

"I thought O'Neill was totally set on keeping the town," I reasoned.

"Remember how he had the civilians out on the front lines," he reminded me. "I believe he had pulled his troops so that if they had to withdraw he would have a trained army to retreat with."

"Coward!" I said in disgust.

"Politician!" Hank corrected.

"It's all the same thing," countered Dean from the back. His voice dripped with sarcasm. "They can stand on the capital's steps in solidarity but did they or any of their families fight in Afghanistan? Nice photo-op as they stay safe and secure."

Henry and I let Dean continue his rant. Although I had to agree with his point, it all seemed moot in this new world. I doubted anyone was safe and secure at this point.

We drove on as the rain abated. The night was getting quite chilly. Goosebumps rose on my arms as my body and the car's heater worked at drying our clothes.

"Are there any blankets back there?" I asked Dean, interrupting his tirade. "I'm freezing."

"There're a couple of containers," he replied. I could hear metal and plastic latches popping open as he searched. "Two bottles of Kentucky's finest, some MRE's, a couple of walkie-talkies, beef jerky, and water. Sorry. No blankets. But the booze might warm you up."

"It will actually make you colder," Henry informed us.

"No it doesn't!" argued Dean, leaning back over the seat. "It always makes me feel warmer."

"Here we go," I groaned. Dean, by this time, should know better than to get Henry going.

"Sure," my husband began. "It makes your skin feel a little warmer; but, in reality, it makes your blood vessels dilate. This causes your core temperature to fall."

"My pappy always told me-" our friend started, but Hank wasn't listening anymore.

"That's it!" Henry cut him off.

Chapter 34
Henry

As I was arguing with Dean about alcohol warming the body, it dawned on me.

"Alcohol restricts the flow of blood to the brain," I blurted out, cutting my friend off in mid-sentence.

"What does that have to do with anything?" he asked, perturbed at my outburst. I could hear static as he checked one of the walkie-talkies.

"That's why some of the people we encountered turned at an incredibly slow rate," I explained, almost having to stop the vehicle in my eureka moment.

"What do you mean?" Dean asked clearly not following.

I had forgotten that everyone was not privy to the notes I had taken during the interviews. I had to think of common cases they would both know about.

"Bill," I began in my most clinical voice. "He had been bitten days before we discovered him. He had been drinking squeeze."

"What's that?" asked Dean, checking another radio, loud static nearly drowning out his question.

"The product of pressing sterno through some type of cheese cloth. It produces methanol, a type of alcohol which can get you drunk but can just as easily kill you," I explained. "The effects of the methanol dilating the brain's blood vessels would have blocked the transport of the parasite to its destination. Thus, it would have delayed the onset of the subject's turning."

"That's why it took so long for Ted to become one of them!" Melissa added, understanding my line of thought.

"Exactly," I agreed.

"So we should all get drunk?" Dean said, hefting a bottle from the case and grabbing the cap.

"No," I said emphatically. "It would not only impair our judgment, but it's only a slight delay of the inevitable. Besides, the undead typically don't take just a small bite. We would die either way."

"Is that why Julie took so long?" asked my friend in a small voice.

"I believe so, Dean."

We rode on in silence, the tires humming as the two vehicles pulled onto interstate 80. I drove past the exit for the college town of Clarion, preferring to enter the state forest from its more remote eastern side. We wove along back roads that made the ones where we lived seem like cities. In this mid-Pennsylvania area, state forest bordered State Forest, which was then bordered by state parks. Not a living or undead soul was within miles. It was so desolate, I began to wonder if they noticed the zombie outbreak.

As we drove down a particular dirt road, a big, gray primer-colored Chevy truck passed by. Spray painted on its side in red was, *The Hillbilly Headshot Posse*. I somehow got the idea that the infected had arrived.

As we pulled back onto a paved road, Melissa sleepily asked, "Are we there yet? I need a ladies' room?"

"Can't you wait?" I asked, irritated.

"I haven't gone in a long time," she replied, straightening in her seat.

"Why didn't you go earlier?"

"I didn't know there was going to be a zombie apocalypse, so I didn't empty my bladder," she replied, rounding on me. "I gotta pee!"

I started to pull off the road, a field to either side. "Don't even think about it!" she said vehemently. "I'm not peeing out in the open!"

I pulled back on the road. I could imagine Drew driving behind us. He must think we're crazy; slowing, speeding, pulling off the road and then veering back again. I could hear Frank and Ben now. They probably were trying to convince the others that we turned into zombies.

A few miles up the road, we saw a lone gas station. It was dark and dingy, but the restroom doors were plainly visible by our headlights. I pulled the vehicle around and hit the high beams so the full power would illuminate the woman's room if I held the door open.

Melissa hurried out of the Humvee, gun first, joined immediately by a duck-walking Amber.

Drew hurried over, saying, "Where are we going?"

Dean tossed him a radio, which Drew couldn't manage to

catch. It dropped to the ground, the back cover popping off, batteries rolling all over the place.

"Fanboys!" my neighbor muttered under his breath. "Up near the dam. There's a secret squirrel CDC base up there."

I fished out a pair of flashlights and handed them to the girls. As we started toward the doors, I could hear Drew telling Dean that Frank almost had them all believing that we were in the throes of reanimating into zombies.

"Do you want me to go in first?" I asked, feeling bold.

"No!" Mel cut me off. "We're big girls. We don't need some big macho man checking on monsters under the bed."

I let them go, watching as Amber grabbed the door handle while Mel aimed her gun at the opening. I kept alert as Amber gave the door a pull.

"Oh," Melissa cried in disgust, wrinkling her nose and turning her head slightly as she carefully walked to the opening. Gun still raised, she looked down at the restroom floor and signaled Amber to let it close.

They then tried the men's room. This time, my wife stalked up to the open door with a weapon in one hand and flashlight in the other. She scanned the room for danger, then directed her friend inside.

"You can at least stand guard," Mel commanded voice full of mirth. "Isn't that what you guys are for?"

"Sure," I replied, taking a place outside the door.

Frank and Ben quickly relieved themselves near the Humvee and immediately hopped back inside. The two others joined me outside the door to the men's room.

"Where are the girls?" Drew asked. I pointed over my shoulder as the pair exited the men's room.

"Ummm..." Drew stammered. "That's the-"

"We know!" Amber said sarcastically, answering his unspoken question. "You don't want to see that!"

Melissa explained what she saw. "It looks like she slit her wrists. She isn't one of them. It looks like she just couldn't take it. Maybe she was trapped."

"She didn't turn?" Dean asked, hand unconsciously going to the gun tucked in the waist of his jeans front.

"No, she's dead," she continued. "It's really quite sad. Every one of these people has a story that will go untold."

We all took a moment, letting that thought sink in. It was true. Even in the future, if we survive this event, everyone's personal experience will just fade away.

Amber leaned into Drew's shoulder. "It's quiet here. Why don't we stay the night in the Hummers?"

"Humvees," Drew corrected.

She frowned, "Whatever. We're all tired and we don't know what's ahead. Is it smart to go there in the dark?"

Melissa placed a hand on my shoulder. "She's right," she agreed. "If there's any sort of trouble ahead, it would be best if we were rested."

We passed out some of the food and water. Each vehicle would be responsible for their own watch. Everyone would stay inside. Even though it was very remote here, we couldn't chance a guard being outside. One slip up and we would all be vulnerable.

The night passed with no incident. The birds' stirring woke us with their songs. If you didn't think about the woman in the bathroom, you would think this area was completely untouched.

Everyone used the bathroom one last time and we ate and drank a little before resuming our journey. The day was cooler, a cold front from the north having followed the storm. It left the air crisp and pure-feeling.

As I started up the military vehicle, I could see Dean's telltale mark on the woman's restroom door. *Dead inside. Not a zombie, just dead*, written in permanent marker. Hopefully, his little guide would save someone the shock that the girls experienced.

The pavement was still mostly dark on the right side, the shadows from trees slowing evaporation from the sun. We traveled north.

Nature seemed to continue as normal. We saw a three deer cross the road and the occasional groundhog munching plants beside the berm. Squirrels and birds darted about in search of food.

"Do you think they will get infected?" asked Melissa absently as she watched the scenes unfold outside her window.

"I doubt it," I assured her. "Most pandemics rarely make a cross-species jump. Even then, sometimes the virus can be present in the blood stream but has no infectious hold on its host."

An abandoned ranger's booth provided us with a map of the

196

Allegheny National Forrest. The dam was clearly shown. Several campgrounds speckled the area, indicating possible places of concern for undead.

We could see the large reservoir appear before us, marking our approach to the Kinzua Dam. Sunlight reflected off the water, looking tranquil. The surface was like glass, undisturbed by the almost nonexistent breeze.

All eyes were on the body of water as our goal came into view. The dam loomed ahead. A long and empty parking lot ran all the way up to the man-made structure that created flood control for the Allegheny River.

"Where's this top secret facility?" asked Dean.

"Up there," I said, indicating a mountain directly beside the reservoir. "She said there was an old road that goes up to another reservoir above this one. That's where the hydroelectric generating station is."

"They put all those deadly diseases near a water source?" he groaned.

"It would provide excellent backup power following a prolonged outage," I proposed. "You wouldn't want the freezers keeping things like bubonic plague losing power."

"No," he agreed. "But, if it did fail, it would contaminate the entire waterway."

"That wouldn't happen," I countered. "These types of facilities have various fail-safes in place, all with redundancies. If the freezers reach a certain temperature, the room or rooms are control-burned at temperatures far beyond what the contents can survive. It is really quite safe."

We found the old road and followed it uphill until we saw a smaller road veer off to the side. Following the smaller one, we came to a fortified metal gate. The high fence was topped with razor wire and ran off in both directions disappearing in the trees. A metal box with a mechanism for swiping coded cards was on the left, but not necessary. The gate stood wide open, one side leaning out at an odd angle. Plastic car moldings and some glass indicated the cause.

"It looks like it was rammed from the inside," Melissa observed.

"Man, someone wanted out in a hurry," Dean added.

Melissa looked at me seriously as our vehicles idled in place outside the gate. "Maybe we shouldn't go in there, Hank."

"We need to see if there's anyone here with some answers," I reasoned. "They may need our findings. They might need help."

The three of us agreed to investigate the facility. As Dean cleared the entrance of debris, I walked back to the other Humvee. Drew lowered the driver's side window.

"We are going in to look around," I informed them.

"I don't think that's a good idea!" Frank called from the back.

"We're with you," Drew assured me.

Frank and Ben shot forward in their seats, nearly climbing over to the front. "Can't you see the gate?" Frank reasoned.

Ben added, "Something bad happened in there!"

"What would Batman do?" Drew challenged the two. Heads lowering, they both retreated to their seats.

"I thought you were Batman," I teased.

"I am," he verified in a serious tone. "But they think I'm Bruce Wayne because I own a comic book store."

Drew's Humvee followed ours as we proceeded through the fence to the main building. Being used to the Atlanta site, I was looking for a large, modern piece of architecture. What we found was a parking lot and a door leading into the mountain, cars parked in orderly rows. It looked like a normal day at the office.

The only thing out of the ordinary was the door hanging open. We parked not far from the entrance.

"I have a bad feeling," Dean said softly to me as we gathered the others in the lot.

"We have to be sure," I answered in low tones. The door had scorch marks on the inside. Gathering my courage, I said in my most commanding voice, "I know this doesn't look like what we expected. We have to know what happened here. We have to keep hope alive and, if necessary, give assistance where needed. Now, if any of you want to stay outside or leave altogether, we will understand and support your decision."

There was silence, the group exchanging worried looks with each other. I began to fear that I might be alone on this excursion.

"I've been with you from the start, Hank!" Dean spoke, hoisting his M16.

"I'm in!" Drew said, joining Dean at my side.

In the end, five of us stood in a group. Frank and Ben deciding

198

to stay in the safety of the vehicle. With weapons ready, we entered the facility.

The door gave off a slightly smoky smell as we passed through the threshold and into a reception area. The room was well lit, which meant the generators were still running, but it also revealed long-dried pools of blood on the floor. A long, reddish-brown smear trailed down a hallway and out of sight.

"Which way?" Amber asked, edging around a congealed, dark crimson puddle.

"Toward the main elevators," I said, motioning straight ahead.

"How do you know where they are?" asked Dean.

"I read the sign," I said while casually pointing at it with the automatic handgun Frank had lent me.

Dean breathed out loudly in disgust as he saw the sign indicating the various departments. Personnel, communications, and financial departments were all on this level. Security and various labs were on the third floor.

We silently crept down the dirty, carpeted hall, paralleling the bloody smear. The lines made by the bodily fluid looked like an abstract painting; fingers absently crossing, creating a random, yet fluid, composition full of irregular rhythm and pattern. If I didn't know what the medium was, it wouldn't have horrified me at all.

When we reached the elevators in the middle of the hall, Dean said, "I guess we go down."

"I don't like elevators," Melissa said in a serious tone.

"These places don't have stairs. One way in and one way out," I explained. "It's a security thing."

I understood her comment. She had told me earlier about her experiences at her office, about how exposed you are when you travel in one. We all readied our weapons, aiming at the double doors and waiting.

The bell chimed and the doors rolled open. It was empty. The faint sound of Muzak could be heard from inside.

We entered, turning to face the closing doors. "I really don't like this," Melissa said with a slight tremor in her voice.

"What floor?" asked Drew, hand hovering near the numbered buttons.

"Third," I responded.

Mel's hands shook as she leveled her weapon at the closed

doors. The rest of us joined her, raising our own guns in anticipation of an attack. I could feel sweat making the handle of my gun slippery. It felt like I couldn't get a firm grip, like the discharge would make the weapon fly out of my grasp.

This prompted me to add my other hand. Doubt made me want to stop the elevator, but I pushed on. My friends were all at my back. We were going to make a difference. I knew it.

The chime sounded, signaling our arrival two floors down. It might have been a dinner bell, except that no zombies were around. The hallway was empty. There was blood and other bits of matter, but not one undead walker.

A sign indicated that security offices were to the right. The left hallway led to the labs. The sound of the Muzak diminished as we exited the elevator and started left. The group moved in precision. We covered each other as we moved down the hall as one unit, weapons always scanning any area, which might pose a threat.

Weeks of living in a hostile situation ingrained safe behaviors. We needed no prompting. We just understood. Never lower your guard. Move as a group. Watch for the unexpected. It was amazing to experience.

We saw nothing until we stalked by a window, which offered a passing view of one of the laboratories. Immediately, zombies approached the glass dividing the hall from the room in which they were trapped. The clear divider was smeared with secretions better left undetermined, blurring our view of the ghastly occupants.

"Which room?" Dean asked over his shoulder, never letting his eyes stray from the point area in our formation.

"Look for some type of research and development lab, some place they might have been developing an antitoxin. We need to find where they might have been trying to create a cure or prophylactic drug," I answered, not sure where we needed to go. "Maybe that one."

I was indicating a laboratory, which looked empty. The room looked well illuminated and totally undisturbed.

The door was locked. I noticed a card slide on the right and produced Pamela Mason's ID card from my front pocket. I slid it through the slot and entered the code she had whispered in my ear. The information I had so fearfully gained paid off as the doors slid apart, revealing an entrance to the lab.

We spread out once inside the room; fanning in different directions, each keeping our guns trained on where our eyes looked. We were a well-honed unit.

I headed straight for the computer desk. Sitting in the chair, I slid forward, only to meet some early resistance. Pushing the chair back as hard as I could, I cleared the desk's opening and bouncing off of the wall directly behind it. There was something under the opening.

My gun trained on the area, I could see a set of legs and the bottom of a white lab coat. "Come out of there!" I demanded.

The rest of my friends, having found nothing, sped to my side, weapons coming to bear on the hidden occupant of the desolate lab. I felt more confident with the extra firepower.

"I'm not one of them!" the hidden woman replied. "Not yet, at least."

I could see by the hastily bandaged hand that she was telling the truth. Blood stained the white fabric as she extended her hands in a gesture of surrender.

Chapter 35
Melissa

It was a woman dressed in a white lab coat, her hand covered in a hastily wrapped bandage. She looked completely terrified.

"It's going to be alright," I soothed, taking her in my arms. I could be reasonably sure she was a good distance from turning at this point, so I didn't fear her embrace. Her skin still bore the rosy hue of a healthy, living human being. Her body was warm, alive, as I held her in my arms. I could feel the tension leaving her limbs as she returned my hug.

We released our hold. I immediately could see a difference in her. She seemed a little less tense, but not relaxed. I stepped aside to let my husband take over. This was his arena. She spoke his language. We needed to know what they knew. If there were any answers found, this was where they would be kept.

"Have there been any breakthroughs?" Henry said, taking the opening. "Has the research here yielded anything?"

"Not much! The parasite is quite virulent," she responded, falling back to her trained way of thinking. "We cannot isolate a way of killing the organism without killing the host."

"Is there a way of inoculating people from the invading life form?"

"No," she said, her voice soft. "Not that we could formulate."

"What about the introduction of iron, we have found that-"

"Listen, we have tried everything. If there was a cure..." she said, lifting her hand and looking at the bloodied bandage. Her eyes became unfocused for a moment. "We have no more time. It's over."

"Maybe we can get the others?" Hank said, trying to bring her back around.

"There are no others!" she said angrily. "I was with them when it happened. We were in a meeting comparing our findings. We didn't know. As we were leaving, we were attacked. I barely made it here. The others..." She stopped, not able to find the words. "We failed."

I looked at the others in the room. Drew held Amber's hands. They were looking deeply into each other's eyes, sharing unspoken words of concern and love. Dean absently rubbed his eyes. I could see the despair in his stance. We were all defeated.

"Was anything else said in the meeting? Something that might give us a chance?" Henry probed gently, trying to keep hope alive.

"There was a report..."

The lights cut out. Red backup lights washed the room in crimson. A mechanical voice immediately informed, *Emergency battery power override. Ten minutes until emergency fail-safe detonation.*

A low-pitched, intermitted buzzing marked the passage of the countdown. The door slid open on its own, revealing the hallway.

"We gotta go!" Dean screamed over the noise, snapping into action. He spun and sprinted to the door.

I raced to his side, peering down the hall as I felt Drew and Amber join us. Looking back, I could see Henry, listening as the woman spoke to him.

"Henry!" I urged as the first of the zombie scientists stumbled into the hall. "It's now or never!"

He hurriedly extended a hand, pointer finger extended up, indicating for me to wait a minute. I felt frustration flooding my anxious body as I shot the first, only to watch as two more replaced him. All wearing the same white, blood-covered coats, they kept coming, stepping over their own as I dropped two more with three shots.

Looking back to see his progress, I saw the woman he was speaking with lean heavily on the desk.

"Hank!" Drew screamed as I turned back to the hall and the growing crowd ambling our way. Some were missing arms, while others dragged legs. They all reached toward us with grasping hands, anticipating a fresh meal.

I fired my weapon until the slide locked back. Frank had explained that this meant there were no more bullets. Amber bravely slid in front of me, shooting into the crowd as I dropped back to reload. Shaking hands fished fresh rounds out of my pocket as I slid them into the empty clip.

"Let's go!" a familiar voice commanded. Henry had joined us in the hall. Instantly, we began slowly moving back toward the elevators. We fought as a group, trying to hold back the gathering hoard. Somehow, the undead bathed in the red warning lights seemed to become even spookier. As I replaced Amber, it looked like we were losing ground quickly.

Nine minutes until emergency fail-safe detonation.

"Can we hurry it up a little up there?" I screamed to the front. Rapid firing confirmed my fear.

"We're a little bottled up here," a voice that sounded like Drew answered.

"In about eight more minutes, we won't have to worry about these zombies!" I urged.

I noticed a marked increase in gunfire toward the front, which was also realized in our movement toward the elevators. The hallway in front of the dead was littered with corpses. This served to slow them down, their already precarious gait impeded with the freshly fallen. The only problem was that as we moved forward we were literally walking on the dead that the people in front had freshly dropped.

As I was reloading again, Amber fell to her knees, stumbling over a prone body. Her gun spun away from her as she dropped. As she reached for the weapon, a zombie dressed in blue scrubs threw herself at my friend. I stepped beside Amber and kicked the creature in the face, sending it backward into the surging crowd.

Reaching down, I grabbed Amber under the upper arm, roughly throwing the woman to her feet. The time I used was too great. I knew I had come too close, maybe got too cocky. As I tried to regain my place in our group, I stepped on a slain zombie's arm. The skin rotated, dropping me to hands and knees. I tried to crawl forward as fast as I could but my heart sank as an iron grip locked on my exposed ankle.

Eight minutes until emergency fail-safe detonation.

I kicked back and forth, trying to free my limb with no luck. Fearing to look backward, I looked forwards and up. Amber had just resumed her position. Her eyes went wide as she saw me and registered my predicament. Her gun swung toward my attacker just as intense pain registered from my calf.

It was over.

Chapter 36
Henry

It was hard to make headway. The undead poured from the labs into the cramped hallway. We actually had to walk over the dead we shot.

Seven minutes until emergency fail-safe detonation. The mechanical voice warned.

"Time's running out!" I yelled. "We got to make it to the elevators."

"We're almost there!" Dean said, encouraged. "I can see them about ten feet to the right."

We pushed on ahead, gaining precious inches but using too much ammunition.

"I'm almost out of bullets," Drew informed. "What are we going to do?"

"Keep going," I encouraged. "We'll fight hand to hand if we have to. Just keep moving!"

We sped up recklessly, risking a misstep or just closing the distance too quickly. We were putting everything into merely reaching the elevators. There was a finite amount of these undead workers, but I also realized that we had a finite amount of ammunition.

My slide locked back and I knew I had few bullets left, so I pulled my revolver to keep up as much firepower as possible. We made the elevators as I fired my last shot.

I could hear Amber from the rear. "I'm empty!"

As we waited for the doors to open, it came down to hand-to-hand combat. We instinctively formed a protective, clear area around the doors. The doors would need to have time to close. I bashed the zombies nearest with my revolver's handgrip, swinging it about and catching my assailants on the side of the head. I never tried punching them in the face for risk of cutting my knuckles on their teeth and getting infected.

As the doors opened, followed by the chime, we maintained our positions, waiting for the last moment to dart through the closing doors and into safety.

Six minutes until emergency fail-safe detonation.

As one, we retreated through the doors, which closed just before cold, undead hands met the solid metal outside of our escape vehicle. The small room filled with the sound of heavy breathing as it lifted upward. Blood coated our clothes from our close quarters battle. We had a little reprieve as we passed the second floor and closed on the first.

A Muzak version of "Stairway to Heaven" began to play over the elevator's speaker system.

"They shouldn't do that to rock classics," Dean remarked disgustedly.

"It is appropriate, though," I answered.

"I have a shot or two left," offered my friend, sounding exhausted.

"Me, too," added Drew who sounded worse.

The rest remained silent, obviously out of bullets.

The doors rolled open, revealing three zombies drawn by the sound of the bell. They turned toward us, extending their arms and moaning. I knew this was it. We had too little stamina left and even fewer bullets.

A burst from an automatic weapon ripped through the air. It knocked two down, dropping them to the floor with their heads nearly torn off. Another weapon fired rapidly, destroying the third and clearing the way.

"You're all clear, kid!" Ben yelled, leveling another undead walker we couldn't see. "Now let's blow this thing and go home!"

Five minutes until emergency fail-safe detonation.

The floor was littered with dead zombies. Ben and Frank had been busy. As I passed each of them, I thanked them, in turn. If they hadn't come out of hiding, we would have died a short hallway's distance from the exit.

We fled, Amber helping Melissa as the rest of us cleared the way. Mel must have twisted her ankle, because she hopped along with Amber's help, favoring one leg. As we entered the receptionist area, another burst from one of the automatic weapons roared, dropping another animated corpse at the door.

Four minutes until emergency fail-safe detonation.

"We aren't going to make it!" Amber cried in despair.

"Just keep going!" I yelled, pushing everyone beyond his or her limits of endurance.

206

The machine guns belched out more rounds outside, joined by the last of the handgun rounds. We piled into the Humvees as more of the living dead shambled into view. They came because of the loud sounds, shuffling towards what they hoped would be dinner.

Two engines came to life; and in seconds, we were careening down the drive toward the gates, unfortunate zombies bouncing off or under the powerful vehicles as we raced to gain a safe distance from the imminent explosion.

Tense moments ticked by as we flew at breakneck speed, tearing onto the old road and heading downhill. The anticipation was maddening. I took turns at speeds far exceeding what would normally be safe.

A loud boom erupted from behind. Seconds later, the blast radius reached our position, blowing vegetation almost horizontal. Loose branches and other debris joined us in being thrown outward from ground zero. I could feel the heavy vehicle being tossed out of my control, the contents and passengers thrown about, spilling in all directions.

Spinning the wheel, I compensated for the blast wave and brought the Humvee to a halt. The other skidded to a stop behind us. I exited the driver's seat and joined by most of the others outside.

Immediately, I looked for Melissa. She wasn't in my Humvee, so I was on my way toward the one driven by Drew. Amber leapt out of an open doorway and met me a few steps away. Placing a hand on my chest, she ended my progress.

"Melissa needs to talk to you," she said to me quietly.

I looked about, not seeing her. "Where is she?"

The woman just pointed, head lowered. A tear rolled down her cheek.

My heart was in my throat as I hurried to where she sat. The door was now closed.

Through the open window, I gently prodded, "Honey?"

"I'm so sorry," she said between sobs.

"It's ok," I assured her, not understanding. "We made it. It's going to be alright."

The door opened and Melissa extended her wounded leg. "It happened downstairs. I am so sorry."

I haven't cried since the first grade. I wept as I took her in my arms, shushing like I would a child. "You have nothing to be sorry for," I answered.

"You risked so much for me," she breathed.

"And I would do it again," I soothed. "I love you and-"

"Outta my way!" Dean commanded, roughly throwing me to the pavement.

I jerked around, recovering, only to see him climbing across Mel's wounded form. Rage erupted in me. He was going to kill her. This was wrong. She was no danger yet. I had so much I wanted to tell her, so much I needed to say. He wasn't going to take that from me.

Scrambling to my feet, I grabbed double handfuls of his shirt and hauled him out. He staggered backward, staying upright but propelled away from the vehicle and my injured wife. I balled up both fists and approached him in rage.

"Hold it, Hank!" he said, extending both hands forward. Still snarling, I noticed that he held two bottles of whiskey. "If we get her drunk, won't that slow down the effects of the bite?"

My hands dropped to my sides, understanding slowly. I snatched a bottle from his outstretched hand. Twisting the cap and breaking the seal, I offered the alcohol to my wife. "Drink this!" I demanded.

She looked at me like I was crazy.

"Remember? It will do something to your blood vessels! It will keep you from turning!" Dean added, explaining what we had talked about in the Humvee earlier.

Mel immediately lifted the bottle to her lips and drank deeply.

Chapter 37
Melissa

The whiskey burned horribly as I gulped down as much as I could take. Excess liquid ran down my chin and dripped off onto my shirt. I lowered the bottle and coughed, nearly vomiting. How did people drink this stuff?

I wasn't a drinker in the normal world. Sure, I had a little wine on the right occasion, but that was about it. When you have an academic as a husband, you tend not to drink that much.

After further encouragement, I took a few more pulls on the vile liquid. Each time, I felt the same queasy feeling in my stomach. I really didn't want to continue drinking this stuff, but I dearly wanted to spend just a little more time with Henry.

"We heard," Drew spoke from behind. "Is there anything we can do?"

"No," I said, trying not to sound mournful. "But thank you all."

I took another swig. Almost immediately, I regretted it, following the mouthful with a series of coughs.

"I don't think drinking will help," offered Ben.

"Actually, it will," Henry corrected, wheeling angrily on the unsuspecting man. "It will slow the onset of the..." He couldn't continue. "We have to go!"

"Where?" Frank asked sarcastically. "In the middle of the apocalypse, I don't think-"

Henry cut him off. "Someplace special. You don't have to come, any of you. But, I have to get Melissa someplace and it has to be fast!"

Everyone just stared at him for a moment.

"I'm going," Dean said.

"We're all going!" Drew added, sharing a challenging look with his two friends.

They just looked sheepishly at their leader.

"Just follow us," my husband said determinedly.

Henry climbed into the driver's seat while Dean sat on the opposite side from me. We tore down the road and, turning again, sped past the lower reservoir, a warm feeling spread through my body.

"I feel warm," I informed Henry.

"Good," he replied. "That means it's working. Just keep drinking. We'll be there soon."

"Where are we going?"

"It's a surprise."

We drove on at breakneck speeds, taking turns hazardously wide and using both lanes. With effort, I looked behind us. Drew and the others raced to keep pace with us as we drove on ahead.

Every time I looked over at Dean, he was watching me, never looking away. I knew he was keeping alert, waiting for any sign of danger.

Henry poured everything out, telling me how much he loved me and lavishing praise and heartfelt feelings about me. And I, in turn, told him the same. As we went on, it was hard for me to speak. My tongue felt sluggish and I slurred my speech, but both men seemed not to notice; they just kept encouraging me to drink more.

The last thing I saw before falling asleep was Dean, wiping tears from his face. I knew he was thinking about Julie and what she meant to him, how he wished he could have said these last things to her. I looked into his eyes and said in a low voice, "She knew."

Chapter 38
Henry

I was driving as fast as I could. The heavily armored vehicle wasn't built for speed. It took turns wide and leaned dangerously as we sped through them.

On a straightaway, I looked in the rear view mirror. Drew had fallen further behind. They were now out of sight.

Through the beginning of the journey, Dean had remained silent, letting Melissa and I speak without interrupting. We each expressed our feelings. It must have been hard listening to our exchange.

Now, an hour later, he was still silent. Mel had fallen asleep, the half empty whiskey bottle slipping to the floor. I chanced another gaze in the mirror and saw my friend holding his pistol in one hand while intently watching my wife.

"How does she look?" I asked, concern in my tone.

"She's ok," he answered. "A little gray, but the alcohol seems to be doing the trick. Where are we going?"

"Presque Isle," I said as we pulled off Route 79 and headed down a double lane road lined with stores. "She always loved it there. Even better than the ocean."

Undead wandered about, but I was able to avoid them for the most part. Using all four lanes, I swerved around most of the walking corpses, suddenly afraid of getting one stuck in a wheel well or anything else that might slow us down.

Dean got on the walkie-talkie and informed Drew of our destination. He said that Amber knew how to get there so I should continue on ahead. They would meet us there.

After turning, we drove down the hill toward the park. The zombie population had dropped dramatically. Ahead, we saw why. Two police cars blocked the road. Their drivers, standing behind the vehicles, brought their weapons to bear on us. I didn't know what to do, so I continued forward.

"Do you think these guys are ok?" Dean said, making quick glances at the pair of officers pointing their shotguns at us as we approached.

"I'll find out," I said, slowing the Humvee. I brought it to a halt about thirty feet from the blockade.

Exiting the vehicle, I raised both hands and walked toward their position. I could see by their uniforms that they both were policemen, sunlight winking off of their badges and sunglasses.

"It sure is good to see other living humans," I called as I moved closer. "Especially policemen. This is great!"

From behind the cars, one called back, "Drop the gun and lay face down on the ground. Spread your hands and legs out wide!"

"I don't see-"

"Just do it!" the other demanded, agitated.

I did as instructed. The pavement was warm. Stray bits of gravel made lying there uncomfortable. I could hear, rather than see, them approach. Sand grinding under their rubber soles marked their arrival.

"Have you been bitten by any of the Z's?"

I quickly deduced their inference of the term Z's. "No," I responded curtly.

"Are there any others in the vehicle?" the same voice interrogated.

"Yes," I said, quickly understanding my folly. Dean was fine, but Melissa was dying. I worried about what they might do if they found that out. My worry turned into full-blown fear as one scooped up my revolver while the other searched me for hidden weapons.

"Call back to the vehicle and have the others dismount," they said as we started back to the Humvee.

"My wife is drunk and passed out in the back seat," I informed them, trying to cover for her condition.

"Fine. Have the other get out!" the other officer said roughly.

I, once again, did as told. Dean reluctantly slid from the military vehicle and they instructed him to drop his weapon and lay spread eagle on the ground.

"What's going on?" my friend asked as he complied.

"This area is under the protection of Congressman John R. Noble!" he explained, keeping his shotgun trained on both myself, and the prone man. "We're a forward unit. It's our job to keep watch over the park's entrance."

I made a mental note that they at no time had mentioned anything about helping. Weren't they supposed to help people like

212

us? What if they discovered Melissa's condition?

I edged closer to the officer at my side. He seemed more relaxed, passing us off as mere survivors and not a threat.

"He's clean," confirmed the other, rising to his feet and brushing dirt from the pavement off of his lower pant legs.

"Check on this man's wife."

The officer opened the door Dean had just exited from and leaned in. "Crap!" he said in disgust. "I think she's a Z!"

The man at my side reflexively raised his shotgun and looked over his shoulder at me. "Are you sure?" he asked.

The other tentatively leaned back in. "She could be drunk, but it sure smells like one of them zombies," he explained. "And her skin's all gray."

Still looking at me over his shoulder, the policeman offhandedly said, "Shoot her!"

I inhaled slowly as the man at the door raised his weapon. Dean had gotten to his feet and was quite casually brushing cinders from his knee.

The loud roar of the second Humvee made us all snap around with a start. I lunged the short span between us and grabbed the gun's stock and barrel. The other man was younger and stronger, but I was full of fury. The gun fired into the air once as I twisted the lawman to the ground.

Dean feigned disinterest. When the patrolman nearest him swung toward the approaching vehicle, Dean launched himself at the gunman, pulling the barrel away from Mel and dragging him out of the doorway.

The shotgun blasted again as I rolled onto my back, bits of debris poking at me through my clothes. I ignored the discomfort and tried to regain the top position.

Dean kneed his opponent in the groin. His assailant went slack from the blow. Ripping the weapon out of his weakened enemy's grip, my friend brought it back across his face.

I kicked and twisted as hard as I could; but it was no use, my opponent was too strong. His stamina was going to win out. I was growing too weak.

There was a dull thud as Dean brought the butt of the shotgun down on the back of the policeman's head. I swung the slack form away from me as he dropped, unconscious. My friend offered me a hand, and I gladly accepted his help getting to my feet.

"Thanks!" I said sincerely. "I guess I owe you one!"

"One?" he shot back smartly.

"Hey," I said, feigning anger. "Ok, two."

The others were piling out of the other Humvee and rushing to our side. I pushed past to check on Melissa. The commotion had brought her back around. "Are you ok?"

"You should have let them shoot me," she said weakly.

"I didn't bring you all this way for them to rob you of my surprise," I stated.

Dean drove us to the shore. The others stayed with the unconscious policemen. I hadn't noticed the smell in the car before, but having been outside for a while, I now understood the officer's reaction. We must have gotten used to it. I didn't care, though.

We drove over the sand and up to the shore. Dean remained in the vehicle as Melissa and I went to the water's edge. We sat for a short while, letting the water wash over our bare feet. I held her and softly repeated much of what I told her in the car. She was burning up with fever, sweat running down her brow.

"I feel cold," she whispered, her head on my shoulder.

"Do you want to dry off?" I said, sliding my feet back from the latest wave.

"No," she said mournfully. "You need to go."

"Just a little longer."

"I can feel it inside me," she said absently. "Trying to get me to do things I don't want to do."

"A little longer."

"Please don't let me become one of them," she said, crying gentle tears.

I felt myself crying now, knowing the time was upon us. "I won't let that happen!

Let's just stay a little while longer."

"No!" she said firmly. "I will not put our friends in danger another moment. Thank you for this gift; for saving me! But, most of all, for loving me so very much."

I was speechless. The time had come, and I didn't know if I could do it.

"There may be more of them. If someone comes to check on those policemen… You have to go now!"

I kissed her on the forehead, feeling cheated at not being able to kiss her lips.

I rose behind her and pulled my revolver.

"I love you," she said.

"I love you more," I answered, covering the click of the hammer drawing back with my words.

My hand shook; the gun's sight waving all about, uncontrollable. Tears ran anew over my cheeks. I tried to pull the trigger, but my finger wouldn't respond.

It wasn't right. There should be a way for her to live. This wasn't fair!

"Please don't let me become one of them," she whispered, urging me on.

Bang.

Chapter 39
Dean

I watched the two of them down by the water. I understood what Hank was going through. The ghost of Julie visited me in my mind, leaving me sad and drained of hope. To busy myself, I checked my gun.

Henry had changed. I watched him become a leader. This apocalyptic time made him into a strong man. But now, as I watched them, I wondered if he could do this final act. What would be required of him? I wondered if I could have, had it been Julie there instead of Melissa.

I watched him rise, gun held outstretched, waiting. As doubt took hold of me, I reached for the door handle. Then, the sound stopped me. Melissa dropped gently to one side and the gun lowered. Hank turned and immediately walked back to our Humvee.

"Are you ok?" I asked, immediately feeling dumb.

"No," he said softly.

"Do you want to bury her?"

"No," he said once again. "There isn't time. Besides, this way she'll be washed out with the tide. She would want it that way."

We returned to the rest of the group. Amber, giving over to grief, rushed up the Hank and enveloped him in a tight hug, her shoulders heaving with each sob, his matching hers.

"We gotta go!" I spoke up.

"Where to?" asked Drew.

"I know a place," Hank said, breaking the embrace and wiping his eyes. "We aren't done yet!"

We all just stood there. *We aren't done yet? What did that mean?*

"What do we still need to do, Hank?" I asked gently.

Henry produced a flash drive. "This parasite didn't evolve on its own!" he said, a fire glowing in his reddened eyes. "A man did this. I want revenge!"

###

This is the end of Parasite. Thank you for reading my book. Please look for the other titles in The True Story of the Zombie Apocalypse series. The next installment is called "Symbiote." The following is a sample of what you'll be missing if you don't get your copy.

Below is a sample from the next book in the series *Symbiote; The True Story of the Zombie Apocalypse.*

Chapter 1
Henry

I sat beside the water's edge, thinking of Mel. It was all so unfair. I had pulled her from the roof and now she was gone. We had such little time after the dead took over the world. Our relationship had bloomed again, and now she was gone; taken from me by this cruel world, this world of the dead.

Waves washed the shore, leaving small pools behind. I could see tiny life forms scurry about, trapped in these small, watery satellites. Wave upon wave washed up, giving brief windows of opportunity for the captive creatures to escape. I watched as some propelled themselves out, freeing themselves as the moment allowed. Other tiny creatures, for whatever reason, remained behind. They were content in their diminutive surroundings.

I wondered at how much like humans they seemed; languishing in the familiar, simply unwilling or unable to leap at an opportunity when it presents itself. Melissa, and others I knew had died trying for the only opportunity that presented itself; survival.

Many people were unable to accept this new world. My friends and I weren't those types of people. We had survived this parasitic invasion, dooming ourselves to a life of fear, constantly on the run. Living on a planet where nearly all technology was now rendered useless, we were thrown back into the dark ages.

The only thing that kept us going was the need to live; to discover a way to rid ourselves of the undead population and to begin the rebuilding process.

It's funny. In the natural world, the need to procreate and spread

217

future generations of one's species is the sole driving force of life. To spread offspring bearing one's genetic code is the primary need, which gives purpose to every organism on our world.

The human species was in trouble. Through some madman's manipulation of a parasite, we were on the brink of extinction. Man's intelligence was the mechanism of our demise. The parasite hadn't naturally evolved into this form. It hadn't randomly become an organism that animated the dead to spread its young through a bite. It had been created by one of us; a human, and a very sick one at that.

The woman in the CDC lab had explained to me that they had received classified documents leading to a place near our present location, a site where a renowned biologist was conducting bizarre experiments. This place and person were what I needed to find.

I needed to track this pandemic to its origins, to possibly find this person and find a way to undo what he had done.

His name was Dr. Spaulding Fleming. He's the person we were searching for. His lab would, hopefully, hold the answers to what we were looking for. The paper suggested that he was operating somewhere in the area we now occupied.

I heard the sound of one of the Hummers pulling down the gravel road. Loose stones pinged off the wheel wells as the vehicle neared the cottage. Hefting my twelve-gauge shotgun, I checked my revolver in its holster and went to greet them.

The cottage was near the shore of Lake Erie. Set back enough to be safe from high water, it was also situated next to a trout stream. We had been supplementing our meals with fish for some time now.

I knew about this cottage because Mel and I had looked into buying it a while back. We hadn't purchased it due to it being on a land lease. We'd heard stories about people losing their homes when the lease was terminated. The cottage was roomy enough for us all to stay in comfort but small enough for us to defend if the need arose.

These cottages were seasonal, which means the water is shut off in the off-season, keeping the owners away. Although the season had just begun, I didn't feel like we were going to get many visitors in the near future (at least not the living kind). We had seen a helicopter in the distance a few times, although I don't think it saw

218

us.

Having the great lake at our doorstep meant we also had a new form of transportation. We could travel by boat. We hadn't tried it yet, but we took the initiative to secure a newer fishing boat to facilitate scouting missions as well as a possible escape route.

As I approached the Humvee, I noticed a few more blood spatters on the side. "I told you to wash and wax it!" I joked as Dean and Ben exited the military vehicle.

"Sure ya did," Dean replied sarcastically while turning to empty the contents of their scavenging. "You want it to look nice while you're driving your date to the prom, right?"

I watched as boxes of canned and dry goods were stacked beside the fender. My former neighbor tore open a box and tossed a small Mylar-wrapped package to me. Catching it, I looked at my prize in disgust.

"A Twinkie?" I gasped. "If I eat any more of this crap..."

Dean laughed, "Hey. At least, they're food."

"And they'll never go bad," added Ben.

"That's just an urban legend," I explained while unconsciously tearing the package open and taking a large bite. Between mouthfuls, I said, "They're made of unstabilized dairy products. My guess is they might last a month but could still be edible for some time afterward."

Ben, having crossed to the other side of the car, snatched the box from Dean's hands and pulled one of the snacks free. With a look of desperation, he tore into the treat moments after freeing it from its wrappings.

"Better eat 'em while we can," he said between cake-coated teeth, immediately pulling another from the box.

"Did you see anything interesting?" I asked Dean Walker.

Watching Ben shove most of a Twinkie into his maw, he absently said, "Nothing. At least, not as interesting as this."

"How about any undead?" I inquired in an attempt to draw his attention from Ben's feeding frenzy.

"Zombies? Oh, we had to take care of two at the CVS. I hit a couple more on the way back here. Five, I guess."

"That's not bad!" I replied. "I knew we'd be somewhat isolated out here."

The cabin was located just north of Fairview, Pennsylvania.

From our observances, the undead creatures weren't particularly fond of water. They would shuffle up to the water's edge, but they didn't seem to want to walk into it. Maybe it was the currents? The "Walkers", as Dean ironically called them, had enough trouble navigating dry, even land. Any waves in the water would most certainly cause them to pitch over and be caught adrift. This would minimize the potential of spreading their larvae to new hosts. They might have been unwilling to risk this outcome in favor of a dry land approach to propagating their species.

The evening was winding down, the sun slipping closer to the horizon. Dean and I stood out near the water while Ben retired to the cabin to try to sleep off his sugary binge.

"I hope everything's ok!" he voiced, a look of concern on his darkening features.

"Me too," I agreed. "It's getting late."

As our surroundings became darker, we moved inside. Ben expressed similar feelings over and over as we sat in the candle-lit building and waited.

Chapter 2
Drew

The day hadn't been too fruitful. We had headed out west from the cabin toward Conneaut, Ohio, but had a little bit of a problem near a place called Lake City. Five or six deer leapt to the road in front of us. Amber screamed and I almost put us into a drainage ditch. When we got out to investigate, three rabbits, an adult, and two young ones, followed the deer toward the other side of the pavement.

"I don't like this," called Frank, still seated in the back seat. "We should get out of here."

"Amber," I said as I watched a groundhog hurry across the road. "I think Frank's right!"

That's when the first zombie emerged from the undergrowth. He was a big one, easily three hundred pounds and about six and a half feet tall. His plaid, flannel shirt and jeans were stained black with gore and other unknown substances.

Two more averaged-sized creatures followed in his wake; one missing an arm from the elbow down, the other just plain hideous.

"Shoot 'em!" Amber yelled, her shotgun barking twice before I could bring my gun to bear.

She caught the big one on the shoulder, the powerful blast taking a good-sized hunk of flesh, but the zombie didn't even slow down. The other shot missed completely.

Hastily aiming my 9mm, I fired a wild first shot, merely grazing the huge monster on his right cheek. Before I could fire again, he was on me. I stood, trying to push the behemoth away as I heard more shots ring out from my girlfriend's position and also from the Humvee.

The giant was slow but strong, and relentless as he tried to sink his teeth into my flesh. Blood flew wildly from his wounds as he fought for a bite. It spattered my clothes and face as we wrestled for position.

His clothes crunched as I gripped them, the dried gore giving way under the pressure of my hands. I was losing ground quickly as my heels hit the edge of the road's berm. The gravelly surface caused me to slide, pitching me backward as the behemoth fell with me.

A loud boom sounded to my right and all went black, my ears ringing from the close proximity of the loud explosion. In a panic, I squirmed under the pressure of my assailant's large bulk, waiting to feel his teeth find their mark. Then, I realized he was all dead weight.

It seemed like an eternity before my friends pulled the still corpse from on top of me. My clothes were soaked with his dark, foul blood. A salty taste filled my mouth and I spit a huge gob on the road. As I followed it to the ground, I dropped to my knees, putting my face inches from the phlegm. There was no mistaking it. My spit was red with the creature's blood.

Amber, unnoticed by me, had also come down and was examining it closely. She roughly jerked my face around, pulling my lips away from my face in search of a wound. There was nothing. The zombie's blood that had sprayed on my face was what had been in my mouth.

I tore out of her grasp and crawled into the weeds, heaving uncontrollably. I emptied my gut, hacking out long strands of stomach lining. My eyes watered fiercely with the effort.

As I regained my composure, I could hear Amber crying loudly behind me. I felt like a man on death row. I returned to my girlfriend, the first one I've ever had, and took her in my arms. She was still sobbing as I gripped her tightly, never wanting to let her go.

"Guys," came a shaky voice from our transportation. "I really think we should get going. There may be more."

Even as Frank said those words, the emaciated form of a woman shuffled into view. Her worn pantsuit clung to her scrawny form, plastered with grime and bodily fluids.

I stood quickly, dragging Amber to her feet with me. As one, we ran, never breaking our embrace. At the front of the Humvee, we separated, hands touching until the last second, breaking only to enter on our own sides.

I moved mechanically, turning the ignition and starting us down the road. Three more zombies joined the woman, and I rammed right through all three. The woman, who I had missed, followed behind us, arms outstretched as if to try to grab our fleeing vehicle.

We drove on in silence. I maneuvered the Humvee woodenly, following the road instinctively as my mind pondered what was going to happen to me. I felt fine. Well, as fine as a man who just wrestled an undead giant and vomited the entire contents of his body could feel.

We passed very few houses. They all looked abandoned, grass growing wildly and going to seed. I wondered how many of them held hidden survivors, people barricaded inside trying to wait this plague out. I'd been trying to do the same thing, but now that I was out, I was quite possibly going to turn into one of them; a zombie.

"What happened back there?" asked Frank, breaking our long silence.

"I … " I couldn't finish my response.

"Drew might have gotten some of the big zombie's blood in his mouth," Amber finished my sentence.

I could see Frank shift in his seat, his handgun nonchalantly shifting to point at me. I understood his reaction.

"I feel fine," I assured him.

"Should he be driving?" Frank asked Amber.

"I think it's ok," she answered.

222

"Do you think he'll turn?" he asked her.

"I hope not," she said mournfully, looking at me.

"He looks a little pale and red around the eyes," he pointed out.

"Stop talking about me like I'm not here!" I said angrily.

"He seems to be getting irrational," Frank continued.

"That's it!" I barked. "If I turn, I'm going right for you Frank Frawley! I'm gonna eat your brains!"

"Stop it!" Amber shouted.

"Not that it'd be more than a mouthful," I mumbled.

"Drop it!" she warned. "Drew's gonna be just fine!" she said with passion. She loved me. I finally have a girlfriend who loves me and now I'm going to become a zombie. How's that for irony.

As we passed the national game lands on the right, the desolate landscape gave way to dirt roads cutting through the woods. We explored the roads, driving past what looked like empty camps. Some were small buildings that were roughly constructed and made for weekend getaways, while others looked pristine and well built. I made a mental note that they would be great places to move to in the event our present place got overrun.

My present condition brought the realization that mental notes may not stay with me very long, so I shared my thoughts with the others. They nodded and agreed with the idea. I wondered what I would remember when I did turn. Would I remember this place? Would I come here in search of my friends to try to eat them? Pushing those thoughts from my mind, I tried to relax, hoping it would delay the progress of the disease.

"Maybe we should be getting back," Amber blurted, voicing her thoughts.

"It's still early," I said, emerging once again from my self-pity.

"Henry's still at the cottage," she said, her head bobbing up and down as if silently agreeing with her own statement (or maybe it was a sympathetic response to get me to accept the idea). "He might be able to do something."

"There's nothing to be done. If the ghoul's blood contained the parasite, it was probably too late from the first instant. I really do feel fine, though," I assured her. "Honest!"

Conneaut was a town about the size of Slippery Rock. The virus had ravaged them also. I don't know why I expected anything else. As we drove through the outer reaches of the town, zombies were drawn to the noise of our Humvee. They streamed from everywhere all at once; front yards, woods, even exiting through ruined doors. It was like we were ringing the dinner bell.

What looked like an entire little league team emerged from a local park. Gloves and bright yellow caps were still worn by many of them as they continued on their intercept course. I drove straight through them, catching most in my deadly strike.

As we drove on, I felt cold. It was one thing to kill an undead person, but killing those children... "Children!"

"It's ok. They were all zombies," Amber reassured. "You didn't do anything wrong."

"No. Where are the children?"

"I think he's starting to turn," Frank mumbled, sitting forward and repositioning his gun.

"You just drove through a bunch of them, Honey."

"No!" I said, having trouble making my mind work in sync with my mouth. "Back at the cabin. We haven't seen children since we arrived. Where are the kids?"

It was true. We'd been at the cabin for about two weeks and made many scouting and foraging missions. I hadn't seen a single child while I was on any of those expeditions. That's weird. Why hadn't I noticed it before?

"What do you think it means?" asked the beautiful woman sitting next to me.

"Maybe they're eating their young?" said my friend from the back seat.

"I don't know what it means. And, no, I doubt they are eating their young!"

"I was just sayin'," he said apologetically. "It's happened before."

Amber spun about. "It's happened before?"

"Cannibalism, not zombieism," I corrected while avoiding a large woman dragging a leg. "But, if they were eating their dead, wouldn't it be happening everywhere? There were kids everywhere else. This place is teeming with them."

As if to emphasize the point, a once-cute little girl in a Catholic school uniform shambled into our path. I couldn't do it. Spinning the wheel, I narrowly avoided striking her full-on. Grazing her shoulder, she spun to the road.

224

It was amazing. The longer we spent in this world, the more accustomed to it we became. A few zombies lurching around our moving vehicle brought little concern. Maybe if we were in a small hybrid car it would've been different, but in this heavy military vehicle, we were provided with little comfort but lots of protection from the clawing hands of death all around.

"It's getting too thick," Frank said, perched forward in his seat. "Maybe we should turn around?"

"My thoughts exactly," I said, spinning the wheel to the left and making an arc through someone's front yard.

The Humvee's turning radius wasn't great. I guess you had to give some things up for safety. Comfort, turning radius, and fuel consumption were all sacrificed.

As my long orbit returned to its origin, I heard a thump on the left side. Checking the side view mirror, I saw the undead schoolgirl lying still behind us. For some reason, my heart sank.

She was so young. When the outbreak started, she probably didn't understand. She was probably so scared. Her parents, I could imagine, tried to protect her, to defend her. But, at some point, she had succumbed. What terrors had she gone through? What horrors had she witnessed?

She was probably better off this way. Her nightmare was over. Now, she could rest.

I might've been thinking these thoughts because I felt my own demise approaching. She was a mirror that I was looking full on into. Was I going to be joining these legions of undead?

"Where to now?" Amber said anxiously. "I think we should go back. Let Hank have a look at you."

"All right!" I grumbled, a little short. Maybe she's right. My stomach was a little queasy.

We were nearing the state game lands when we saw a police car in the distance ahead. It was coming our way. The roof mounted lights turned on, strobing dizzily.

"Crap!" I exclaimed.

"What are we going to do?" said my girl hastily.

"Maybe they won't remember us," Frank cried in desperation.

"See that side road ahead?" I said flatly. "When we get there, hang on. We're gonna make a run for it!"

"But, what if they're the good guys?" Frank begged, sliding

back into his seat and buckling his safety belt.

"I'm not going to take that chance!"

We were going to make it to the side road just before the cops would. Not speeding up, I tried to make it look as nonchalant as possible.

At the intersection, I veered right and pushed the gas peddle to the floor. A road sign reading *Rudd Road* caught my eye. The diesel motor roared as we surged forward. A moment later, I heard tires squeal as the law enforcement vehicle made the correction and gave chase.

It seemed like we were in slow motion as the powerful police cruiser flew up behind us. Lights still blazing, its motor was designed for this type of situation. I remembered the list of stuff we'd given up for these heavily armored Humvees. Comfort, turning radius, fuel consumption and exactly what we needed right now; speed.

A single shot ricocheted off the driver's side door. "We're not gonna get away!" Frank screamed while hunkering down in his seat.

"We're going to make it!" I barked, looking for a way out.

"We're not gonna make it!" he said again as another shot sounded.

We flew down the road in a deadly chase, our vehicle pushed to its limit.

"We can't outrun them!" Amber said, strangely calm.

"I don't think we'll have to," I informed them.

The bridge ahead was blocked by a bunch of disabled cars. It looked like a small pileup had occurred, possibly at the beginning of the outbreak. To the side, a small dirt pull-off lead down to the trout stream that the bridge spanned.

"Everybody hang on!" I warned in a loud, commanding voice as we swerved onto the dirt track and plunged into the water.

The windshield became a blur as the stream's flow splashed across it, obscuring our vision. The Humvee slid a little to the right but almost immediately found traction and pushed on ahead. Its wheels were completely submerged, indicating the depth of the water.

Almost instantly, the police cruiser plunged into the current behind us. The much lighter vehicle floated for a second, then

226

submerged, water nearly halfway up its windows.

I found a dirt egress on the other shore and drove up, out of the stream. Water poured from the Humvee onto the path as we continued up the other side. A last wild, parting shot sounded from behind as we pulled onto the road and accelerated out of reach.

"That was close!" Amber said, pulling her fingers through her hair.

"What happened?" remarked Frank, rising from his crash position. He'd tucked his head between his knees in an effort to survive.

"We left them stranded at the riverside," I informed him, mimicking the lyrics from an old Rush song.

We followed the road and at the next intersection made a left, heading east once again, toward the cottage. We had never explored this road. As we drove on, we passed a few homes, mostly spread out with no nearby neighbors. We also passed a school.

"Talk about rednecks!" Frank said, looking at the abandoned elementary building. "Who puts a school right next to a pig farm?"

He was right. Situated right next to the single story school were about a half dozen long buildings. The sign out front had the image of a large hog with a dust-covered nameplate. The smell was horrendous. The odd thing was that there was no farmhouse.

"Oh," Amber said, covering her nose. "That's horrible."

"I'll bet the school got the land for free," I surmised. "The farm must have had some way of masking the smell."

"I sure hope so," she said in a nasal voice, pinching her nose closed with her thumb and pointer finger. "Those poor kids."

"I wonder what their team mascot was," Frank joked. "The Fighting Pork Chops?"

I knew when school was in session it couldn't have been this bad. It was probably coming off the pigs. Not being taken care of for over a month, the animals were probably dead and rotting. This image brought me back to my own dilemma.

Not a hundred feet down the road, a sign came into view.

"There's a gas station ahead," I announced to no one in particular.

"Do we need gas?" asked Amber cautiously, leaning close to check the gauge. I could see by her actions that she was wary of my condition.

"We could use some, but we should check it out anyway and see if it has a good supply," I answered. Mainly, I wanted to get out of the vehicle and see if it had been damaged. Back in Conneaut, we'd driven through a lot of ghouls, and I just wanted to make sure there weren't any stuck in a wheel well or something.

We pulled into the fueling area, twigs and cinders crunching under our tires. The place looked empty and completely untouched by the zombies, although showing no evidence of undead didn't mean it was pristine. It was amazing how fast our normal buildings and grounds went to pot as soon as we couldn't maintain them anymore. Rain and wind made debris pile up quickly. If left for a year or more, I wondered how much of the paved lot would be totally obscured by nature.

I located the round cover where fuel tankers deposited their load and quickly jimmied it open. Dean had rigged two pond pumps that we had scavenged from a local hardware store with hoses so we could pump gas. I lowered one end of the hose into the hole and put the other in the Humvee's tank. Plugging the pump into one of the receptacles in our vehicle started the homemade contraption. Within seconds, we were filling our tank with diesel.

It didn't take long to top off our supply, so we filled both of our two five gallon portable tanks for good measure. Frank and Amber, all the while, covered my back.

"All done," I said, switching off the pump. I retrieved the hoses and hung them outside to dry out.

Returning to the driver's side, I cut the engine. Silence.

The world probably sounded much like this when Native Americans were the only ones living here. The only sound was of distant birds and the soft breeze. To me, it was unnerving. I was used to noise, used to the sound of cars and people. In the former world, there was so much background clatter that we never really experienced true quiet. Natural quiet. The low din of human existence was so normal to us that this complete silence felt strange. Spooky.

"Should we check inside?" asked Amber while shifting her shotgun toward the building.

"I think we should leave altogether. Get out of here!" objected Frank.

"Let's have a look," I answered, taking command. "It couldn't hurt."

This is the end of chapter 2 in the exciting sequel called Symbiote; The True Story of the Zombie Apocalypse. Look for it at your favorite eBook retailer today.

About the Author
Doug Ward currently lives in Western Pennsylvania. He is a graduate of Slippery Rock University. He has a BFA in Fine Art. Doug spends much of his time doing oil paintings which incorporate mythology and science.

Connect with Me Online:
Facebook: http://www.facebook.com/doug.ward.754
Smashwords:
http://www.smashwords.com/profile/view/DougWard
Twitter: https://twitter.com/ZombieDoug

39225042R00129

Made in the USA
Middletown, DE
08 January 2017